MAKE THEM PAY

MAKE THEM PAY

A Brock and Poole Mystery

Graham Ison

This first world edition published 2012
in Great Britain and 2013 in the USA by
SEVERN HOUSE PUBLISHERS LTD of
19 Cedar Road, Sutton, Surrey, England, SM2 5DA.
Trade paperback edition first published
in Great Britain and the USA 2013 by
SEVERN HOUSE PUBLISHERS LTD.

British Library Cataloguing in Publication Data

Ison, Graham.
  Make them pay. – (A Brock and Poole mystery)
  1. Brock, Harry (Fictitious character : Ison)–Fiction.
  2. Poole, Dave (Fictitious character)–Fiction.
  3. Police–England–London–Fiction. 4. Murder–
  Investigation–Fiction. 5. Detective and mystery stories.
  I. Title II. Series
  823.9'14-dc23

ISBN-13: 978-0-7278-8238-7 (cased)
ISBN-13: 978-1-84751-467-7 (trade paper)

All Severn House titles are printed on acid-free paper.

Severn House Publishers support the Forest Stewardship Council [FSC], the
leading international forest certification organisation. All our titles that are printed
on Greenpeace-approved FSC-certified paper carry the FSC logo.

MIX
Paper from
responsible sources
FSC
www.fsc.org   FSC® C018575

Typeset by Palimpsest Book Production Ltd.,
Falkirk, Stirlingshire, Scotland.
Printed and bound in Great Britain by
MPG Books Ltd., Bodmin, Cornwall.

ONE

When the man arrived in Birmingham, he stopped at the first newsagents he saw. Alighting from his Volkswagen Polo, he entered the shop and spent a few minutes browsing the shelves. Finally he found what he was looking for: a copy of a local newspaper.

Returning to his car, he sat for a few minutes perusing the columns of small ads that listed rooms to let. Selecting an address at random he set his satnav – a recent add-on extra to his old car – for a road in Sheldon.

Parking his car some distance away from the house he had decided upon, he walked the rest of the way. It was an old house with paintwork that needed some attention and brick-work that was overdue for pointing. What had once been the front garden was now overlaid with concrete to provide hard standing for an ancient Toyota saloon car and a motorcycle. He made his way towards the front door, carefully avoiding a couple of wheelie bins and several black rubbish bags. It was not the ideal sort of place at which he would have chosen to stay, even in the short term, but he had no intention of staying there at all.

'Mrs Patel?' the man asked, when a woman opened the door in response to his knock. He immediately detected a strong smell of curry. Not that it bothered him; in fact he enjoyed a good curry, but he would not be taking advantage of the land-lady's culinary skills.

'Yes, I am Mrs Patel.' She was wearing a sari and her long shiny black hair was fashioned into a plait that, when she turned, he could see reached almost to her waist.

'I understand that you have a room to let.' The man extended a finger to indicate the advertisement in his folded newspaper.

'How long do you want a room for? It has to be at least a month otherwise it's not worth my while.' Mrs Patel looked searchingly at the man, as though assessing his ability to pay. But he was neatly dressed in a blazer and a collar and a striped tie, and that satisfied her. In fact, he appeared to be a little more respectable than most of her usual paying guests.

'It'll be at least a week, Mrs Patel, perhaps even a little longer.' The man told the lie easily.

'I'll show you the room,' said Mrs Patel, and led the way upstairs.

'Oh yes, this will do nicely,' said the man, having given the sparsely furnished bed-sitting room a cursory glance. That the accommodation comprised only a bed, a chair and a wash-hand basin didn't matter; it would serve the purpose for which he wanted it.

He agreed the rent with Mrs Patel and paid for a week in advance from a roll of banknotes. Mrs Patel gave him a rent book in which she had entered the man's name in block capitals together with the address. She took a large ledger from a drawer and made an entry in it. 'For the tax people,' she said, by way of explanation. 'We are very particular to keep good records.'

'Thank you, Mrs Patel.' The man put the rent book in his pocket. 'I just have to go to New Street station and collect my baggage. I'll see you later.' But he never returned.

Instead, he drove to a gun club, the address of which he'd found on the Internet.

The club secretary and the armourer were talking in the office when the man entered.

'Can I help you?' enquired the secretary, glancing up at the well-dressed man. The armourer particularly noticed the man's tie; it could have been that of an army regiment, but the armourer had been in the Royal Air Force and was not able to identify it.

'I'm considering applying for membership, if that's possible,' said the man.

'Always glad to recruit a new member,' said the secretary warmly, and took a form from a drawer in his desk. 'Just a few particulars and a chat with the armourer-instructor, and then you're in. Do you have anything to say who you are?'

As evidence of identity and place of abode, the man produced the rent book that Mrs Patel had given him.

The secretary recorded the applicant's name and address and returned the book. 'This is a very active club,' he said. 'We're open for practice most weekday evenings and on Saturdays and Sundays.'

'Have you handled firearms before?' asked the armourer.

'Yes, I was in the army,' said the man, preferring not to mention the circumstances under which he'd left.

'Good, but I still need to see if you can handle a weapon safely,' said the armourer. 'Perhaps you'd come out to the range.'

'Of course,' said the man, and followed the armourer. Once on the range, he took off his jacket and rolled up his sleeves.

The armourer unlocked a cabinet and handed the man a pistol.

'What sort of weapon is this?' asked the man, examining the pistol closely. 'I've never handled one of these before.'

'It's a Rohm Twinmaster Action CO2-charged air pistol.'

'Don't you have any proper automatics? A Walther or a Beretta perhaps?'

The armourer looked at the man and shook his head in disbelief. 'Being ex-military, I'd've thought you'd've known that the law doesn't allow us to hold automatic pistols that fire lethal ammunition. Not since the Dunblane massacre in 1996. It was that that caused the change, and the following year every lethal sort of handgun was banned. It's made life very difficult for anyone hoping to qualify for the Olympics.'

'I didn't know that. I've been abroad for quite a long time. Not that I'm much interested in the Olympics.' Disappointed, the man grasped the weapon in a two-handed grip and competently fired off a few shots. 'Thank you,' he said, as he returned the pistol.

'Well, you obviously know how to handle a firearm,' said the armourer, 'but if you want to fire automatic pistols, I'm afraid you'll have to go abroad to do it. Germany's a very good place, I'm told; they've got gun clubs all over the place. Practically every village has a club.'

'Germany, eh?' said the man thoughtfully. He had spent a lot of time there.

'See you again soon,' said the armourer, as he and the man returned to the secretary's office.

'Yes indeed,' said the man, but he never came back.

As it happened, the acquisition of a firearm did not turn out to be at all difficult. The man knew Germany well and he spoke the language with a reasonable degree of fluency.

The gun club he selected, within a short distance of Essen, welcomed him and enrolled him as a member after a few desultory enquiries that consisted of little more than glancing at his passport.

He attended the club's well-appointed range three or four times, but after that he was never seen again. It was only when the armourer checked the arsenal that he found that a point-two-two calibre High Standard Supermatic Trophy pistol was missing. The matter was reported at the local police station and details of the weapon were recorded on the national computer of the *Bundeskriminalamt*. But there the matter rested.

The man was slightly apprehensive when a customs officer took an interest in him at Harwich; usually they did not bother. In the event it turned out not to be a problem. The officer had asked the usual routine questions, poked about in the boot of the man's Volkswagen Polo, and sent him on his way. His only interest was in any excessive amount of alcohol or tobacco, or any drugs that the man might have had in his possession, but he found nothing of importance. He didn't examine the vehicle closely enough to discover that the pistol the man had stolen from the German gun club was secreted beneath the car, securely attached to the chassis.

Cyril Jefferson alighted from his car and opened the rear door. A large red setter jumped out and then stood waiting for his master.

'Off you go, Raffles,' said Jefferson.

The dog bounded off, tail wagging, lolloping across the grass towards a clump of trees. It was the route it followed every time that Jefferson took it to Richmond Park. Every so often the dog would stop and turn its head, waiting for Jefferson to catch up.

It was when he reached the edge of the group of trees that

Jefferson heard the sound. It was a noise like a cork being removed expertly and gently from a bottle of champagne, but that much louder. There followed two more similar sounds.

He moved closer, his curiosity aroused. In the centre of the group of trees he saw a man wearing an anorak with the hood raised. And he was firing a pistol at a tree.

The dog's sensitive hearing had heard the shots long before Jefferson, and it crouched and emitted a low growl. The man turned in panic, pocketed the pistol and ran very fast out of the cover of the trees, making his way towards the road.

'Heel, Raffles,' said Jefferson, fearful that the man would shoot his dog. The animal obeyed and Jefferson made his way quickly in the direction the man had run, but being careful to keep a safe distance. Nevertheless he lost sight of him. Moments later, he saw a car – he thought it was a Volkswagen Polo – driving out of the park at quite high speed. He was unable to see if it was the gunman driving it, but he did notice that one of the car's side windows was broken and the missing glass had been replaced with cardboard.

Being one of that rare breed, a concerned citizen, Jefferson took his mobile telephone from his pocket, called Kingston police station and told the operator what he had seen.

'Is the man still in the park, sir?' enquired the sergeant to whom the call had been transferred.

'I don't think so,' said Jefferson. 'When he heard my dog bark, he ran off. I did see a car, a Volkswagen Polo I think, leaving the park at high speed though, but I don't know if the driver was the man I'd seen with the pistol.'

'Did you happen to get the car's number, sir?' asked the sergeant.

'No, I'm sorry.'

'Well, thank you, sir, we'll make a note of the incident.' And that, as far as the Kingston police were concerned, was the end of the matter. People were always telephoning the police to report something they thought they'd seen.

The man parked his car outside a fashionable house in a street in Pimlico and mounted the steps to the front door. He looked around furtively before pressing a button on the intercom.

'Yes, who is it?' asked a woman's distorted voice.

'It's me,' said the man, hoping that the girl would recognize her caller. She did.

'Well, well, the wanderer returns, but if it's more money you want, darling, you're out of luck. The well's dried up.'

'Let me in, Lavinia, it's important,' said the man crouching over the intercom.

'It'd better be,' said Lavinia, and buzzed him in.

With a last surreptitious look around, the man entered the house and ran up the stairs.

'This had better be good, buster.' Lavinia stood in the doorway of her apartment. She was attired in a black jersey dress that stopped well above her knees and clung to her figure like it was glued on to every alluring curve.

'I'm in trouble,' said the man, following her into the seating area and flopping into a chair.

'So, what's new? D'you want coffee?'

'Please.'

'So, what's this big problem of yours?'

'I was doing a bit of target practice at a tree in Richmond Park and a guy saw me.'

'You were doing *what*?' Lavinia held the cafetière in the air in an act of suspended animation, and her eyes opened wide in a combination of surprise and disbelief. 'D'you mean you had a gun?'

'Of course I had a gun. What d'you think I was using, a bow and arrow?'

'What were you doing with a gun? And what the hell were you shooting at trees for? Have you got it in for trees all of a sudden?' Lavinia skirted the kitchenette counter and joined the man in the seating area, handing him a mug of coffee. 'Are you out of your mind?'

'Why I was doing it doesn't matter, and it doesn't concern you.'

'So, what the hell d'you want me to do about it, then?' Lavinia leaned back on the sofa, spreading her arms along the top and crossing her long legs.

'I could use some money,' said the man. 'How about a couple of hundred, Lavinia darling?'

'Oh the hell with you!' exclaimed Lavinia, but nevertheless took four fifty-pound notes from her handbag. 'There you are. And that's it. No more. Daddy doesn't approve of you and he doesn't approve of me keeping you.'

The man ignored that comment; he'd heard it all before. 'D'you think I could stay here just for a few days and lie low, darling?' he asked, swiftly pocketing the cash without a word of thanks.

'No, you bloody well can't, *darling*. You ran off once and you're not coming back. Anyway, I've got a new guy in my life now. And he's got his own money. And he drives a Ferrari.'

'Just for a day or two.' The man adopted a wheedling tone.

'No way.' Lavinia swept a hand through her long blonde hair. 'But you can screw me if you like, just for old time's sake.'

The man knocked at the door of 17 Clancy Street in a fashionable part of London's Paddington.

'Yes?' The Nigerian who answered the door peered into the gloom outside.

'Hello, Samson.'

'Oh, it's you.' Samson Adekunle looked at his caller and smiled. 'Have you come to take up my offer? We could certainly use you.'

'In a manner of speaking, Samson. We have certain matters to discuss.' The man produced a pistol and pointed it straight at Adekunle. 'I know how to use this, so step back inside and keep your hands where I can see them.'

'What on earth are you doing?' asked the panic-stricken Adekunle. Although adept at using the telephone to extract money from defenceless elderly people, he was not a physically brave man. His eyes widened in terror and he began slowly to walk backwards, his hands raised in the air. He would have been even more terrified if he'd known that he had less than an hour to live. And that that hour would be filled with unspeakable agony. But the man with the gun had a score to settle.

'We'll start with your computer, Samson,' said the man. 'There are a couple of our mutual friends I want to get in touch with: Hans Eberhardt and Trudi Schmidt.'

'I don't know where they are,' said Adekunle. 'I think they've moved house.' He glanced at the man's menacing pistol and knew instinctively that his lame denial was pointless. He was in little doubt that his assailant was pursuing a personal vendetta. When they had first met, Adekunle had convinced himself that this man was possessed of an uncontrollable streak of viciousness. He remembered what had happened when he'd lost his temper with a naked Trudi Schmidt, just because she'd teased him. And that brutality had terrified him then, and now terrified him even more because he suddenly realized why the man was here.

Forcing Adekunle into the kitchen, the man ordered him to bring one of the chairs back to the living room. Once there he instructed Adekunle to strip naked, before securing him to the chair with several lengths of rope that he took from a shoulder bag.

'And now, Samson, you're going to tell me all I need to know.'

'Like hell!' exclaimed Adekunle, but it was destined to be his last act of bravado.

Three days later, the man parked his car a yard or two away from the camper van. It was exactly where he had instructed the driver to park, on the grass verge and facing north, opposite 21 Bendview Road. That he had selected that address was merely coincidental; the man had no idea who lived there and cared even less. It just so happened that that was the house opposite a suitable grass verge.

Taking a jerrycan full of petrol from his car, he placed it on the grass close to the van. Creeping stealthily along the left-hand side of the vehicle he slid open the door to the rear of the driver's seat. Taking out his pistol, and moving rapidly he got in and sat down immediately behind the driver.

Hearing the noise, the driver turned in alarm. '*Wer sind sie?*' The sudden intrusion caused him to pose the question in his native language.

'Who *are* you?' translated the man mockingly. 'I'll tell you, my friend. Right now, I'm your worst enemy.'

The woman turned in her seat. 'My God, it's you,' she said in faultless but heavily accented English. 'What are you doing here?'

'I've come to settle a debt,' said the man, fitting a suppressor to his pistol. 'In a manner of speaking.' He fired a round into the back of the man's head.

The woman cried out in horror as the gun turned towards her. '*Nein, liebchen, bitte.*' But her plea was to no avail. Roughly seizing the woman's hair, the man turned her so that she was forced to look out of the windscreen. Then he fired a round into her head too. 'And that's for you, you whore,' he said. He had actually enjoyed killing Adekunle and these two.

Removing the suppressor from his pistol, he pocketed both. Gathering up the shell cases that had been ejected, he alighted from the camper van. Unscrewing the cap of the jerrycan, he spread its contents liberally over the interior of the vehicle and the two dead bodies. Finally he threw the jerrycan into the van, struck a match and ignited the fuel before returning to his car and driving away.

TWO

The sign on my office door informs any interested party that the occupant is DETECTIVE CHIEF INSPECTOR HARRY BROCK HSCC(W).

I'm attached to a unit called Homicide and Serious Crime Command West that has its headquarters at Curtis Green, a turning off Whitehall in central London and which was once a part of New Scotland Yard. But that was before our beloved parliamentarians claimed the building for themselves and shifted the police to a concrete pile in Broadway that has all the aesthetic charm of a grain silo. Not many people know the whereabouts of Curtis Green, including a large number of police officers, and we're responsible for investigating weighty crimes from Westminster to far-flung Hillingdon and all the dens of iniquity that lie in between.

So much for my professional side. As for my social life, what little there is of it, I'm in a wonderful relationship with a gorgeous blonde resting actress called Gail Sutton and we've been together for a few years now. I'd met her while investigating a murder at the theatre where she was working. The victim had been Gail's friend and fellow dancer.

As Gail and I had both been married before, we'd decided against risking matrimony again. We even lived apart; I had a flat in Surbiton and Gail lived in a townhouse, a mile or two away in Kingston, although I seemed to spend more time at her place than at my own.

Gail had been married to a theatre director called Gerald Andrews. I'd never met the guy, but from what Gail told me, he sounded a thoroughly dislikable character. However, the union had ended in divorce when, feeling unwell, she'd returned home early from Richmond Theatre one afternoon – she'd been appearing in a revival of Noël Coward's *Private Lives* – and surprised her husband in bed with an attractive young woman. The girl, an exotic dancer, usually performed in the nude and this occasion was no different. I'd often thought, since hearing the story, that Andrews must've been crazy to let a girl like Gail escape. Just to emphasize the separation, Gail had reverted to using her maiden name.

But with typical male chauvinism, Andrews had resented Gail's justifiable objection to his philandering – something that she'd long suspected – and had done his best ever since to thwart her attempts to get decent acting parts. Consequently, she'd been hoofing, as she called it, in the chorus line of a second rate revue called *Scatterbrain* when I met her.

My own tale of marital woe was a result of my marriage to Helga Büchner, a nymphomaniac German physiotherapist who'd massaged my shoulder back into working order after a physical confrontation with a gang of youths in Whitehall when I was a uniformed constable. Contrary to the predictions of my colleagues at the nick, the marriage – but not the nymphomania – lasted sixteen years. However, well before that a tragedy occurred that marked the beginning of the end.

Against my wishes, Helga had continued to work at the hospital after the birth of our son Robert. She had left him with a neighbour while she went to work, but the boy had fallen into the garden pond and drowned. He was four years of age.

The day that the superintendent had called me into his office to break the news is forever etched in my memory. The police are very good when it comes to personal tragedy.

'I've got some bad news for you, Harry,' said the superintendent. 'I'm afraid your son has died.' Without any frills, he went on to tell me exactly what had occurred, just as though he were giving evidence. But that's the way we coppers prefer it. 'Take as much time off as you need,' the superintendent had said. 'I'll square it with the guv'nor. Give me a bell if there's anything you want.'

The death of our son, together with the ensuing adultery on both sides, finally succeeded in cancelling out the promise of 'until death do us part'. It was inevitable really; Helga had been carrying on an affair with a doctor at the hospital for quite a few months before I found out. It was no comfort that a colleague told me that the husband is always the last one to find out.

The last murder in the HSCC West area of responsibility had fallen to a colleague of mine and I knew that I was next on the list. Consequently, I'd decided to take the weekend off secure in the knowledge that it would probably be the last free time I'd have for a while. I'd hoped to spend some of that time with Gail, but she'd gone to Nottingham to visit her parents George and Sally. George was a property developer whose only overt vice was an obsession with Formula One motor racing and the land speed record, both of which he talked about incessantly. Until his wife Sally, herself a former dancer, told him to shut up.

As a result I was condemned to spending my temporary freedom mooning about the flat, and doing some essential shopping in Kingston.

Strangely, and to a certain extent unnervingly, things continued to be very quiet for me. Murder and mayhem in that part of the capital for which HSCC West was responsible seemed to have died. To coin a phrase.

I took advantage of that lull to call Gail and suggest a quiet dinner somewhere.

We took a taxi from her place to a restaurant a few miles away that served good meals and had a decent wine list. We both knew it well and had been there on several occasions in the past.

'Ah, Mr Brock, how good to see you again,' said the unctuous proprietor, almost bowing. 'And you too, Miss Sutton. A table for two?'

The owner knew I was a police officer hence, I suspect, the excessive servility. He also claimed to have seen several of the shows in which Gail had appeared and was convinced he'd seen her on television, but she'd never appeared on TV. I'd come to the early conclusion that he was a consummate liar with an eye to the main chance: money and staying on the right side of the law. But he employed a first-rate chef and that was all that mattered.

'You seem to have had a lot of time on your hands recently, darling,' said Gail, once we were settled at a discreet table. A candle illuminated the space between us.

'Don't tempt providence,' I said, little knowing that she'd just tempted it once too often. We ordered an aperitif and mulled over the menu.

We enjoyed our meal, despite frequent solicitous enquiries from the proprietor wishing to know if we were satisfied. My only regret was that I could no longer complete my enjoyment with a cigarette. But Gail was unsympathetic; she was always encouraging me to give up the habit, even though she occasionally smoked herself.

'A nightcap at my place?' asked Gail.

I knew what that meant and readily agreed. Somehow, I finished up staying the night. Again.

On Thursday the seventeenth of July, a red and white California T5 Volkswagen camper van parked on a patch of grassland just off Bendview Road in Richmond, Surrey. The tourists, if that's what they were, had probably stopped there because the location afforded a magnificent panoramic view of the curve in the river Thames, from Richmond Bridge in the north to Marble Hill Park in the south.

The presence of the vehicle had first been noted by the crew of a patrolling police car at a quarter past eleven the previous night. The crew had paid it scant attention other than to note that lights were on behind the curtained windows. The driver's colleague saw that the van was rocking slightly and made a coarse comment.

At ten to one in the morning of Friday the eighteenth of July, the crew of the same police car received a call from the despatching sergeant at Richmond police station to a fire in the camper van they'd noticed earlier. Acknowledging the message, the operator turned on the blue lights and the driver accelerated away.

When the police car arrived the van was burning furiously, the flames leaping some ten feet into the night sky. The fire brigade was already in attendance, but despite the efforts of its crew little could be done to save the van or the occupants. By the time the firefighters had quelled the flames all that remained of the vehicle was a blackened burnt out shell with blown-out windows and deflated tyres. Black smoke still rose into the air and black flecks of debris were spirited away in the slight breeze.

And that's when it got complicated.

'Well, that's it, mate. We've done our bit,' said the fire chief, 'but you might be interested to know that there are a couple of charred bodies inside.'

'Wonderful,' said the police car driver, hands in pockets as he surveyed the smoking debris. 'That's all I need. We'll be lucky if we get off duty by seven.'

'Well, it's not my problem, pal. By the way, the van's got German number plates.'

'Even better,' said the PC. 'You're enjoying this, aren't you? Anything else to cheer me up?' he asked.

'Oh yes,' said the fire chief, laughing as he removed his helmet and wiped his brow with a grubby handkerchief, 'there seems to be a strong smell of petrol. More than I'd expect in the circumstances.'

'What are you suggesting?'

'Could've been started deliberately, but it would need an arson investigator to say for sure.'

'It's all too much for me, mate.' The policeman turned to his colleague. 'Better put in a call for the CID,' he said.

* * *

I just hate being woken up at half past three in the morning by my mobile phone playing a silly little tune. However, it's one of the penalties of my job that wherever I go, it goes. My late father tried to encourage me to become an accountant, but I knew that I'd've died of boredom if I'd pursued a career in bookkeeping. After leaving school, I spent three weary years as a clerk with a water company, but on my nineteenth birthday, I decided that the commercial world was not for me and I joined the Metropolitan Police. Even now I'm not sure I did the right thing, but I might as well hang in there for my pension.

Not that the old man was a great judge when it came to career choice; after a lifetime spent driving an Underground train on the Morden Line, he died of pulmonary emphysema four weeks into his retirement. He left me nothing but a pile of pornographic magazines, a clapped out vintage motorcycle and a crop of unpaid bills.

However, back to the present problem. Hoping to reach my wretched phone before it disturbed Gail I grabbed at it, but managed only to knock it to the floor.

'Damn the bloody thing!' I muttered, leaping out of bed, stubbing my toe, and only just restraining myself from using an obscene epithet.

'What *are* you doing, darling?' asked Gail in her sleepy, sexy voice as she turned and stretched sensuously. She always stretches sensuously.

'Trying to answer my bloody phone,' I said, as I scrabbled about on the floor in an attempt to find it. 'Harry Brock,' I snapped, having finally reunited myself with the small black box that is the bane of my life.

'It's Gavin Creasey, sir, at the incident room.'

'D'you know what bloody time it is, Gavin?' I asked, somewhat testily. Sitting naked on the floor with my back against a bedside cabinet is not a position conducive to good humour when conversing with a detective sergeant.

'Yes, sir, it's twenty-five to four. In the morning, that is.'

'I hope this is important, Gavin.'

'A burnt-out Volkswagen camper van has been found in Richmond, sir. There are two dead bodies inside. And you're next on the list.'

'Why should that concern me? It's just a fire, isn't it?' I was doing my best to avoid getting involved in this distant tragedy, hoping that it was an unfortunate accident, but I knew instinctively that I was on a hiding to nothing. 'What's the SP?' I asked, culling a useful bit of jargon from the sport of kings that, when used by a CID officer, was a request for the details.

Creasey explained, in a masterpiece of brevity, what had occurred, including the comment by the fire chief about an excess of petrol fumes. Then he added the crippler. 'The commander has directed that you investigate.'

That was all I needed. The day had started early and badly and could only get worse. The one redeeming feature was the thought of the commander being roused in the wee small hours, and the earbashing that he would undoubtedly have received from his harridan of a wife at being disturbed by something as trivial as a couple of dead bodies in a fire-ravaged camper van.

I'd never met Mrs Commander, but I'd seen her photograph on the commander's desk, and that was enough. I'd always regarded it as an awful warning against matrimony.

'Dave Poole is on his way, sir,' continued Creasey. 'Doctor Mortlock is the duty Home Office pathologist and he's en route to the scene as I speak. And I'm just about to raise DI Ebdon and the rest of the team.'

'Don't bother Miss Ebdon, Gavin. There's no point in all of us turning out, at least not yet,' I said. 'And arrange for a traffic car to pick me up,' I added, finally admitting that I was lumbered.

'Right, sir. Would you by any chance be at Miss Sutton's place?' Creasey enquired with cunningly feigned innocence.

'You know bloody well I am,' I said. It was an open secret among my team that I spent a lot of my time at Gail's house. And knowing how CID officers' minds worked they'd probably deduced that much of it was spent in her bed. And they'd be right.

'I've been called out, darling,' I said to Gail, who was now wide awake. 'It seems that a couple have been barbecued in a camper van in Richmond.'

'I'll make you a cup of tea,' said Gail, completely unfazed by this momentous announcement. Slipping out of bed completely naked apart from Chanel Cristalle, she sashayed across the bedroom and made for the door. Deliberately waggling her voluptuous derrière, she glanced over her shoulder and shot me a lascivious smile. I do wish she wouldn't do that just when I've been called out.

I drank my tea, pecked Gail on the cheek and left. Reluctantly.

'Mr Brock is it?' asked the traffic car driver, as I sleepwalked out of Gail's house.

'That's me.'

'Where to, guv?'

'Bendview Road, Richmond.'

The traffic guys, known to us of *the Department* as the Black Rats, got me to my destination in a hair-raising siren-filled seven minutes.

'Sorry it took so long, guv,' said the driver, grinning broadly. 'Always have to be a bit careful at night. People tend to take chances, jumping traffic lights and that sort of thing.'

'Yeah, thanks a bundle,' I said, shakily alighting from the car. If the journey had taken less time, it would've been positively suicidal. I know I shouldn't have worried – the Met's drivers are among the finest in the world – but I'm only human despite what my subordinates might tell you.

The road had been closed and police officers, male and female, normally scarce during the daytime, seemed to be there in abundance, most of them doing not very much.

'And you are?' An officious uniformed inspector approached me clutching a clipboard and waggling a pen. He was what the Metropolitan Police likes to style 'the incident officer'.

'Detective Chief Inspector Brock, HSCC West,' I said.

'Right, sir.' The inspector carefully recorded my details without which an investigation couldn't possibly begin. Once again, I reflected that solving crime is easy, but paperwork's the tricky bit. 'Your people are already here, sir,' he added helpfully.

'I should hope so,' I muttered, ducking under the inner tape.

'Morning, guv,' said Dave Poole, all bright and perky as usual.

Of Caribbean origin, Detective Sergeant Poole is my assistant, what in the trade we call a bag-carrier. What I don't think of, he does, and we enjoy an excellent working relationship, unlike that invention of fiction, the oppressive senior officer who is always rude to his subordinates. That most definitely does not work in practice.

Not that all senior officers are as agreeable as me; in some I've known the similarity to an orang-utan springs to mind: the higher they go the more of their less attractive features become apparent. Even so, an overbearing senior officer will often dig himself a big hole while his acolytes stand round silently waiting for him to fall into it. But in Dave's case he frequently spotted something I'd missed, thereby saving me a great deal of aggro, to say nothing of veiled hints from the commander of neglect of duty.

Dave's grandfather came to this country from Jamaica in the fifties and set up practice as a doctor in Bethnal Green, and Dave's father was a chartered accountant. But Dave, after graduating in English from London University, spurned a professional career and decided to become a policeman thus making him, in his own words, the black sheep of the family. He then compounded the offence by marrying a delightful white girl called Madeleine who is a principal dancer with the Royal Ballet. The suggestion that Madeleine occasionally assaulted Dave was put down to canteen scuttlebutt. Dave is six-foot tall and well-built, whereas his wife is a petite five-two. Nevertheless, ballet dancers are renowned for their strength, so perhaps . . .

'How far have we got, Dave?'

'Not very far, guv. Doctor Mortlock's just finished poking about.' Dave indicated a black saloon car parked behind an ambulance, the presence of which was clearly unnecessary. Unless, that is, a callow young policeman happened to faint from the sight of dead bodies. It never seemed to affect the women officers; they just gritted their teeth and got on with the job.

'Good morning, Henry.' Mortlock, our pet forensic pathologist, was sitting in his car making notes. I slid into the passenger seat beside him.

'There's nothing bloody good about it,' muttered Mortlock testily, 'and before you ask, I can't tell you a thing, other than that both bodies are well and truly done to a turn. What the French would call *bien cuit*. I'll need to get them on the slab before I can come up with anything. Try to get your people to move them in one piece, there's a good chap. From the state of them they'll likely fall apart when they start to shift them, and it's a bloody nuisance trying to put them together again.'

'When are you going to do the post-mortem?' I asked.

'This afternoon, I suppose. Once I've had some sleep.' And with that pithy rejoinder, Mortlock whistled a few snatches from some obscure aria, started the engine and drove off. I only just managed to get out of his car in time.

'I understand that this job's all yours, guv.' The local detective inspector looked extremely pleased with himself, presumably because he was aware that what had all the signs of being a tortuous investigation had been taken over by HSCC.

'Yes, it is,' I said. 'What do we know?'

'Couple of bodies seriously overcooked, but we haven't found any ID so far. By the way, the camper van's got German number plates. The index starts off with a letter E and the dealership's details on them show it was supplied by a firm in Essen, so I suppose that's where it's registered.' The DI was obviously a detective who quickly got to grips with the basics.

'Thanks very much,' I said with a hint of sarcasm. It was as well that I spoke German fluently, the only advantage of my marriage to Helga, because it looked as though I was going to need it. 'Who called the fire brigade?'

'A man called Guy Wilson at number 21.' The DI pointed at a house opposite the scene of my latest investigation.

'Anyone spoken to him?'

'Not as yet, guv. By the way, the fire brigade reckoned there was an excess of petrol fumes. The chief thinks the fire was started deliberately.'

'Yes,' I said. 'That much I've heard.'

Making a mental note to have Wilson interviewed later in the day, I crossed to the camper van and gave it a cursory visual examination. There was nothing much to see beyond what I'd been told already. The fire had left little of the van's interior intact, so much so that there was hardly anything to learn just by looking at it. Two blackened corpses, their sex not immediately apparent, occupied the front seats and from their posture appeared to have been overtaken by the flames before they could do anything. A strong odour of petrol still pervaded the air, but given what the fire chief had said that was to be expected.

The presence of an abandoned jerrycan on one of the rear seats caused me to wonder why it was there and why the cap was open. Not for the first time I was to discover that things aren't always as they seem.

A smart white van had been parked just inside the tapes. It was emblazoned with the words EVIDENCE RECOVERY UNIT, a snazzy slogan doubtless created by the boy superintendents who staff the funny names and total confusion squad at the Yard.

Linda Mitchell, the senior forensic practitioner, walked across to join me. Unlike the crime scene investigators in American television shows, she was not wearing high-heeled shoes or attired in one of the latest designer creations to emerge from New York. Neither had she come straight from a fashionable hairdressing boutique. She was instead dressed in unflattering white coveralls. 'Is it all right for me to make a start, Mr Brock?'

'By all means, Linda,' I said, 'but from what Doctor Mortlock said, I doubt you'll find very much.'

'He's a pathologist, not a forensic scientist,' said Linda dismissively. 'And unlike TV, he doesn't try to do my job and I don't try to do his.' This was a sharp and uncharacteristic reaction from the normally equable Linda, and I got the impression that she was no happier than the rest of us at having been called out this early in the morning.

But on this occasion, Mortlock was right. Very nearly.

'There's nothing we can do until we get the vehicle to the lab, Mr Brock,' said Linda, having made a brief visual examination of what remained of the camper van and its gruesome contents. 'I'll arrange for a low-loader to take it to the Amelia Street lab in Walworth. I think the best idea would be to move it as it is, bodies and all, and then they can be shifted to the mortuary in sterile conditions.'

I wasn't about to argue with that, and it would mean less hanging about in Richmond, even on a warm summer's morning as this one was turning out to be. The first fingers of dawn had already crept over the eastern sky.

THREE

'd decided to go straight to the office and Dave and I arrived at about seven o'clock. Dave immediately disappeared to rustle up two cups of coffee.

My first job was to establish the identity of the two bodies that had been found in the camper van. I presumed that any identification documents the couple might have had were destroyed in the blaze. I set Gavin Creasey the task of finding the telephone number of the Essen police in North Rhine Westphalia.

A few minutes later, I was talking to their duty officer, *Kriminalhauptkommissar* Horst Fischer, and told him who I was and what little we knew of the two deaths that were about to occupy a great deal of my time.

'Perhaps you would give me a description of this vehicle, *Herr* Chief Inspector,' said Fischer, 'and its registration details.'

'Ah! One moment.' I paused, realizing that I'd started the conversation without having this vital piece of information to hand. But fortunately Dave handed me a slip of paper on which were the requisite particulars. As I've already mentioned, he thinks of things I don't. 'It's a red and white Volkswagen California T5, *Hauptkommissar,*' I said, and gave the Essen policeman the registration details.

'One moment, *Herr* Chief Inspector, while I interrogate my computer,' said Fischer.

I heard the telltale tapping of keys and twenty seconds later Fischer came back with the information.

'The Volkswagen is registered to a *Herr* Wilhelm Weber. According to our computer, he lives with his wife Anna in Kettwig. I will give you their address.'

Although I would never have admitted it to Helga, you've got to go a long way to beat German efficiency.

'Whereabouts is this place Kettwig?' I asked, as I wrote down the names and addresses.

'It is a town on the Ruhr between here and Düsseldorf, but it is part of outer Essen, a suburb if you like.' I wasn't surprised I'd not heard of it. My visits to Germany had been confined to Cologne, where my ex-wife Helga came from, and I'd only been there a couple of times to visit her parents. And that was under duress. The Büchners were not the most likeable of people and regarded a lowly British uniformed constable as a highly unsuitable match for their daughter. In the fullness of time that became my view too.

'Are you able to contact the Webers' next of kin, *Hauptkommissar*,' I asked, 'and inform them of the deaths of Wilhelm and Anna Weber? Assuming that's who they are.'

'It will be done immediately. I will call you back.' Fischer paused. 'You speak excellent German, *Herr* Brock,' he said eventually, and somewhat hesitantly.

'Thank you, *Herr* Fischer.' I forbore from telling him that fluency in his language was the only benefit of my marriage to Helga. On reflection it would've been cheaper to have gone to night school. I replaced the receiver.

'Got a result, guv?' asked Dave.

'Of sorts, Dave,' I said. 'At least we know who the dead people are.' But that assumption proved to be short-lived.

I decided it was time that Dave and I had some breakfast. An empty stomach is definitely a drawback when it comes to investigating suspicious deaths.

Deciding on a brisk walk, we cut across Parliament Square and into Victoria Street where we adjourned to the upstairs restaurant of the Albert public house. I had breakfasted there many times and knew that we'd be assured of a good meal.

Contrary to prevailing dietary advice, and sly hints from Gail, I indulged in their excellent kedgeree, bacon and eggs with mushrooms, hash browns, and freshly brewed coffee. But Dave appeared to be consuming twice as much as me. It's a wonder that he manages to keep so slim, but he'd probably say that it's because he's always running about after me.

Now replete and more or less ready for the inevitable long day ahead, we returned at half past eight. Kate Ebdon and the rest of the team had arrived and were catching up on the night's events.

Detective Inspector Kate Ebdon is a flame-haired Australian who had come to HSCC on promotion from the Flying Squad. It was strongly rumoured that she had given pleasure to a number of the Squad's officers, male ones of course, but you shouldn't believe everything that policemen tell you.

Kate usually dresses rather provocatively in tight-fitting jeans, a man's white shirt that strains at the buttons, and high heels. It's a mode of attire that displeases our beloved commander, but he hasn't the bottle to tell her. When she first arrived at HSCC he asked me to have a word with her about her dress, but I pointed out that it could amount to sexism or even racism, given that she hailed from the Antipodes. The commander is very keen on diversity, whatever he means by that, and the matter was quietly dropped. That said Kate can turn out in a stunning and very feminine outfit when she gives evidence at the Old Bailey. She certainly knows how to charm the menfolk, and although that includes High Court judges, she doesn't seem to have much sexual impact on the commander.

I explained to the team what we had learned so far, but everything now hinged on Henry Mortlock's findings at the post-mortem, and what the fire brigade's arson investigator had to say about the cause of the conflagration. Until we had that essential information, together with Linda Mitchell's input, there wasn't a great deal more we could do, except to start on a few local enquiries.

'Kate, would you arrange for house-to-house enquiries in the area. Get someone to start with a local resident named Guy Wilson who called the brigade. Dave will give you the address.'

'I'll speak to him myself, guv,' said Kate. 'He might have something important to tell us as his house is right opposite the scene of the incident.'

By now, Detective Sergeant Colin Wilberforce, the day-duty incident room manager, had arrived. He immediately set about organizing everything, as only he can do. Wilberforce is an absolute wizard at office work and it'll be a sad day if he ever gets promoted and is transferred. His desk is a classic example of administrative efficiency; even his pens and pencils are arranged with military precision. And God help anyone, including me, who interfered with his little empire.

At midday, Wilberforce came into my office. 'I've just had a call from Linda Mitchell, sir. The remains of the bodies have been delivered to the Horseferry Road mortuary.'

'A bite of lunch, Dave,' I said, 'and then we'll be off to Henry's carvery.'

Dr Henry Mortlock was sitting at his desk tapping away at his computer when Dave and I arrived at the mortuary.

'When are you going to start, Henry?' I asked.

'I've finished, dear boy,' said Mortlock, swinging round on his office chair, 'and you'll be delighted to learn that both your victims – a man and a woman – had been shot. A single round to the back of the head in each case. But there was no exit wound. A low calibre bullet, I should imagine.'

'Oh bloody hell!' I exclaimed. Two suspicious deaths had now become a double murder enquiry.

Mortlock afforded me an owlish grin. 'I was lucky to find the rounds,' he said, pointing at a kidney-shaped bowl containing two bullets, 'given the state of the bodies.'

'I almost wish you hadn't,' I said. 'So it wasn't the fire that killed them.'

'I thought that's what I just said.' Mortlock shot me the sort of patronizing glance that forensic pathologists reserve for explaining things to thick coppers.

'Any chance of getting a DNA sample, Henry?' I asked.

'That shouldn't be a problem, Harry. How lucky can you get, eh?' Mortlock peered at me over his spectacles. 'But there's not a cat in hell's chance of getting fingerprints. There isn't much left of the fingers.'

At four o'clock, I received another telephone call from the highly efficient Horst Fischer of the Essen police.

'*Herr* Brock, I have some interesting news for you. One of my officers called first at the Webers' address in case there were relatives who shared the house with them. But Wilhelm and Anna Weber were there, as alive as you and me.'

'The bodies we found were not the Webers, then?' I said, half to myself.

'That is so, *Herr* Brock,' said Fischer, politely avoiding any hint of sarcasm. 'It seems that *Herr* Weber lent his Volkswagen camper van to a friend of his. This friend was called Hans Eberhardt.'

'It looks as though he's our victim, then.'

'I would think that is a possibility.'

'And was Eberhardt's wife the woman who was with him?'

'Not as far as we know. *Herr* Weber does not think that Eberhardt was married. He believes the female to be *Fräulein* Trudi Schmidt, a girlfriend of Eberhardt. We are now trying to trace this couple's next of kin to inform them of the tragic accident. There is likely to be some delay because *Herr* Weber does not know of any relatives of either Hans Eberhardt or Trudi Schmidt.'

'I see.' I paused before committing myself, but I was talking to another copper and there is a trust between policemen, no matter what their nationality. 'I'd be grateful if you kept this to yourself for the time being, *Herr* Fischer,' I said, 'but we now have evidence that this couple had been murdered.'

'Are you able to give me the details, *Herr* Brock?' Fischer responded calmly to this announcement, as though it came as no surprise.

'Yes, the pathologist found that each of the people in this Volkswagen had been shot, killed by a single round to the head.'

'It sounds very much like an execution, a revenge killing perhaps,' said Fischer. 'I shall find out what I can about this Eberhardt, discreetly of course, and keep you informed.'

'Thank you for your assistance, *Herr* Fischer,' I said. 'I'll keep you up to date with our investigation.'

'One other thing, *Herr* Brock . . .'

'Yes?'

'Is it possible to obtain a DNA sample from the bodies of your victims? Just to be certain of the identification. Also we might have a record of these people in our DNA database.'

'They were badly burned, but the pathologist said that he is fairly confident. There's no possibility of obtaining fingerprints though.'

'That is hardly surprising in the circumstances, but thank you. If there is anything else we can do to assist from this end, please tell me.'

'Does this mean a trip to Germany?' asked Dave, once I'd finished talking to Fischer.

'I doubt that the commander would sanction it,' I said.

'The DAC might though.' Dave obviously knew, as did I, that the commander had a fear of making such a decision without reference to higher authority. Or, for that matter, any decision.

FOUR

Three hours after *Kriminalhauptkommissar* Horst Fischer's last phone call, I received another from him. I was not surprised to find that he was still on duty. Having been saddled with my enquiry in the first place it was obvious that he was now seeing it through. Like me, he was a detective, and once tasked with a job our periods of duty knew no bounds.

'There are some interesting developments, *Herr* Brock. After we spoke earlier, I learned from our records that Hans Eberhardt is of interest to this department.'

'Oh, in what way?'

'He has a criminal record, *Herr* Brock. Three years ago he was before the court in Düsseldorf for being a confidence trickster. He was imprisoned for eighteen months for selling tickets for a lottery that did not exist. But now it would seem that he has moved up in the world; into what I think the Americans call "the big time". We visited his house today and of course received no reply. I empowered my officers to force an entry and we found what you would call an Aladdin's cave.'

'D'you mean you found stolen property, *Herr* Fischer?'

'No, a sophisticated printing press.'

'Is he a forger, then?'

'Yes, but in a specialized way, you understand. In the basement we found a great many forged share certificates, and the printing press was for producing them. It looks as though he is making a lot of money from selling bogus shares. On his computer we have found what could possibly be a list of those persons he has defrauded, but it appears to be in some sort of code. One of our technicians is passing the details to the *Bundesamt für Verfassungsschutz.*' Fischer paused. 'You know of this organization perhaps, *Herr* Brock?'

'Yes, I do. The *BfV* is your counter-espionage service, is it not?'

'Exactly so. We are hoping that one of their cryptanalysts will be able to decode the list. By the way, we have also arrested Wilhelm Weber, the man who owns the van and lent it to Eberhardt. He is a businessman here in Germany.'

'Is he involved in this share forging business, then?' I was surprised at Weber's arrest. Fischer had previously mentioned that Weber had lent his camper van to Eberhardt, but it now looked as though the German police suspected that he might be connected in some way to Eberhardt's criminal pursuits.

'Maybe, maybe not, but we are interrogating him all the same. It seems unlikely that he was in ignorance of Eberhardt's activities, but he is making strong denials. All he has told us so far is that his friend Eberhardt went several times to the Bahamas. But he claims to know nothing of the fraudulent share certificates.' Fischer paused, ominously I thought. 'Perhaps he tells the truth, but we shall see.'

From what little I knew of the German police, I imagined them to be very good at interrogation. 'What about Trudi Schmidt?' I asked.

Fischer chuckled. 'Ah, yes, Trudi Schmidt. She too is known to us and also to our colleagues in Hamburg. We understand from the Vice Squad there that she was a dancer in a nightclub on the Reeperbahn in Hamburg. You know of this area?'

'I've heard of it, *Herr* Fischer.' The Reeperbahn is the infamous red light district of Hamburg and most people with even a slight knowledge of Germany know of its existence and what goes on there. I'd even suggested taking a holiday in Hamburg with Gail so that we could see it, but she obviously knew of the area's reputation and promptly vetoed the idea.

'But we have also heard that Trudi Schmidt was arrested several times for unlicensed prostitution in Hamburg and also in Essen after she moved here.'

No surprise there, I thought. The terms nightclub dancer and prostitute are often synonymous, but it was news to me that the Germans licensed their hookers.

'Did she live with Eberhardt?'

'We don't think so. There was no sign of female habitation in Eberhardt's house – no women's clothing, cosmetics or anything like that – but we are still making enquiries. It is possible that we shall find her fingerprints there.' Fischer paused. 'Are you thinking of coming to Germany to see for yourself, *Herr* Brock?'

'Not at this stage,' I said, 'but it might become necessary at some time in the future.'

'You will be most welcome.'

'Incidentally, our pathologist *was* able to get DNA samples from the victims. I'll have the readings sent to you.'

'Thank you. We are satisfied that the two people you have in your mortuary are Eberhardt and Schmidt, but the DNA would confirm it. Now then, you will wish to know of the travel arrangements of Eberhardt, I think. On the computer of Hans Eberhardt we found booking details of his journey to England. He and Trudi Schmidt were booked on the overnight ferry from the Hook of Holland to Harwich on Tuesday the sixteenth of July. The registration number of the van on the ferry company's computer was the same as the one you have found on the burnt out Volkswagen.'

'They must've travelled overland, then,' I said. It was more of a conclusion than a question.

'Yes. One supposes that Eberhardt drove from Essen to the Hook of Holland, about two hundred and sixty kilometres. There must have been a good reason for his journey to England, but *Herr* Weber was not told of this. In fact, he did not even know the van was to be taken abroad. But I don't believe him. A vehicle could not be taken out of the country without the necessary documentation which Weber would have had to provide.' Fischer emitted a throaty chuckle. '*Herr* Weber is very upset about the loss of his van. Apparently he and his wife had intended to use it for a holiday in Bayreuth next month. But this statement was perhaps what you would call a smokescreen.'

'I imagine he would be upset,' I said, although in all honesty

I couldn't've cared less. In fact it would've been far better for me if he *hadn't* lent Eberhardt his damned van. 'That means that Eberhardt and Schmidt arrived here the day before they were murdered, although it was actually ten minutes into the next day,' I said, aware that the Germans were sticklers for accuracy. 'Were there any details of a hotel booking in England on the computer, *Herr* Fischer?' I doubted it, but a search of a hotel room might yield something useful.

'No, but as they were using *Herr* Weber's camper van, I imagine that they intended to live in that. Perhaps being a criminal Eberhardt was in your country to commit a crime and did not wish to leave a trace of his movements in England.'

'I think that's very likely.' Leaving a paper trail was something that criminals generally preferred to avoid whenever possible; particularly if they were embarking on a criminal enterprise.

'But I do not think that to be the case,' said Fischer. 'It would seem that an email was sent from a man called Adekunle to Eberhardt's computer at oh-nine-thirty on Tuesday the fifteenth of July, in which it was said that Eberhardt should come to England urgently. This man Adekunle said that something very serious had occurred that Eberhardt could only deal with in person. Without going into details, it was suggested that someone had been milking his account in Lichtenstein.' Fischer paused for a moment. 'It also said that Eberhardt shouldn't stay anywhere that could be traced. I suppose that's why he borrowed the camper van.'

'Was that email in English, *Herr* Fischer?'

'Yes, it was, *Herr* Brock.'

'And was there a reply?'

'Within half an hour. Eberhardt emailed back to say that he would arrive in the UK on Thursday the seventeenth of July in a camper van, and asked where he should meet Adekunle. He also asked a question about the Lichtenstein account, but there was no reply.'

'I wonder who this Adekunle is,' I said, half to myself.

'I can't help you there, *Herr* Brock, but after the first email there was another one from Adekunle telling Eberhardt that under no circumstances should he come to Adekunle's house.

He then went on to specify that Eberhardt should park in Richmond,' continued Fischer, 'and gave an address: number twenty-one Bendview Road, as the one opposite which he should park for the night.'

'It looks as though this Adekunle might've committed my two murders,' I said.

'*Ja*, perhaps so. Are you any further with your investigation, *Herr* Brock?'

'Not yet, *Herr* Fischer, but your information will be a great help to me.'

'Perhaps it was gang warfare. I understand that you have gangs in London. We have them also in Germany.'

'There are a few, certainly, but these are early days. At the moment we don't know why they were murdered. I'll keep you informed of our progress, *Herr* Fischer,' I said, hoping that there would be some progress to report. 'By the way, my name's Harry.' I wasn't sure whether it was a good idea to mention that; Germans are often much too formal to use first names until they've known you for some time.

But Fischer wasn't one of them.

'OK, Harry. I'm Horst. If you come to Germany we'll have a few beers in my favourite *Gasthof*, *ja*?'

'You can bet on it, Horst,' I said, and we left it at that for the time being.

'Mr Wilson?'

'Yes, I'm Guy Wilson.' Smiling with the air of a serial womanizer Wilson slowly appraised the attractive flame-haired young woman in jeans and a white shirt. 'Hello,' he drawled.

'I'm a police officer, Mr Wilson,' said Kate sharply, and produced her warrant card. She'd met men like this before, many times. 'Detective Inspector Ebdon of New Scotland Yard.'

'Oh!' Wilson's smile faded immediately. 'It'll be about the fire in that camper van, I suppose. You'd better come in, Inspector.' He escorted Kate into the elegant front room of his house. 'Please take a seat.' He indicated a luxurious sofa with a wave of his hand, but remained standing in front of an ornate York stone fireplace.

'I understand that it was you who called the fire brigade, Mr

Wilson.' Kate settled herself into the sofa, crossed her legs and took out her pocketbook. 'Perhaps you'd start by telling me how you came to notice it? It was quite late, I believe.' She knew the exact time that the fire brigade had been called, but always wanted to hear what a witness had to say. She'd come across variations before, but the fire brigade was as accurate as the police when it came to recording times and details of incidents.

'It was just after midnight, if I remember correctly. I'd been doing some cataloguing.' Wilson paused. 'I deal in antique books,' he added diffidently and shrugged, almost as though it was something he was ashamed of. 'There's always a lot of catching up to do when one has clients worldwide as I do. That's why I was working late.'

'Yes, go on.' Kate glanced up from her pocketbook. If Wilson had expected her to say what an interesting job he must have, he was disappointed.

'I'd been working in my study at the back of the house, and I'd noticed this camper van parked there earlier, maybe around eight or nine o'clock.'

'If you were working in the back of the house, how was it that you saw the van, Mr Wilson?' Kate stared quizzically at him.

'Ah, yes, I see what you mean.' Wilson rapidly concluded that this woman police officer was not only attractive, but had a very quick brain as well. 'I'd come in here to check on one of my more valuable books that I keep in the safe.' Wilson waved a hand at an oak cupboard on the far wall. It didn't look very secure, but Ebdon was not here to offer crime-prevention advice. 'Anyway, as I said, I saw the van and thought about ringing the police to make a complaint. We have a good view of the river from this house and I don't like seeing just anyone parking there, least of all travellers or gypsies, or whatever they were. Well, none of us around here likes to see that sort of thing. People who seem to be camping tend to lower the tone of the neighbourhood, if you see what I mean. They're prone to leave rubbish strewn about and God knows what else.'

Kate Ebdon thought that Wilson's attitude was fairly typical of the people who lived in the area. He had the unmistakable

air of an insufferable snob who was inclined to ostentation.
Although he was expensively dressed in an orange shirt, designer
chinos and a pair of Loake Anvil boots, his shirtsleeves were
rolled to the elbows to display a chunky gold Rolex watch.
Furthermore, Kate was convinced that he dyed his hair and,
gravest crime of all in her opinion, he sported a gold neck chain.

'But then, I presume, you had another look. Later on.'

'Yes. If the van was still there, I certainly *did* intend to lodge
a complaint. But in view of what happened, I wish I had. I
might have prevented it.' Wilson spread his hands, as if to
apologize for his previous boorish attitude. 'Did the people in
the van manage to escape?'

'No, Mr Wilson, they were burned alive,' said Kate, forbearing
to mention that they had in fact been murdered. She had not
intended that her statement should sound so dramatic, but that
was the effect it had.

'Oh my God, how awful.' Wilson contrived to look guilty,
but it was not convincing. 'If only I had complained, I might've
prevented it,' he said again.

'Was there anything else that caught your attention when you
were looking at this vehicle?'

'No, there wasn't, apart from the fact that the van was rocking
slightly.' Wilson paused and his lascivious smile returned. 'I
wonder what they were doing,' he said, half to himself.

But his sexist comment evinced no response from Kate, not
even a smile. 'Anything else?'

'I don't think so. Oh, just a minute though . . .' Wilson clicked
his fingers. 'I did see the van again at about midnight it must've
been. I'd come into this room to pour myself a Scotch, and I
saw a car pulling away.'

'Can you describe it?'

'It was a small car, a family saloon, I suppose you'd call it,
and it was a sort of silver-grey. As there was a bright moon last
night it showed up quite clearly.'

'I don't suppose you got the number or the make of this
vehicle.' Kate's tone was almost accusing.

'No, I couldn't see the number, and all small cars look much
the same to me.' Wilson afforded Kate a smile that was a carefully contrived combination of apology and condescension. This

woman inspector's incisive questioning was succeeding in making him feel quite inadequate; an unusual emotion for him when he was talking to women. But this attractive young police officer was not reacting to him as attractive women usually did, and that hurt his ego. He had always assumed that his charm and his ability to 'pull a bird', as he put it, was irresistible.

'But you came back into this room ten minutes later, and that was when you saw the fire. Why did you return here so soon?'

'To refill my glass,' said Wilson. 'Er, would you like a drink, Inspector?'

'Thank you for your assistance, Mr Wilson,' said Kate, ignoring Wilson's offer as she rose to leave. 'You may be called to the inquest, in which case I'll inform you of the date.'

'Will there be anything about this business in the newspapers, Inspector?' Wilson suddenly assumed a concerned look.

'Probably.' Kate had the impression that such publicity would not be to Wilson's liking, perhaps fearing that his comments about disliking 'travellers and gypsies' might be repeated in court. And they certainly would be if she had the opportunity to repeat them.

The murderer opened the newspaper and eventually found what he was looking for. At the bottom of page seven there was a small article headed TRAGIC FIRE; the byline read *by our own reporter*. It went on to report that a fire in a Volkswagen camper van in Richmond in the early hours of Friday the eighteenth of July had claimed the lives of its two occupants. It is believed, the article continued, that they were a German couple on holiday in the United Kingdom and that the gas canister in the vehicle had exploded with fatal results. The murderer was not to know that the piece about the gas canister was pure supposition on the reporter's part.

He folded the newspaper and smiled in satisfaction. There now seemed no way in which the bumbling police would connect him to the incident.

FIVE

On Saturday morning, Linda Mitchell, dressed in jeans and a tee shirt, arrived in the incident room.

'There's nothing to report that's of much use, I'm afraid, Mr Brock. There were no fingerprints in the vehicle itself that were capable of comparison, neither were there any shell casings, which points to a revolver having been used. Or a careful killer. Unfortunately the fire consumed any useful evidence there might have been, except for a mobile phone in one of the man's pockets.'

'D'you think that you'll be able to get anything from it, Linda?'

'We'll certainly give it our best shot. I've sent it to the lab at Surbiton in the hope that they may be able to develop some latent fingerprints. And we'll see if they can turn up any useful numbers if the SIM card has survived. Insofar as the rounds that were recovered by Dr Mortlock are concerned, they weren't misshapen, and the ballistics examiner is positive that they're point-two-two calibre. If the weapon is recovered, she should be able to prove that the rounds came from it, sufficient to satisfy a court.'

'That's assuming we ever get to court,' commented Dave gloomily.

'Did the ballistics examiner suggest a particular weapon that the rounds might've come from, Linda?' I asked, even though it was hoping for a lot. But this murder was beginning to look like one of those cases that would remain forever open and ongoing, as we say in the Job when we can't solve it and have more or less given up.

'She seemed to think that it might be a competition weapon, the sort that is used by members of gun clubs,' said Linda.

'But ownership of such weapons is illegal, ever since the Dunblane massacre. Even gun clubs aren't allowed to hold that sort of weapon.'

'Perhaps the killer bought it from an underworld armourer, guv,' suggested Dave. 'Either that or the weapon was illegally held after the type was banned. Of course, it could've been nicked. That's assuming, of course, that Eberhardt and Schmidt were murdered by someone living in this country. Like this Adekunle guy that Mr Fischer mentioned.'

'Don't complicate things, Dave,' I said, even though I suspected he might be right.

'I've also got the fire brigade's arson investigator's report here,' Linda continued. 'He's prepared to give evidence that an accelerant was definitely used, almost certainly petrol, and probably about twenty litres.'

'What's that in English?' asked Dave.

Linda gave Dave a disparaging glance. 'About four and a half gallons,' she said.

'I wonder if the killer brought petrol with him,' I mused aloud.

'I don't think so, Mr Brock,' said Linda. 'We found an empty can in the camper. But there were no fingerprints on it,' she added, before I could ask.

'Yes, I noticed the can,' I said, 'but the cap was open.'

'Yes it was,' said Linda, 'but fire does peculiar things to evidence. It could've been left there by the killer, though,' she added, as an obvious afterthought.

'We're going to have fun with this one,' said Dave, expressing what I was thinking, although 'fun' wasn't exactly the word I'd've used.

It all now depended on what further information Horst Fischer had for us. It looked as though a trip to Germany wasn't out of the question after all, but that was something I'd have to take up with our beloved commander at a later date.

As Linda left the office, she almost collided with Kate Ebdon on her way in.

'I've seen Guy Wilson, guv. He was the man who lived opposite the scene of the fire, and who called the fire brigade.'

'Did he have anything useful to say?' I asked.

'Of sorts,' said Kate, accepting my offer to sit down in my only available armchair. 'About ten minutes before he saw that the camper van was on fire, he claims to have seen a car driving away from the scene. The best he could do was to describe it as a silver-grey family saloon. No index mark, nothing.'

'To be expected, I suppose, and he probably wouldn't be able to recognize it again.'

'Not a chance,' said Kate.

'Anything else?'

'Yes, he was a self-opinionated galah.'

Later that day, Horst Fischer came up with more information.

'I've just received an email from the German police officer in Essen, sir,' said Colin Wilberforce, handing me the printout as he entered my office.

'Is it good news?' I asked, although I didn't hold out much hope.

'I wouldn't know, sir, it's all in German,' said Wilberforce.

'Fischer was getting the German counter-espionage service to decode a list he'd found on Eberhardt's computer,' I said, running my eye over the email. 'He thought it might contain details of Eberhardt's targets and it appears from this that they succeeded.'

The list contained over twenty names of people in the United Kingdom who had been swindled by Eberhardt. Nine of them were in the Greater London area, five in Birmingham and five in Manchester. The rest were scattered around the country, but that there were none in Scotland didn't surprise me. The Scots are a canny lot. Fischer went on to say that he had omitted the names of people in other parts of the world, but was willing to forward them if I felt we needed them.

I walked out to the incident room and gathered the team together. Bringing them up to speed on what Horst Fischer had passed on, I explained about the list that he had discovered and which had been decoded by the *BfV*.

'I'm going to split you up into nine pairs,' I said, 'and allocate one of these London addresses to each pair. Pay them a visit, starting tomorrow morning.' I noted their looks of surprise. 'Yes, I know it's a Sunday, but this is a murder enquiry. Don't give any indication that that's what we're dealing with, but merely suggest that we're investigating a large-scale fraud involving bogus share certificates. I want you to keep your eyes open and report anything that you think might warrant further enquiries. If that doesn't yield anything, then we'll have to go further afield. Oh, and one other thing . . .' I told the team about the silver-grey car that Guy Wilson claimed to have seen. 'If any of the scam victims has a car, just make a note of it, but don't ask any questions.'

Detective Sergeant Lizanne Carpenter and Detective Constable Sheila Armitage had been allocated an address in Pinner in what was once the county of Middlesex. Some sixteen miles from Whitehall, Pinner was a place that the residents liked to style 'a village' even though it was now a part of Greater London.

It was a moderately sized detached house, built probably between the wars, and had survived the redevelopment of its particular area. It now stood alone and slightly forlorn among the blocks of new flats that had proliferated to accommodate the young upwardly mobile professionals who wanted easy access to central London. And the Metropolitan Line of the Underground railway provided it.

The grey-haired woman who answered the door must have been well into her seventies, was stooped and leaned heavily on a walking stick. She was dressed in a sweater and a skirt in the pattern of an invented tartan. Her pair of flat suede shoes looked as though they had been selected for their comfort rather than their style. Despite the warm weather she wore a heavy cardigan.

'Catherine Fairfax?'

'Who wants to know?' The woman spoke with a refined accent and regarded the young women who stood on her door-step with a measure of suspicion.

'We're police officers, Ms Fairfax,' said Lizanne, producing her warrant card. 'I'm Detective Sergeant Carpenter and this is Detective Constable Armitage.'

'What's it about?' Catherine Fairfax still sounded sceptical at the arrival of two policewomen on her doorstep on a Sunday morning.

'It's about certain investments we believe you to have made, Ms Fairfax.'

'You'd better come in,' said the woman, and opening the door wide led them into a sitting room. 'I'm sorry I'm only hobbling along, but I've had an arthritic hip for some years now and the damned doctors don't seem to be able to do anything for me,' she added, seemingly irritated both by her disability and the medical profession.

'We must apologize for calling on a Sunday morning, Ms Fairfax, but police work's a bit like that.'

'That's all right, my dear. I gave up going to church some years ago. There didn't seem to be much point in it any more. Please sit down.'

The two detectives settled themselves on a large sofa. The room was sparsely furnished, but the remaining items appeared to be of good quality. The impression was of a woman who had been obliged to sell various cherished pieces in order to make ends meet. On a side table there was a silver-framed photograph of a handsome man in army uniform with red tabs on the collar.

'That's my late husband, General Sir Michael Fairfax,' volunteered his widow. 'He died about five years ago.' There was a momentary pause. 'And that makes me Lady Fairfax,' she added, in a tone that was almost apologetic and certainly didn't imply censure for having been addressed incorrectly.

'I'm so sorry, Lady Fairfax,' said Lizanne. 'The list we got from the German police merely named you as Catherine Fairfax.'

Lady Fairfax waved a hand of dismissal. 'You weren't to know, my dear. Anyway, my husband always referred to the title as something that came up with the rations. Generals get it automatically, you see.' She smiled at the recollection. 'But why have the German police taken an interest in me?'

'Without wearying you with the details, it was as a result of an incident in this country.' Lizanne had been instructed not to mention the murders. 'We had to get in touch with the police in Essen and one thing led to another. However, they sent us a list of names of people in this country who had allegedly been swindled out of large sums of money.'

'And there's little doubt that I was one of them,' said Lady Fairfax, with a sad shake of her head. 'It would never have happened when Michael was alive.'

'How *did* it come about, Lady Fairfax?' asked Sheila Armitage.

Catherine Fairfax did not immediately answer the question. 'I'm so sorry, I haven't offered you girls a cup of tea. And as you've come from London you could probably do with one.' She made it sound as though the capital was a hundred miles away instead of less than an hour's drive.

'There's no need, Lady Fairfax, unless you were having one yourself.'

'I was about to put the kettle on when you arrived, as a matter of fact.'

'Let me help you, then,' said Sheila, leaping to her feet.

'That's very kind of you, my dear. It'll certainly get it made quicker. I have a nasty habit of dropping things these days. I've given up using my best crockery. What little of it I have left.' Catherine Fairfax displayed her gnarled hands. 'It's the arthritis, you see.'

Once the three of them were settled again, and the tea had been poured, Lady Fairfax began her story.

'I had a telephone call from a very nice young man who introduced himself as a share broker located in the City; at least that's what he led me to believe. He said that he was sure I'd got some spare cash just sitting in a bank, and he could make it work for me and produce a substantial profit.'

'Did you wonder how he knew you'd got some capital to spare?' asked Sheila.

'I did at first, but then I imagined that being a share broker he somehow had access to my account. I don't have a computer myself, but I understand that one can do something called hacking. I seem to recall something about a newspaper doing that sort of thing.' Catherine Fairfax glanced at Lizanne. 'Have I got that right?'

'It is a possibility,' said Lizanne, without mentioning that hacking into a bank account required a high level of computer expertise. 'And presumably you took this young man's advice?'

'Unfortunately, my dear, yes I did,' said Lady Fairfax ruefully. 'You see I had a nest egg of some forty thousand pounds tucked away. And it was quite true when the young man said it wasn't doing anything. Ever since the banking crisis and this Eurozone nonsense, I was getting hardly any interest and, despite what you may think, the pension of a general's widow doesn't amount to very much. Michael retired from the army thirty-one years ago, and in real terms the pension has been diminishing all the time. And a widow only gets half of that anyway.'

'And how much did you invest, Lady Fairfax?' asked Sheila Armitage, making notes in her pocketbook.

'Twenty thousand at first.'

'At first?' Sheila looked up, carefully disguising her astonishment.

'He came back to me again, and said that the launch of this company was looking very promising and that there had been great interest worldwide. He went on to say that he wanted me to get in on the ground floor, so after a bit of persuasion I invested another twenty thousand. He assured me that I would more than double my money.'

'Did you take any independent advice before investing this amount of money, Lady Fairfax?' asked Lizanne.

'No, I'm afraid I didn't, my dear, and I suppose you think I'm just a foolish old woman.'

'Not at all. Even experienced financiers have been tricked by people of this sort,' said Lizanne. 'Have you any idea where this man had his office? You said he was in the City.'

'I presumed that's where it was. It was certainly a City of London address on the letter that came with the certificates. Let me show you what they sent me.' The old lady rose unsteadily from her chair and crossed to an escritoire that stood in the corner of the room next to a small television set. She spent a few seconds ferreting about in an untidy accumulation of paper before producing a large envelope. 'It's all there,' she said, handing it to Lizanne.

The envelope contained a sheaf of ornate share certificates purporting to show an investment in some emerging international company of information technology developers based in Buenos Aires. And to add a hint of authenticity it claimed that the company was linked to an unnamed corporation in North California, the area known colloquially as Silicon Valley. Accompanying the shares was an impressive letter headed with an address in the City of London and dated eighteen months

ago. The letter was signed by someone who called himself
Anthony Cook. Lizanne Carpenter was in no doubt that the
name and the address were as false as the share certificates that
would probably match those that had been found in Hans
Eberhardt's basement in Kettwig.

'Presumably you didn't receive any dividends, Lady Fairfax,'
said Lizanne.

'Not a brass farthing, my dear. I tried telephoning, but the
number had been disconnected, and I'm too old and infirm to
go traipsing up to the City. So I suppose that's that.'

'How did you pay this man the money, Lady Fairfax?'
enquired Sheila Armitage.

'I wrote cheques to the account shown in the letter and paid
them into my bank.' Lady Fairfax gestured at the documents
Lizanne was holding.

'Well, we'll certainly follow that up,' said Lizanne.

'I doubt if the money's still there, my dear. In fact, when I
spoke to some girl at the bank she told me that the cash had
already been forwarded, and that the account that it had been
sent to had been closed.'

'I'm afraid that's standard procedure in this sort of case,
Lady Fairfax,' said Lizanne. 'Even so, you might be eligible
for some compensation under the Proceeds of Crime Act if
any monies are recovered, but first we have to find the fraudsters and convict them. I don't want to buoy up your hopes
because these people tend to move their money from one
offshore account to another and it's very difficult, if not impossible, to trace it. The likelihood of recovery is remote to say
the least. What's more, anything got back would have to be
shared out among all the parties who've been defrauded by
this particular individual.'

'I suppose you think I'm just a silly old woman,' said Lady
Fairfax, once again.

'Not at all. These people can be very persuasive.' Lizanne
left unspoken her opinion of people who combined stupidity
with avarice. 'I'm sorry to say that people fall for this sort of
fraud almost every day.' She tapped the envelope containing
the certificates. 'May I hold on to these? I'll give you a receipt,
of course.'

'Certainly. They're no good to me. I'm glad that Michael's not still alive. He'd've had something to say about it, I can tell you. But then if he'd still been here it wouldn't have happened.'

'Did you discuss this with anyone, Lady Fairfax?' asked Sheila Armitage. 'Once you'd realized that you'd been swindled.'

'I spoke to my solicitor and he had a look at the certificates, but he said what you've just said. In short, that I'd been seen off by a clever fraudster. He suggested I should tell the police, but that I'd probably be wasting my time and theirs. Funnily enough I mentioned it to a friend of mine, and he'd fallen for it too.'

'The same shares?' asked Lizanne.

'Yes, and the same letter. He was in the army, as well. He's a retired sergeant major I meet at our social club. He's about my age, I suppose, perhaps a little older, and he claimed to have remembered Michael. He said the general was highly respected by the men, but he would say that wouldn't he? You know how crafty old soldiers can be.' She smiled. 'But there again perhaps you don't.'

'Is this club local?' asked Sheila, still busily making notes.

'Yes, it's here in Pinner. He's become a good friend over the years and he collects me in his car every Tuesday to go to the club.'

'That's very good of him. Perhaps you'd give me his name and address. We'd like to have a word with him, in case he's able to give us some more information.' Following Brock's instructions, Sheila asked no questions about what sort of car the man drove.

'It's William.' Catherine Fairfax paused. 'I'm just trying to remember his surname. Ah, yes, I've got it, it's Rivers, William Rivers, but he told me he was always known as Billy in the army, after Billy Two Rivers. The army's very good at giving one nicknames. I know my husband had one, but I can't remember what it was now.'

'Do you have an address for Mr Rivers?'

'I'm afraid not, my dear. I only know he lives locally, but I couldn't tell you where.'

'Thank you, Lady Fairfax,' said Lizanne, as she and Sheila

Armitage rose to leave, 'and thank you for the tea. I'd like to
say that we'll have good news for you next time we meet, but
if I'm honest I very much doubt it.'

SIX

'**M**r Brock, a moment of your time, if you please.'
'Yes, sir,' I said, and replaced the receiver.
Why the hell couldn't the commander just wander
into my office for a chat like any real detective instead of
telephoning me? But I knew the answer: he wasn't a real detective. He had been the beneficiary of what in the Job is known
as a 'sideways' promotion. In other words, he'd spent his entire
career in the Uniform Branch until some administrative genius
high in the ivory tower of New Scotland Yard decided that the
CID were deserving of his talents. Most other senior officers
to whom this transition had occurred just sat back and let the
detectives get on with it, but our revered commander actually
thought he *was* a detective. The only drawback, as far as he
was concerned, was that he could no longer wear his uniform
and that meant that people might not know how important he
thought he was.
'Ah, Mr Brock, close the door, and bring me up to date about
this suspicious death in Richmond.' The commander always
referred to any death we were investigating as suspicious, just
in case it turned out to be manslaughter instead of murder. Or
even suicide. But he is something of a pedant.
'Deaths, sir, plural.'
'Ah, yes, quite so. Deaths.' The commander hated getting
things wrong and disliked even more being corrected by a junior
rank. But a commander who'd come up through the ranks of
the CID wouldn't have had to ask for that information in the
first place; he'd've been in the incident room the same day,
poking about and finding out for himself.
'They'd both been murdered, sir. A single shot to the head
in each case, and then the camper van was deliberately set on

fire.' I started to tell him about the information we'd received from the Essen police, but the moment I mentioned it, he interrupted me.

'There'll be no question of you going to Germany, I hope, Mr Brock.' Any suggestion of unnecessary expenditure was anathema to the commander, and to him all expenditure was unnecessary. I don't know why he was so uptight about it. He'd already got a Queen's Police Medal, and he'd been appointed an Officer of the Order of the British Empire in the last Honours List. What more was he hoping for? Promotion? I wish! So long as it was back to some Uniform Branch post. If I were in his position, I'd just coast happily towards my retirement and let my minions get on with the nastiness of everyday detecting.

'That remains to be seen, sir,' I said, just for the hell of it. I couldn't really see the necessity for a trip to Germany, but I enjoyed planting the seed of doubt. 'As I was saying, sir, it appears that we've stumbled on a scam of monumental proportions—'

'A scam?' The commander abhorred criminal argot, even though he knew what I meant. He peered at me over his half-moon spectacles. I'm sure he only wore them because he believed that they lent him an air of importance. And I'd put money on them containing plain glass.

'Yes, sir,' I said, declining to explain what 'scam' meant. 'We'll probably have to involve the Fraud Squad, but at the moment my priority is to discover the murderer or murderers of Eberhardt and Schmidt.' I then told him what Horst Fischer had found in Eberhardt's basement. 'The German police are interrogating Wilhelm Weber as well, sir.'

'Who is this Weber, Mr Brock?'

'He's the man who lent the camper van to Eberhardt, sir. But all he's told them at the moment is that Eberhardt travelled several times to the Bahamas.'

'I hope you're not thinking of going to the Bahamas either, Mr Brock.' The commander looked quite distressed at this latest piece of information.

'I doubt it, sir,' I said, without wishing to antagonize him further, but I was by no means sure that a trip there was out of the question.

'Very well, Mr Brock,' said the great man, 'but keep me informed.' He turned enthusiastically to a pile of files in his in-tray and moved the topmost one to the centre of his desk. He loves paperwork does the commander and devours it with all the enthusiasm of a dedicated bureaucrat.

I returned to the incident room and began to read the statements about the team's visits of yesterday. They all told the same depressing story of naive people taken in by unscrupulous fraudsters.

'This Lady Fairfax, Lizanne . . .? Did she know the address of William Rivers?'

'No, guv,' said Lizanne Carpenter. 'She just said that he picked her up in his car every Tuesday to take her to this social club they belong to. But she did say that he lived locally.'

'Rivers was on *Herr* Fischer's list, sir, and he was interviewed by Charlie Flynn,' said Colin Wilberforce, proving yet again that he was well and truly conversant with every aspect of the enquiry. 'His statement's the third one in the file you've got.'

'Where is Charlie, Colin?' DS Flynn was a former Fraud Squad officer and it was beginning to look as though he would be a useful man to have on this enquiry.

'He's just slipped out for a haircut, sir. Should be back any minute.'

'Ask him to see me the moment he gets back.'

Charlie Flynn appeared in my office five minutes later. 'Sorry, guv, but I needed a quick trim,' he said apologetically.

'No problem, Charlie.' I knew that my detectives, working the hours they did, rarely had time off when civilized establishments like hairdressers were open. 'Tell me about Rivers,' I said, waving Flynn to a chair.

'His story's much the same as the one Lizanne got from Lady Fairfax, guv, and from the documents I obtained from Rivers it appears to be the same bogus company that the poor old fool invested in. Some IT company in Buenos Aires.'

'Did you find out what sort of car he's got? Apparently he picks up Lady Fairfax and takes her to this club.'

'Yeah, it's a red Renault Twingo, about five years old, I should think. And it's registered to him. I checked.'

'That doesn't tally with the description of the car that Guy Wilson saw near the van. The one he told Miss Ebdon about.'

'I shouldn't think Rivers is capable of committing a murder anyway, guv. He must be at least eighty and he looked as though he was at death's door.'

'He's a former soldier, according to Lady Fairfax.'

'Yes, he said he'd been a sergeant major. There was a shield on the wall of his sitting room that looked like it was one of those regimental things, a bit like the Met Police shields we give away. I don't know what it was, but it had what seemed to be a flaming dagger on it. Anyway, I took a photo of it while he was upstairs looking for the documents.' Flynn fiddled with his mobile phone and held it up for me to see.

'That's not a flaming dagger, Charlie,' I said. 'According to a book I read it's a downward-pointing Excalibur wreathed in flames on a crusader shield.'

'Yeah, well, whatever, guv,' said Flynn.

'It's the crest of the Special Air Service, Charlie.'

'Blimey, the SAS. I wonder if he took part in the Iranian Embassy siege back in 1980. He's about the right age.' Every policeman knew about the siege; it was the only time the SAS had been called in to assist the Metropolitan Police.

'Whether he did or not, if he's ex-SAS he's a trained killer, Charlie. Not the sort of bloke you'd like to meet on a dark night if you'd upset him. Like if you'd defrauded him. How much did he lose in this scam?'

'Ten grand, guv.'

'Did he indeed? I think it's worth me having a chat with him.'

'But the car isn't the one that Wilson saw, guv.

'There is such a thing as hiring a car, Charlie.'

'Possible, I suppose,' said Flynn.

'By the way, there is a job you can do when you've got a moment.' I gave Flynn details of the bank into which Lady Fairfax had deposited her two cheques totalling forty thousand pounds. 'The cash got moved on a bit sharply according to the enquiries that Lady Fairfax made, Charlie. See if you can get any more details. Not that I think you will.'

*   *   *

William Rivers's house at Pinner was nothing like the house
in which Lizanne Carpenter had said that Lady Fairfax lived.
The old soldier's abode was a two-up-two-down semi in one
of the less salubrious parts of the Harrow suburb.

I hammered on the door, but there was no reply.

A woman in a flowery apron immediately appeared from the
adjoining house and stood on tiptoe, peering over the dividing
fence. She had frizzy bottle-blonde hair and an excess of
make-up.

'If you're looking for Bill Rivers, he's gone away,' she said.

'D'you know when he went?' I asked, silently thanking God
for nosy neighbours.

'Late last night. Can I give him a message when he gets
back?'

'I'm a police officer, madam,' I said. 'I rather want to talk
to him urgently.'

'He's not in trouble, is he?' But the woman's attitude gave
the impression that if Rivers was in a spot of bother with the
police, it would be something to gossip about to her
neighbours.

'No, not at all,' I said, although I wasn't too sure about that.
'Have you any idea where he went?'

'He said he was going on holiday for a week or two. He
usually goes to Brighton. He's very fond of Brighton, is Bill.
He mentioned several times that he always goes there. I think
he even goes sea-swimming. Not something I'd care to do at
his age, but he's a tough old nut.'

'Have you any idea where he might be staying. If he always
goes to Brighton, he might be putting up at the same place.'

'No, love, he never let on. He tends to keep himself to himself
does Bill, if you know what I mean.' The woman smiled and
touched her hair. It was black at the roots.

'Did he take his wife?' asked Dave.

'No, dear, Bill is a widower. His wife died about twenty
years ago, I think.'

'Did he take his car?' asked Dave.

'Yes, I think so,' said the woman. 'At least it's not outside
where it usually is.'

'That'd be the Renault, would it?'

'I think that's what it is,' agreed the woman. 'He used to have a Volkswagen, but then he bought that French thing he's got now.'

We left it at that and returned to our car.

'Have you got an address for Lady Fairfax, Dave?' I asked.

'Yes, guv,' said Dave, and read out the address from his pocketbook. It was only a ten minute drive from where we were.

Lady Fairfax appraised the two of us somewhat nervously. Dave, being six foot tall and black, tended to have that sort of intimidating effect on people.

'I'm sorry to bother you, Lady Fairfax,' I said, once I'd told her who we were, 'but I'm anxious to speak to William Rivers.'

Catherine Fairfax showed us into her sitting room. 'I'm afraid I don't know where he lives, Chief Inspector.' Being an army officer's widow, Lady Fairfax obviously knew about ranks and didn't leave out the 'chief' as did the actors who appeared on television. I'm always irritated that fictional TV chief inspectors not only allow themselves to be called 'inspector', but even introduce themselves as such. There's a difference of about eight grand a year in pay, and real coppers don't make that mistake or allow others to do so.

'We know where he lives, Lady Fairfax,' said Dave. 'We've just called at his house, but I was told that he's gone on holiday. Quite suddenly it seems. According to a neighbour he went late last night, probably to Brighton.'

'Oh dear!' said Catherine Fairfax. 'He didn't say anything about that to me. I wonder how I'm going to get to the club tomorrow morning.'

'I'm afraid there's not much we can do to help you there.' In view of what DS Carpenter had told me about the amount of money the woman had lost, I didn't like to suggest a taxi.

'There were two nice young lady police officers here only yesterday, Chief Inspector, a sergeant and a constable. Is it something to do with the enquiries they were making?'

'It is connected, Lady Fairfax,' said Dave, smiling almost beatifically and as usual oozing charm as he did whenever he dealt with old ladies. 'Those officers are colleagues of ours.'

'It's such a dreadful business. I don't know how I was so

stupid as to get mixed up in it. But they threatened to go to the police if I didn't make the second payment. They said I'd entered into a parole contract, whatever that is.'

'It's legal jargon for a verbal agreement,' said Dave, 'and in these circumstances not worth the paper it's not written on.'

Lady Fairfax appeared bemused by this bit of Dave Poole doubletalk and smiled. 'I see,' she said, but I doubt that she did.

'What are we going to do about Rivers, guv?' asked Dave, once we were back at Curtis Green.

'Supposing Rivers has in fact gone to Brighton, Dave, it might be worth asking the local police to keep a look out for his car. Charlie Flynn will give you the details.'

'If that's where he has actually gone,' said Dave pessimistically.

'We just have to hope that his neighbour was right,' I said. 'If the local law down there are lucky enough to spot it ask them to let us know, but to take no other action. If they do manage to locate him, we'll take a trip down there and have a word. It could be that he really has gone on holiday.'

'Yeah, maybe, guv, but it seems all too convenient to me that he vamooses straight after Eberhardt and Schmidt were murdered. There we have an ex-SAS geezer who suddenly takes it on the toes just after Charlie Flynn called in to see him.' Dave regarded everyone involved in an investigation as a suspect until proved to be innocent. 'Guilty knowledge, no doubt about it,' he added, just to make his point.

'You might be right, Dave. It seems odd that he took off straight after he'd had a visit from the police. However, there are some loose ends to be tied up.' Although I knew damned well that the address on the letters sent to the 'investors' was false, I had to show in the final report that this had been checked. And that meant a trip into the foreign territory cared for by the City of London Police.

The address on the letter received by Lady Fairfax turned out to be premises occupied by a firm of solicitors. In my view, not the smartest move on the part of the share-pushers. But as it happened, the lawyers hadn't even opened the letters that had arrived at their address.

'Yes, we had quite a few letters addressed to this fellow Anthony Cook,' said the senior partner, after he'd consulted his office manager, 'but we sent them back to the post office marked "Not known at this address".'

'You weren't interested in why letters for this man kept arriving here?' I asked, just for the hell of it. 'Didn't you open them to find out?'

'They were not opened because so to do might have constituted an offence under Section 84 of the Postal Services Act 2000,' said the solicitor. He was a smug sort of character, mid-forties and expensively suited. 'And lawyers are not in the habit of breaching the law, Chief Inspector, as I'm sure you appreciate.'

Really? I've certainly known a few who'd bent it, to say the least.

'If any such letters arrive in the future, perhaps you'd let me know.' I handed the lawyer one of my cards. 'I'll arrange for an officer to seize them as evidence in a case of double murder I'm dealing with. I'm sure you'll agree that such action will exonerate you from any allegation of interfering with Her Majesty's mails.'

'Quite so,' said the solicitor acidly.

So much for that. Now we had to look into the matter of the discontinued 0845 telephone number that Lady Fairfax, and doubtless the others, had tried calling. But I knew what the outcome would be.

Back at the office, I set Colin Wilberforce the task of discovering details of the subscriber from British Telecom. Or BT as it now styles itself in the prevailing fashion of using abbreviations for everything. It took him about ten minutes.

'According to the director of security at BT the number has never been issued, sir,' said Wilberforce.

'But Lady Fairfax said that it came up as disconnected,' I said.

'It would've done, sir. I was told that it's the standard recorded response to numbers that have been disconnected or never issued.'

'But how was our mysterious share-pusher lucky enough to come up with a number that had never been issued?'

'He probably kept dialling 0845 numbers until he hit on one that had been disconnected and then put that on his bogus letterhead,' suggested Dave.

'Sounds right, sir,' said Wilberforce. 'It was a bonus that it hadn't been issued, but in the event it didn't matter.'

'It wouldn't've really have made a difference if he'd picked any number,' said Dave, as usual getting to the nub of the matter. 'After all, he picked a solicitor's address for his letterhead.'

'One other thing, Colin,' I said. 'Get on to the delivery office that serves the solicitor's address and find out what they did with the Anthony Cook letters that were returned to them.'

Later that night we had surprisingly good news from Brighton, although at the time we didn't realize how surprising or that it wouldn't be good. At near midnight, a Sussex traffic-division officer had seen Rivers's Renault Twingo and followed it to a guest house. The driver – a man in his eighties, it was reported – had alighted and gone inside. It was that simple! I never cease to be amazed at how often uniformed constables will find someone for whom the CID had been searching for days if not months. Not that that was the case here. Less than twelve hours was pretty good going.

The Sussex police message had come in straight after the discovery, but the night duty incident room staff had wisely decided not to bother me with it.

SEVEN

The next morning I entrusted myself to what Dave calls his purposeful driving, and we arrived at the guest house at about half past eleven. William Rivers's car was parked outside. The guest house was one of those seedy establishments that had a signboard boasting a sea view, but a sight of the sea could probably be achieved only by standing on a chair in the attic.

Dave and I walked into the entrance hall and I banged a table bell on a desk that bore the optimistic sign 'Welcome'. That the owner was a harridan in her fifties and as dowdy as the guest house itself came as no surprise.

'We haven't got any vacancies,' said this vision of loveliness, viewing Dave with obvious distaste.

'That's all right, this is the last place on earth I'd want to stay,' said Dave, who was quick to recognize a racist when he met one.

'We're police officers,' I said. 'I want to speak to Mr Rivers, one of your guests.'

'I don't know as how he's in,' said the woman, obviously intent upon being as obstructive as possible. I got the impression that she didn't like the police and idly wondered why, but it wasn't my concern. 'He never come down for breakfast this morning, but I've got more to do than run about after guests what can't be bothered to get out of their bed of a morning.'

'Perhaps you'd find out if he's in,' Dave suggested, 'or we could go round knocking on doors until we find him.'

The woman tossed her head as she realized it would be futile not to cooperate. She snatched at the telephone and dialled a two-digit number, but replaced the receiver after a few moments. 'He's not answering,' she said, 'but I'm sure he's in. Perhaps he's asleep. It's Room Five, top floor,' she added tersely and walked away muttering to herself.

We trudged up two flights of worn nylon-carpeted stairs and Dave knocked on the door bearing the number of Rivers's room. The number was a cheap stick-on affair, the sort that people buy at DIY shops to put on their dustbins.

I pushed open the door. Sprawled across the bed was a fully dressed man. There was a pistol in his right hand, and blood had stained the bedclothes and was congealed on his neck from a head wound. His eyes were wide open.

Dave crossed to the bed and felt for a pulse. He looked up. 'He's a goner, guv,' he said. 'Still, he could hardly miss at that range.'

'Bloody hell!' I said. This untoward event introduced an

unnecessary complication into our investigation. Not because Rivers, and I'd no doubt it was him, had obviously committed suicide, but because it would now mean involving another police force.

I took out my mobile phone and paused. 'I don't suppose you've got the number of the local nick, Dave, have you?'

'It so happens I have, sir,' said Dave and reeled it off from memory. It was one of Dave's little foibles that he always called me 'sir' whenever I made a fatuous remark or asked for something I should've known. And he always called me 'sir' in the presence of members of the public.

I called Brighton police station and asked for the detective inspector. Having eventually made contact, I introduced myself and went on to explain our interest in William Rivers and what had happened.

'Oh dear! What appalling bad luck,' said the DI, and laughed before promising to come and take a look.

Twenty minutes later, he strode into the room. There'd been no flashing blue lights, no sirens, and no hordes of policemen stringing out miles of blue and white tapes, just the DI in a small unmarked saloon car. But then this was not the make-believe world so beloved of crime scriptwriters.

'What's the SP, then, guv?' asked the Brighton DI, as he strolled into the room.

I explained, as briefly as possible, the murder enquiry in which I was involved and that it had, in my view, led to Rivers's suicide.

'I don't suppose he left a note or anything,' said the DI as, hands in pockets, he surveyed Rivers's dead body.

'Nothing that I could find.'

'Reckon he's your man for this topping of yours, then?'

'Possibly,' I said, 'but could you arrange for a ballistics test on the pistol? With any luck it'll turn out to be the murder weapon, and it's a point two-two, the same calibre that was used by our killer.'

'You can take it with you if you like, so long as you let me have it back.' The DI glanced around the room, taking it all in. 'Well, I'd better call up the cavalry and get them to clear up the mess. I'll let you have anything we find, guv.'

'Thanks, much appreciated,' I said. 'D'you mind if we take his house keys? I think a look round his drum might be profitable.'

'Not at all,' said the DI, 'so long as you sign for them.' He seemed very keen on paperwork and I wondered if he'd ever met our commander.

The DI produced his pocketbook and made an entry, and I signed for the pistol and the keys.

'There's one other thing,' I said. 'He's got a car outside. I'll take a look inside, if it's all the same to you, but then I'll leave it to you to dispose of.'

'No problem.'

'I'll drop the car key back when I've finished.'

'Right,' said the Brighton DI, and began to make calls on his mobile phone. 'Be lucky, guv,' he added while waiting to be connected.

Dave and I descended to the ground floor.

'What's going on?' demanded the 'chatelaine'.

'Any minute now you'll have hordes of policemen swarming all over the place to investigate the death of Mr Rivers,' said Dave. 'He seems to have blown his brains out.'

'But what will the other guests think?' The woman's face registered horror. 'This is a respectable guest house,' she complained.

'Not any more it's not,' said Dave.

We made a cursory examination of Rivers's Renault Twingo. There was the usual unpaid parking ticket and an empty cigarette packet, but there was nothing to excite our interest. And certainly nothing to point to Rivers being our murderer.

When we got back to London, I took Dave into my office and we settled down to work out where we were going to go from here.

'D'you reckon he did top Eberhardt and Schmidt, guv?' asked Dave, tossing me a cigarette before crossing the room to open a window. We'd both tried to give up smoking and not even the draconian rules that forbade smoking in police buildings, which we were now breaking, had had the desired effect.

'I'm damned if I know, Dave. If the weapon he used to off

himself with is the one that killed them, then yes, I think we might have a result. But this name Adekunle that Horst Fischer found on Eberhardt's computer still bothers me. There's got to be a connection there somewhere.'

'So, what's next?' asked Dave.

'Get the pistol across to ballistics, and then we'll have a look round Billy Rivers's house.'

Colin Wilberforce was hovering when I left my office.

'What is it, Colin?'

'The Anthony Cook letters, sir. The local delivery office returned them all to the senders.'

'Really? I wonder why Lady Fairfax didn't mention that.'

At ten o'clock the following morning, Dave and I arrived at William Rivers's house in Pinner. I had arranged for the local police to be on hand with a rammer with which to force an entry, just in case. But the keys we'd taken from Rivers's body fitted the lock. I dismissed the locals and in we went. But not before the helpful neighbour appeared on her doorstep.

'Everything all right?' she asked, obviously excited by the arrival of the police.

'Couldn't be better, madam,' said Dave.

The inside of the property was exactly as I imagined an old soldier's would be. Despite Rivers having reached an age when most elderly people get slovenly and forgetful, the house was immaculately tidy and everything was lined up and in its allotted place. Even Colin Wilberforce would've been impressed at the man's somewhat ascetically ordered way of life.

We were looking for documentary evidence that might point to Rivers being our murderer. But all we found was an address book, the usual bills and junk mail, and a week-old newspaper. I knew that Charlie Flynn had taken the papers that Rivers had received from the bogus share-pusher, but given the amount of money he'd invested, I did wonder whether he might've had a safety deposit box somewhere. However, we found no evidence to indicate that he had. In short there was nothing in the house to make us believe that Rivers was our killer. Neither was there a letter from Anthony Cook that had been returned by the post office.

'I suppose we ought to let Lady Fairfax know that Rivers has topped himself, guv,' said Dave.

'Might be as well, while we're in the area, Dave, but it's Tuesday and she's possibly found someone else to take her to her club.'

'It's Wednesday, sir,' said Dave.

'Oh, it's you, Chief Inspector.' Lady Fairfax smiled and opened the door wide. 'Do come in.'

'I'm afraid we have some bad news, Lady Fairfax,' I began, and went on to tell her what had occurred in Brighton, but without describing the gory details. I merely said that William Rivers had committed suicide and she didn't ask how.

'I suppose it must've been the realization that he was unlikely to get his money back, Chief Inspector.'

'Quite possibly, Lady Fairfax,' I said, without telling her about the murders of Eberhardt and Schmidt, or that we suspected that Rivers might've been their killer.

'I wondered why he didn't turn up yesterday.' Catherine Fairfax sighed. 'I suppose I'll have to find someone else to take me to the club,' she said. 'Oh dear!'

And that seemed to be her only concern about the demise of William Rivers, her one-time volunteer chauffeur.

'One other thing, Lady Fairfax,' I said. 'Did you ever write to the Anthony Cook who signed the letter you received?'

'No, Chief Inspector, there didn't seem any point once I found out that I couldn't get through to the telephone number on his letter.'

That answered my question about why she'd not had any such letter returned. Not that it made a scrap of difference.

Back at the factory, as we detectives call our place of work, Dave and I started going through William Rivers's address book.

'There's a phone number for a Stella Rivers here, guv, but no address,' said Dave. 'Must be a relative.'

'We'd better let her know,' I said. 'We might learn something.'

'Won't the Brighton police tell her, guv?'

'They probably don't know of her existence, Dave. Anyway they haven't got the address book.'

Colin Wilberforce did a subscriber check on the telephone number and gave us the address.

'Stella Rivers?' I asked of the woman who opened the door of the neat semi-detached bungalow in Hounslow. She must've been in her fifties, and was dressed in jeans and a colourful blouse. She was quite a big woman and had shoulder-length grey hair that didn't really suit someone of her age.

'Not for the past twenty-five years,' she said. 'I'm Mrs Kumar. What's this about, anyway?'

I introduced myself and Dave, and Mrs Kumar invited us into a garishly furnished sitting room that she called her lounge.

'Are you by any chance related to a William Rivers who lived in Pinner, Mrs Kumar?' I asked.

'He's my father. Why, has something happened?'

Now came the bit that policeman hate the most. 'I'm afraid he's dead, Mrs Kumar.'

'Oh, I see.' Stella Kumar remained calm and apparently unaffected by this news. 'Well, thank you for letting me know. Was it a heart attack?'

'He committed suicide . . . in Brighton.'

'Why on earth did the silly old fool do that? And what was he doing in Brighton anyway?'

There was no sign of grief and I suspected that a rift had existed between Rivers and his daughter for some time.

'According to a neighbour he went there on holiday,' I said.

'And he'd lost ten thousand pounds buying worthless shares, Mrs Kumar,' said Dave. 'That might've been the reason for his committing suicide.'

Mrs Kumar's mouth fell open and her eyes widened in astonishment. 'Ten thousand! Where in the name of God did he get that much money from?'

'We don't know, Mrs Kumar,' said Dave. 'We were hoping you might be able to tell us.'

'I've not the faintest idea,' said Stella Kumar, shaking her head in disbelief. 'We certainly didn't see any of it when we were struggling to buy a house.'

'As a matter of interest, when did you last see him?'

'Not for a very long time. In fact I haven't seen him since my mother died, and that was about twenty years ago. We didn't get on, dad and me,' said Mrs Kumar, confirming my suspicions of a family feud. 'You see, Mr Brock, I married an Indian, Ram Kumar, and my father wouldn't accept him as a member of the family, even though he's now a successful restaurateur. My late mother was quite happy about it, but the old man wouldn't even use my married name. Whenever he wrote to me, or sent me a birthday card – which wasn't often – he always addressed it to me as Stella Rivers. The hurtful part was that he wouldn't even acknowledge the existence of his grandchildren. No birthday cards, no presents then or at Christmas, nothing. And to think he had all that money tucked away.' She shook her head sadly at the injustice of it all. 'Not to put too fine a point on it, my father was a racist.'

'And that presumably soured the relationship,' I suggested. I realized now why Mrs Kumar's telephone number was listed under her maiden name in William Rivers's address book.

'I determined to have nothing more to do with him, Mr Brock. I didn't mind him having a go at me, but to take it out on the kids was unforgivable, and I told him so. There was one huge row and that was that. But he could be very bloody-minded when the mood took him.'

'I understand he was in the SAS,' said Dave.

'Yes, that and the Parachute Regiment. He was obsessed with the army. He was always going on about it, muttering about how National Service would straighten out today's youngsters and give them a proper start in life. I got sick of it, I can tell you. And what was worse it indirectly resulted in the death of my brother Leonard.'

'How so?'

'The old man bullied him into joining the army and he was killed thirty years ago on some stupid exercise somewhere in Germany. He was a dispatch rider and got run over by a tank transporter,' said Stella and paused in thought. 'I suppose I'll have to do something about dad's funeral,' she added, returning to the demands of the present day. 'There's no one else . . . apart from my Aunt Gladys, that is, and I have no idea where she is.'

'I suggest you get in touch with the police in Brighton, Mrs Kumar,' said Dave. 'They'll tell you when your father's body can be released.' He gave her the telephone number and the name of the DI there. 'Perhaps you'd let us know when the funeral is to take place,' he added, and gave her the telephone number of the incident room at Curtis Green.

We'd learned a little more about the late William Rivers, but nothing that was going to get us any further in determining whether he had murdered Hans Eberhardt and Trudi Schmidt.

Back at the office, I got hold of Tom Challis.

'Tom, find out what you can about William Rivers's family. His daughter's name is Stella Kumar married to a Ram Kumar, and she had a brother named Leonard who was killed thirty years ago in Germany with the army. Mrs Kumar also mentioned an aunt called Gladys. But she didn't know where she's living now. From what I understand of the Riverses' somewhat dysfunctional family, she might even be dead.'

On Thursday morning, we discovered that our search of Rivers's house and our visit to his daughter had been largely a waste of time. The report from the ballistics examiner stated categorically that the firearm with which Rivers had committed suicide was not the weapon that had killed Eberhardt and Schmidt.

That was a setback. I'd thought that everything so far had pointed to Rivers being our killer; but one of the realities that detectives learn early in their career is that forensic scientists don't always come up with the answers that detectives want.

That Rivers's weapon was most likely illegally held was not our problem. The Brighton police could pursue that if they felt so inclined. In their shoes I wouldn't have bothered.

'And we didn't find any other weapon among his belongings when we searched his house in Pinner, Dave,' I said.

'He could've had another one that he threw in the river, guv,' said Dave, injecting his usual pessimistic realism into the discussion. 'After all, the toppings took place within yards of the Thames.'

'But the car seen by Guy Wilson wasn't the car that Rivers drove.' I know I'd vaguely suggested to Charlie Flynn that

Rivers might've hired one, but I doubted it. That would've left a trail that dogged detective work would quickly have discovered. And I'd already concluded that our murderer was a careful individual.

'So, where do we go from here, guv?'

'There had to be a reason for Rivers committing suicide in his Brighton doss house, Dave,' I said, 'and as we now know, it's unlikely that he'd committed the murders.'

'Despite what I just said about having a second weapon that was thrown in the river,' said Dave, 'I think that Rivers was much too old to have done a job like that, but he might've known a man who wasn't.'

'That's a strong possibility, I suppose. On the other hand it could've been depression that made him top himself. Perhaps, being a bit of a macho man, he regretted having admitted to Charlie Flynn that he'd been swindled out of what was probably his life's savings.'

'Well, it wouldn't depress me enough to top myself, guv, but as I've only got life savings of about twenty quid it wouldn't really matter. Mind you, my bloody great mortgage is enough to depress anyone, and I wouldn't want to leave Madeleine a millstone like that in my will.'

'Colin,' I said, crossing to Wilberforce's desk. 'Did *any* of the nine losers that were interviewed have a car that tallied with the description of the one seen by Guy Wilson in the vicinity of the camper van?' He'd already told me that none had, but more information might've come in since then.

In view of the complexities of the enquiry, HOLMES – the Home Office large major enquiry system – had been installed in the incident room.

Wilberforce turned to it and scrolled up the relevant entry. 'No, sir,' he said, swinging round to face me. 'You already know that Lady Fairfax doesn't own a car and that Rivers's was a red Renault Twingo. None of the other losers had a car that matched the one seen by Wilson, as far as we know. If Wilson's sighting is to be relied on, that is.'

'On the other hand,' I surmised, 'the car Wilson saw might've had nothing whatever to do with the murders. It could've been a coincidence. Perhaps it was some law-abiding citizen who'd pulled up to answer his mobile phone, rather than use it while he was driving.'

'Blimey, that'd be a first,' muttered Dave.

The more I thought about Dave's comment that Rivers might've known the man who'd committed the murders, the more I thought it a strong possibility. The SAS is a close-knit family and I was sure that their renowned esprit de corps continued into retirement. If any one of their number had been the victim of the sort of fraud perpetrated on Rivers, his former colleagues were more likely to deal with it themselves rather than leave it to the police. And their sanctions would've been far more severe than any penalty the courts might have imposed.

'We'll need to go through Rivers's address book, Dave,' I said, 'and see if he'd listed any old comrades.'

'I don't know why it's called an address book,' said Dave, 'because it only contains phone numbers. What's more I expect the crafty old bugger wrote them all in code.'

'Well, he didn't write his daughter's in code, so we'll have to hope that the rest are in clear.' I got hold of DS Tom Challis and gave him the job of finding out the addresses of everyone listed in Rivers's address book. Not that there were too many. I returned to my office and was just about to deal with some necessary paperwork when the call came in.

'Sir, the DI at Paddington has just been on.' Colin Wilberforce appeared at the door with an email printout. 'He was called to the murder of a Samson Adekunle on his patch and his lads have found a bunch of dodgy share certificates in his house. They think Adekunle's topping might be connected to our job.'

'There's no doubt about it,' I said. 'That's the name that Horst Fischer found on Eberhardt's computer. There was an exchange of emails in which Adekunle told Eberhardt where to park.'

'And that was where Eberhardt got topped,' commented Dave.

'Did they say what sort of share certificates?' I asked, certain that I knew.

'Yes, sir. I asked for the details and they're on this email. Some are the same as the ones that were obtained from Lady Fairfax and William Rivers, but the others refer to a cargo of oil leaving Nigeria. Probably just as bogus as the Buenos Aires share certificates.'

'Just my bloody luck,' I said as I scanned the information. 'Has the commander had a copy of this?'

'Not yet, sir.'

I took the printout and made my way to the commander's office, well knowing what the outcome of the interview would be.

'Ah, Mr Brock, I was just about to send for you.'

'I presume it wasn't about the murder of Samson Adekunle, sir. It's only just come in.' I handed him the printout containing the details.

The commander almost snatched it from me. 'This is most irregular,' he said, when he'd finished reading it. 'Why wasn't I shown this before?'

'It's called chain of command, sir. It was quite proper for it to come to me first, and my job to bring it to you.'

For a moment or two the commander stared at me before placing the printout in the centre of his desk. He leaned back, steepled his fingers and pursed his lips. 'Yes, quite so.' For one brief second I was foolish enough to think he was going to apologize. 'In the circumstances, you'd better undertake this enquiry,' he said, making another, and for him uncharacteristic, command decision. 'It seems to be connected to the deaths of Eberhardt and Schmidt.'

'You're absolutely right, sir.' A comment that seemed to please the commander. I turned to go and then paused. 'You said you were about to send for me.'

'Yes indeed. I haven't seen the seating plan for the forth-coming senior officers' luncheon, Mr Brock, but I can see that you'll be much too busy. I'll speak to Mr Cleaver about it.'

'Very good, sir.' I always knew that the commander had a different set of priorities from the rest of us. Whatever was vexing him about the seating plan, he was unlikely to get much change out of Alan Cleaver, the HSCC detective chief superin-tendent. Cleaver had never been too interested in this quarterly bean feast and often made pressure of work an excuse for not going. One of the drawbacks to what would otherwise be an enjoyable function was that the commander took full advantage of his lofty position to lord it over the assembled diners. And to round it off, he could always be relied upon to make a lengthy and pompous speech in the strangulated prose that is a keystone of the teachings at his beloved Bramshill Police College.

I called in at the incident room and told Wilberforce that this latest murder was down to me, and shouted for Dave.

'Right, sir,' said Wilberforce, and turned to his computer.

'Grab a car, Dave,' I said. 'We're on our way to Paddington.'

EIGHT

The houses in Clancy Street, just north of the Bayswater Road, were elegant dwellings. Number seventeen was a terraced property of some three floors. And it was triple-glazed. That and the thickness of the party walls turned out to be a significant factor and one that must have been of advantage to the murderer.

Having passed through the tapes closing off that part of the street, Dave and I mounted the steps and met the incident officer clutching the inevitable clipboard; this time the local nick could only spare a uniformed sergeant. We gave him our particulars.

The next hurdle to overcome before we got on with our investigation was Linda Mitchell waiting to hand us protective suits, gloves and overshoes.

'Where's our body, Linda?' I asked, once we were attired in the functional garb that is vital in preventing contamination of the crime scene.

'Through the front door and first on the right, Mr Brock. And it's not a pretty sight.'

No expense had been spared in furnishing the sitting room. The expensive armchairs and sofa, and the carpet and curtains were all of good quality, and the usual extras were all there: flat screen plasma television set, sound system and original paintings. But there were no personal photographs.

'DCI Brock, HSCC,' I said, acknowledging the local DI who was leaning against the wall. 'And this is Dave Poole, my skipper.'

'Pleased to meet you, guv.' The DI levered himself off the wall and shook hands with each of us.

I'll bet you are, I thought. *You're about to wash your hands of this little lot.*

Dr Henry Mortlock was seated in one of the armchairs, legs crossed and hands linked behind his head, gazing at the black body of Samson Adekunle. It was naked and tied to an upright kitchen chair, and showed signs of having been tortured quite savagely. Judging by the bloody weals, it was obvious that the victim had been whipped repeatedly, and there were several burns on the body that had probably been caused by a cigarette. There were numerous lacerations where deep incisions had been made. A piece of bloodstained rope lay on the floor near the victim's chair together with a blood-encrusted kitchen knife.

'I get the distinct impression that someone didn't like this guy too much, Harry.' Mortlock's dry humour matched that of any detective I'd ever met.

'Any idea how long he's been dead, Henry?' I asked.

'We're talking days rather than hours,' said Mortlock. 'I'll have a better idea when I've carved him up. A bit more than he's been carved up already,' he added with a chuckle.

'A rough idea?' I asked hopefully, sniffing the fetid air.

'There's a certain amount of putrefaction and marbling, and the blood on the body and the carpet has congealed. A week at least, possibly longer, but as I said I'll probably be able to narrow it down a bit when I do the post-mortem. But it's clear that he was tortured quite brutally. He must've yelled his head off, but with the triple-glazing, I don't suppose anyone will have heard anything. Somebody obviously wanted something from him. But what he wanted, Harry, is your problem not mine.'

'Have you finished here, Henry?'

'Yes, you can get the body down to the mortuary as soon as you like.' Mortlock picked up his bag and made for the door. 'By the way,' he said, pausing, 'it looks as though he was shot in the back of the head and that's probably what finished him off. But I'll be able to tell you more when I've done the PM.'

'What do we know about this job?' I asked the local DI once Mortlock had departed.

'We got an anonymous phone call earlier today from an untraceable mobile, tipping us off to the presence of the late Mr Adekunle, guv. We came round and forced an entry and that's what we found.' The DI gestured nonchalantly at the body. 'No sign of a break-in and nothing appears to have been taken. There's some pretty expensive gear lying about, too. It looks as though the murderer was admitted by the deceased and was after information rather than property. I'd guess that the killer was known to the victim.'

'Where did you find the dodgy share certificates that were mentioned in your email?'

'Spread about in the study. There's a lot of sophisticated IT gear up there, too. I did a search on the police national computer re the certificates and found that you had an interest. I guessed you'd be copping this one, so my lads didn't go any further than having a quick look round. Nothing like a pristine crime scene for you to get stuck into, is there, guv?' The DI grinned, probably at his good fortune at not being lumbered with a murder that had all the signs of being complicated and prolonged.

'Yeah, thanks,' I said.

'Anything else I can do?' the DI asked. 'If not, I'll leave you to get on with it.'

'If there is, I'll give you a bell,' I said and paused. 'By the way, d'you know if Adekunle owned this property?'

'No idea, guv. Like I said, we didn't do anything once we knew it was down to you.'

'How did you know the victim was Samson Adekunle?'

'The guy who made the duff phone call obligingly told us who he was. And he added the useful information that Adekunle was a villain, but there's no trace of him in CRO.'

The fact that Criminal Records Office didn't have an entry for Adekunle did not, however, mean that he wasn't a villain; just that he hadn't been caught. It was interesting too, that the murderer had left it as long as he had before informing the police. It looked as though he wanted to make sure of his escape – probably abroad – before telling us about the presence of Adekunle's body.

Linda Mitchell had followed us into the room. 'I'll carry on now that Doctor Mortlock's finished, Mr Brock, if that's all right.'

'Go ahead, Linda. Have you done the study yet?'

'Yes, we've finished in there; it's on the next floor up. There are a host of fingerprints, so it'll take time before we've any chance of getting an ident. Incidentally, I had a quick look at the keyboard of the computer for fingerprints, but we're not going to be able to get any from there. I've taken the victim's prints, but there's no trace of him in records.'

'That much the local DI told us,' I said. 'And that was about all.'

'Incidentally, there's a balcony at the back of the top floor and what looks like a garage with an access via a road from the rear of the property.'

Dave and I made our way upstairs. As the Paddington DI had said, the study was full of hi-tech equipment. The share certificates were strewn about on a desk and on the floor, as though someone had glanced at them and then abandoned them. There was a safe against one wall, but it was locked and I knew from experience that only a skilled locksmith – or a safe-breaker – could get into it. I've tried opening safes before and the widely held concept that you can hear the turning of a combination lock's tumblers with the aid of a stethoscope is an urban myth.

'We'll take the computer with us, Dave, and get one of our boffins to see what he can find. You never know, we might get lucky.'

'In view of Dr Mortlock's estimation of the time of death it couldn't've been this Adekunle guy who topped the camper-van duo, guv,' suggested Dave. 'Given that Adekunle is an associate of Eberhardt, I reckon that he was tortured by the murderer to reveal how Eberhardt could be found. An SAS job, d'you reckon?'

'I'd like to think that the SAS is a bit more subtle than that, Dave.'

We had a quick look round the rest of the house, making sure that we didn't get in the way of Linda's photographers, videographers and fingerprint guys, but found little of interest. We did note, however, that other parts of the house were as expensively furnished as the sitting room.

The top floor consisted of two empty attic rooms and, as Linda had said, there was a balcony that looked down on the rear access and the garage.

Going back downstairs, we found a door that opened straight into the garage. Inside was a new Bentley Continental in grey livery that must have been worth at least a hundred and forty thousand.

'Would you believe that?' said Dave, looking around the garage. 'He's only had it carpeted.'

What Dave said was true. The garage had been covered, wall to wall, with expensive Axminster. The car was unlocked, but the interior contained nothing that would further our investigation.

We made our way back to the street in time to meet Kate Ebdon.

'It looks as though this Samson Adekunle guy lived here on his own, Kate,' I said. 'Once Linda's finished, have another detailed look round, and then get the team to start on house-to-house enquiries. But I doubt they'll turn up very much. And see if you can find out who owns this place. Meanwhile, Dave and I will get back to the factory.'

'Have a look in the garage, guv,' said Dave to Kate. 'Our victim has only had it carpeted.'

As usual we now had to await the results of the scientific examination of the scene of Adekunle's brutal slaying. But at least we had the computer to play with. When I'd told Dave that we'd get a boffin to look at it, I'd meant Colin Wilberforce. He's an absolute wizard at interrogating these mysterious machines.

'Everything had been deleted, sir,' said Wilberforce, an hour later. 'The computer's as clean as a whistle.' He had a disappointed look on his face.

'So much for that,' I said. 'All we've got to do now is find who murdered Adekunle. And it's a racing certainty that he also murdered Eberhardt and Schmidt.'

'How about Guy Wilson, guv?' suggested Dave tentatively. 'Why else would his place have been selected? D'you think he knows more than he's telling?'

'Maybe, Dave. The murderer certainly knew the Richmond

area well enough to give Eberhardt specific directions, and that might give us a lead. I think it's time we had a word with Wilson. Although I doubt we'll get any more out of him than Miss Ebdon did.'

I decided that we'd call on Guy Wilson straightaway. Kate Ebdon had said that he was an antiquarian book dealer, and she thought it likely that he worked most of the time at home.

It was just after three o'clock when we arrived at Richmond, and Wilson answered the door.

'Mr Wilson?' I asked.

'Yes, I'm Guy Wilson.'

'We're police officers, Mr Wilson,' I said.

'What again?' said Wilson, effecting an air of surprise. 'An attractive young lady inspector called on me last Saturday.'

'Detective Inspector Ebdon is one of my officers,' I said.

'One of *your* officers? So you must be the *grand fromage*,' said Wilson, as he opened the door and invited us in.

'I'm Detective Chief Inspector Brock, if that's what you mean, and this is Detective Sergeant Poole.' I could see why Kate had taken a dislike to this man whom she'd described as a galah. I could immediately see a likeness to that colourful Australian cockatoo, although I think that Kate had the other meaning in mind: that he was a fool. My own instant assessment was that he was an egotist with an inflated perception of his own sagacity, and a tendency to make what he thought were terribly witty remarks.

'I suppose this is to do with the fire, is it?' Wilson ushered us into his wood-panelled study at the rear of the house. Thickly and expensively carpeted, the room had been fitted from floor to ceiling with custom-built oak bookshelves and a matching workstation bearing a proliferation of computer equipment. The shelves were full of books and there were several piles on the floor. A shelf above the workstation held a number of trophies apparently to do with skiing, if the little silver man on skis was anything to go by, and a model of *Bluebird*, Sir Malcolm Campbell's record-breaking car. Gail's father would undoubtedly have been able to tell me the year and the speed that this particular model triumphed at Bonneville Salt Flats in Utah.

'Yes, Mr Wilson, our enquiries are connected with the fire,' I said.

'Please take a seat and tell me how I can help you.' Wilson indicated a pair of club armchairs with a nonchalant flourish of his hand, but remained standing in front of one of the bookshelves, relaxed and hands in the pockets of his maroon trousers. If his stance was designed to impress me with some sort of ascendancy, it failed. It'd been tried too often in the past to have any effect.

'The two occupants of the camper van that was parked opposite this house had been murdered in what we're viewing as an execution-style killing,' I began. 'They'd each been shot in the head.'

'Good grief! Are you sure?'

I declined to dignify that question with a reply. After all, I wouldn't tell him how to run an antiquarian book shop. 'Furthermore, Mr Wilson, we now know that the driver of the van was given specific instructions to park opposite your house. In that way the murderer would know exactly where he was and thus be able to kill him. And his girlfriend.'

'Oh my God!' Suddenly Wilson's pomposity vanished. 'I just thought it was an unfortunate but tragic fire.' He paused, shaking his head. 'You don't think that I was responsible for killing these people, do you?' An element of panic crept into his voice as he posed that last question.

'Well, did you, Mr Wilson?' Dave took out his pocketbook and opened it to a blank page. He managed to make it look menacing.

'Of course I didn't. I didn't even know they'd been murdered. Your inspector told me that they'd been burned alive.'

'That was our assumption at the time,' I said, 'but it was subsequently discovered that they'd been shot before the van was set alight.' Kate was always careful not to give too much away to anyone who might prove to be a suspect. And right now Wilson was moving rapidly to the top of my list. It surely couldn't have been a coincidence that the murderer had selected this particular house when telling Eberhardt where to park.

'Do you know anyone called Samson Adekunle?' asked Dave.

'No. He sounds like some sort of foreigner.'

'Have you ever invested in any shares—?' I began, but got no further.

'I don't see that my financial affairs have any bearing on this,' snapped Wilson, recovering his haughtiness and interrupting me sharply.

Any minute now I thought he was going to ask if we'd got a warrant to search his house. I have to admit that the possibility of obtaining one was crossing my mind.

'The only reason I ask is that we're also investigating a large-scale share fraud that's connected with the murders. Have you ever invested in, say, an IT development company in Buenos Aires or in a cargo of oil allegedly being shipped from Nigeria? Both of them failed to yield any dividends.'

'Good God no,' said Wilson vehemently. 'I'm not stupid and that sort of fraud is going on all the time. Well, you'd know that better than me, Chief Inspector,' he added, making a rare concession that someone might know more than he did. 'If you'd care to follow me, I'll show you what sort of investments I make.' He was clearly at pains to distance himself from our probing questions and from the implication that he was connected with the murders.

We crossed the hall and followed Wilson into his sitting room.

'This is my wife Helen,' said Wilson, waving casually at an attractive raven-haired woman wearing tight-fitting white designer jeans and a long white sweater around which was a gold chain, all of which probably cost a fortune.

'Good afternoon, madam,' I said.

'These gentlemen are from the police, darling. They've come to see me about that awful fire last Thursday night or Friday morning or whenever it was. The chief inspector was just telling me that the two people in it were murdered.'

'Oh, really? How interesting. I'll leave you to it, then, Guy.' Helen Wilson finally looked up from the magazine she was reading, appraised Dave and me scathingly, but said nothing to us. Clearly a double murder virtually on her doorstep was not something that excited her. 'Anyway, I've some telephone calls to make.' The ice maiden rose from her chair, ignored Dave and me, and tossed her magazine on to the seat before leaving the room without a backward glance. She appeared to be quite a few years younger than Wilson, but first impressions were that she shared his arrogant attitude. She certainly didn't seem to enjoy having two common policemen sullying her elegant sitting room.

Wilson crossed to an oak cabinet, unlocked a safe that was secreted inside and took out a book in a plastic bag. 'This is the sort of investment I make, Chief Inspector. It's a first edition of John Buchan's *The Thirty-Nine Steps*. It retailed in nineteen fifteen for a shilling.' He paused. 'That's five pence in today's currency, but now it's worth somewhere in the region of twelve thousand pounds.'

Good for him, I thought, *but Guy Wilson was not the sort of man who would admit to having been swindled, even if he had. It wouldn't be good for his image.*

'How fascinating,' I said, but failed to see why anyone would want to pay that much for a book. If I really wanted to read *The Thirty-Nine Steps*, I could probably pick up a paperback edition for a few pounds in a bookshop or even less at a charity shop. But perhaps I'm an iconoclast.

'I could download that on to my Kindle for a few quid,' commented Dave, playing the dim copper, something he's very skilled at doing when the mood takes him. 'It might even be free.'

'Really?' said Wilson scathingly. The mere mention of a Kindle seemed to offend him.

'This silver car you saw on the night of the fire . . .' Dave walked to the window and stared out at the site of the camper-van fire. 'Had you ever seen it before, perhaps during the days leading up to the fire?'

Wilson answered immediately. 'No. At least, not as far as I can recall. I did see a sports car that stopped there about a week ago. But I think the driver was just using his mobile.'

'Did you happen to hear any shots just before the fire?'

'No, I didn't. But he'd've used a silencer wouldn't he?'

'Oh, I never thought of that, sir,' said Dave, turning from the window, but his sarcasm escaped Wilson.

'Have you anything to add to what you told Inspector Ebdon, Mr Wilson?' I asked.

'No, I told her all I know. That I saw a small silver car leaving just before I saw the van go up in flames.'

'Just now you mentioned seeing a sports car,' I said. 'Any idea of its make, colour, anything like that?'

'No, I'm afraid not.'

'Do you own a car yourself?' asked Dave casually.

'Yes, as a matter of fact, I've got a Lamborghini and before that I had a Porsche. But I'm thinking of trading in the Lamborghini for a Ferrari later this year. Unfortunately, and to my chagrin, I just missed laying hands on a 1920 Haxe-Doulton. It was made by an American firm in Detroit that went bust the following year. A good investment if I'd've been able to get it.'

'Really, sir?' Dave sounded enthusiastically impressed. 'You're obviously well up on sports cars, then.'

Wilson preened slightly. 'I think I can safely say that I know my way around them, yes.'

'But you couldn't identify the sports car you saw outside your house a week ago.' Dave shut his pocketbook and tapped it with his pen.

'All I can say is that it was one of the cheaper models,' said Wilson, irritated that Dave had so easily made him appear foolish. 'I'm not awfully familiar with the lower end of the market.'

'Thank you for your time, Mr Wilson,' I said, as Dave and I made to leave.

'What d'you think, guv?' asked Dave, as we drove away from Wilson's house.

'I don't imagine that anyone in his right mind would set up a job like the murders of Eberhardt and Schmidt bang opposite his own house, Dave. Mind you, I don't think he's the brightest star in the firmament, despite his airs and graces and his bluster about clever investments. Nevertheless, it seems an odd co-incidence that his was the address that the sender of those emails singled out for the killing ground.'

'D'you think he's clever enough to try a double bluff, guv?' asked Dave. 'Pretends to be an airy-fairy pseudo-intellectual, but is smart enough to cover his tracks.'

'Possibly,' I said, 'but we'd need more evidence of his involvement. Much more.'

'I wonder if there's anything in his sighting of this sports car,' said Dave.

'I shouldn't think so, but we'll bear it in mind.'

'D'you think he had anything to do with Samson Adekunle's murder, guv?'

'I don't see our Mr Wilson as a torturer, Dave. He's much too squeamish and the sort of barbarism that was done to Adekunle would more than likely make him throw up.'

'Shouldn't we have asked him where he was when Adekunle was murdered, guv?'

'When *was* he murdered, *Sergeant*?' I said, employing Dave's little ploy of formal address. It wasn't often I was able to turn the tables on him.

'Ah!' said Dave.

NINE

I was on the point of leaving the office when I received a telephone call from the detective inspector at Brighton.

'It's about your man William Rivers, guv. The post-mortem showed that he was in the advanced stages of pancreatic cancer. The pathologist reckoned he had only a matter of days to live.'

And that presumably explained his suicide. But it didn't solve the question of whether he'd told a former colleague about being swindled. And if he had, whether that colleague had acted upon the information.

On Friday morning, the first of the scientific reports about Samson Adekunle's murder came in.

When Linda Mitchell arrived in the office she was looking stunningly attractive, something that hadn't really registered with me before. Wearing her day clothes rather than the unflattering protective coveralls in which we saw her at a crime scene, she was attired in a smart grey trouser suit and wore her long black hair loose.

'You're obviously giving evidence in court this morning, Linda?' suggested Dave casually.

'What makes you think that, Dave?'

'Because you're wearing your Old Bailey outfit,' said Dave.

'But I always dress scruffily to go to court, Dave. Like you do,' said Linda, and turned to me. 'We found fingermarks all over the Clancy Street address, Mr Brock. We've identified one set as belonging to Adekunle, but there's no trace of any of the others in records. It's possible, I suppose, that some of them belong to a cleaning woman. Assuming, of course, that he allowed anyone to come in to clean up. Although in view of what he was involved in, I think that that's unlikely. The other possibility is that most of them belong to previous tenants or visitors. The only prints in Adekunle's car were his own.'

'I doubt that any of them belonged to our murderer,' I said. 'He seems to have been very careful.'

'There were no weapons anywhere in the house either,' continued Linda. 'I understand from Doctor Mortlock that the victim was tortured in a variety of ways. But we didn't find a whip, although there was that piece of bloodstained rope we found near the body.'

'Any joy with tracing the rope, Linda?' I asked.

'I'm afraid not. It was fairly standard stuff, the sort you could buy at almost any hardware store or DIY supermarket, and the blood on it was Adekunle's. The killer might've brought it with him or found it in the house somewhere, although we didn't find any similar rope. We examined the rack of kitchen knives and one of them was missing. But the one that was found near the body seemed to match the kitchen set and that, of course bore traces of the victim's blood. There were no cigarette ends anywhere in the house, either.' Linda laughed. 'But we did find a bit of cannabis secreted in the toilet cistern. How original is that?'

'You can forget about the cannabis, Linda. I've got enough on my plate without worrying about that sort of nonsense. But if anything else crops up, you will let me know, won't you?'

'Of course, but there are a couple of other things, Mr Brock. We got our tame locksmith to open the safe. Inside was a bundle of banknotes, ten thousand pounds in used fifty-pound notes to be precise. If they'd been new, we might've been able to find out when and where they were issued.'

'I doubt that that would've helped much,' I said.

'And then there were these.' Linda displayed a sheaf of bank statements. 'They relate to an account in the name of Trudi Schmidt, one of the camper-van victims. The account is at something called *Sparkasse* with an address in Essen. Would that be the name of the bank?'

'Not specifically, Linda. *Sparkasse* is German for savings bank. But that's all very interesting. Why, I wonder, should Adekunle have been holding Trudi Schmidt's bank statements?'

'Perhaps he was the banker for the whole scam, or at least the United Kingdom branch,' said Dave.

'We'll see if Horst Fischer can shed some light on it. Thanks very much, Linda,' I said. 'It gives us something else to work on. By the way, where's the cash now?'

'At the moment, it's in the safe in the property store at Paddington police station. Sergeant Wright took charge of it.'

'Thanks, Linda. I'll have a word with him.' 'Shiner' Wright was the laboratory liaison officer whose task, among others, was to preserve continuity of evidence. 'You said there were two things.'

'I thought I'd save the best bit until last. This was also in the safe.' Linda produced a dark green document and handed it to me. 'Adekunle's Nigerian passport.'

'I wonder when he arrived in the UK,' I said, flicking through the pages of the passport.

'Officially, it appears that he's not here, Mr Brock. There's no entry stamp.'

'So, he was probably an illegal immigrant. Well, there's a surprise. But at least we know how old he is and that he was born in somewhere called Calabar, for what good that'll do us. I'll get checks run with the Border Agency and the Nigerian High Commission.'

'Good luck,' said Dave quietly.

Ten minutes later, Kate Ebdon appeared in the incident room, but unlike Linda, Kate was wearing her usual working outfit: jeans and a man's white shirt.

'After a great deal of messing about with the local authority, the land registry and God knows who else, I've managed to trace the owner of the Clancy Street property, guv.' Kate referred to her pocketbook. 'After a few false starts I eventually tracked down the local estate agency that's responsible for renting out the property and spoke to the manager. The property's owned by a Lucien Carter and apparently he resides abroad. Very much the absentee landlord by all accounts. But the agent has never seen Carter and hasn't got a clue where he lives.'

'None at all?' I asked.

'The best he could suggest was that he thought he might be in France, but he'd got nothing to back it up with. All he could tell me was that Adekunle rented the property on a two-year lease about a year ago. I seized a reference that Adekunle gave the manager when he signed the agreement, but it's almost bound to be duff. It's on expensive notepaper purporting to come from a New York letting agency in East 92nd Street and stated in glowing terms that Adekunle was the sort of tenant anyone would be delighted to have living in their house.'

'Lucien Carter won't think so now that there's blood all over his expensive carpet,' said Dave, and paused. 'Unless it was Carter who put it there.'

'That letter's bound to be a fake, but I'll have a word with Joe Daly,' I said, taking the plastic-shrouded document from Kate. Daly is the resident FBI agent in London whose official title is legal attaché at the United States Embassy. 'Any luck with house-to-house enquiries?'

'No, guv. The nearest neighbours reckoned they'd never set eyes on Adekunle, and certainly never saw anyone entering or leaving the house. Must've been a night bird.' Kate paused to laugh. 'I interviewed one old biddy who lived opposite and who said she definitely thought there was something funny about the house, but as evidence goes, it's crook. I think she just enjoyed a yabber.'

'Perhaps you'd translate that for me, Kate.' I was gradually getting to grips with Australian slang, but some of Kate's more obscure words still eluded me.

'"Crook" means that in terms of evidence it's no good and "yabber" means she just enjoyed having a chat, *sir*,' said Kate, with a cheeky smile. It seemed that she'd caught the 'sir' habit from Dave.

'I'm glad we've got that cleared up. Now perhaps you'd do what you can with this, Kate.' I handed her Adekunle's Nigerian passport. 'See if the Border Agency's got anything on this guy. It looks as though he's in the country illegally. And the Nigerian High Commission might help, but I doubt it.'

'Pity he didn't get deported at some stage,' said Kate. 'It would've saved us a lot of trouble.'

'Couldn't've deported him, guv,' said Dave. 'It might've infringed his human rights.'

Kate scoffed. 'Give me ten minutes with him in a dark cell and I'd've infringed his human rights for him,' she muttered.

'Well, somebody did, that's for sure,' said Dave. 'And he was in no position to appeal to an immigration tribunal.'

The matter of Adekunle's passport being out of the way for the time being, I telephoned *Kriminalhauptkommissar* Fischer to tell him about the bank statements that Linda had found in Adekunle's safe.

'What address was there for Trudi Schmidt on the statements, Harry?' Fischer asked.

'Glockestrasse 59, Kettwig. Does that mean anything to you?'

'That's very useful, Harry, because she no longer lived at the address we had for her in our records. The present occupants of her old apartment hadn't heard of her, and the letting agent certainly didn't know where she'd gone. I'll arrange to have the Glockestrasse address searched and I'll tell you what we find. That's if we find anything that might help the investigation.'

I gave the bank statements to Charlie Flynn. 'See what you can do with those, Charlie. They're in German, but they're much the same in layout as those issued by UK banks and shouldn't be too difficult to read. If you have a problem with the language, come and see me.'

Next up was Tom Challis. It was turning out to be one of those busy mornings when people wanted me to make decisions.

'I've got the details of the subscribers to the telephone numbers in William Rivers's address book, guv.'

'How many, Tom?'

'Twelve, but of those only three were in the Metropolitan Police District.'

'Any near neighbours of Rivers?'

'No, guv, none at all, but there were three in the Aldershot area, one in Bordon and one in Odiham.' Challis gave me a meaningful glance. 'Living in that area could mean they're ex-army, I suppose.'

'Could be,' I said, 'although Odiham is a Royal Air Force station, so I think we can rule that one out. Let me have the addresses and Dave and I will take a trip to the home of the British Army. I just hope we won't be wasting our time.'

'I've also done that search on the Rivers family you asked for, sir.'

'Turned up anything useful, Tom?' I asked, glancing at my watch.

'It's complicated, guv, but it won't take a minute to explain. William Rivers's sister Gladys was married to a guy called Edward Deacon, both now deceased. Their only son is Charles Deacon and he's married to Mary née Webster. They also have an only son whose name is George Deacon, aged twenty-five.'

'Do me a chart, Tom, and then track them down. I suppose we'd better have a word. If George Deacon knew about his great uncle being swindled, he might've decided to do something about it. Any evidence that he is or was in the army?'

'No, sir. Not yet.'

Before going to Aldershot, I decided to make time to call on Joe Daly.

One of the great benefits of visiting the United States Embassy in Grosvenor Square is the quality of its coffee. And the fact that it always seems to be available. If you're lucky enough to be invited to lunch, you can look forward to a T-bone steak that overlaps the plate. And in the centre of the round table there is a Lazy Susan holding every condiment you could possibly want. And a few you've never heard of.

'Great to see ya, Harry.' Joe Daly swept across his huge

office and seized my hand with a vice-like grip. He'd once told me that he'd been a useful baseball player in his youth and the strength of his hand confirmed it. 'Dave, how ya doing?' Dave Poole was subjected to a similar bone-crushing grasp.

'So, Harry, what can I do for my favourite Limey cops today?' Daly waved his hand in an expansive gesture that Dave and I took as an invitation to sit in his deep armchairs. Right on cue Darlene, his secretary, appeared with the coffee. Darlene is pure Hollywood, a svelte American redhead who looked as though she'd stepped straight off the set of an episode of *Sex and the City*. Given that most of the support staff at the embassy was British, I presumed that Joe Daly's secretary being American had something to do with the need for security. Ever since 9/11 the Americans have been justifiably concerned about security. I just hope that one day we might be too, but we won't if the Border Agency has anything to do with it.

'I'm dealing with a triple murder, Joe,' I began.

'Would that be the fire out at Richmond that I read about in the paper, Harry?'

'That's the one.'

'But there were only two bodies in that camper, weren't there? But now you're treating it as a homicide.'

Clearly Daly kept his finger on the pulse. I explained the circumstances surrounding the deaths of Eberhardt and Schmidt and went on to tell him about the murder of Samson Adekunle. Finally, I produced the letter of reference that Kate Ebdon had seized from the estate agent who'd rented out the house where we'd found the body of the Nigerian fraudster.

'You want me to check it out?' asked Daly, once he'd cast his eye over the letter with the New York address.

'If it's no trouble, Joe,' I said. 'But it'll probably come to nothing.'

'Not necessarily,' said Daly. 'For all we know, it might be connected to an ongoing boiler-room scam in the States.' Turning in his chair, he shouted at the open door between his office and that of his secretary. 'Darlene, just hightail your sweet little butt in here one second.'

Daly's secretary reappeared, a notebook in her hand. 'Yes,

Joe?' She smiled at the three of us in turn, sat down in the vacant armchair and crossed her shapely legs. I wondered if there was something going on between her and Joe. And who would blame him . . . or her for that matter?

'Send a coded signal to the SAIC,' began Daly, pronouncing it 'say-ik', 'at the New York office—' He broke off to explain. 'Means special agent in charge, Harry,' he said, telling me something I knew already. He returned to his dictation. 'Attach a copy of this letter of Harry's, Darlene, and ask for enquiries to be made into its bona fides.' He went on to outline the details of my murders and the share-pushing scam in which the victims had been involved.

'That it, Joe?' asked Darlene.

'That's it, honey.'

Darlene closed her notebook, took the letter and stood up to return to her office. Crossing the floor with a provocative sway of her hips, she shot Dave a backward smile. I don't know what it is about Dave that attracts women, but then I'm a man, so I wouldn't know.

'I'll get back to you as soon as I've gotten a reply, Harry.' Daly stood up and shook hands. 'I'm sure looking forward to this lunch at the Yard next week,' he said. 'Alan Cleaver sent me an invite. Will I see you both there?'

'Maybe,' I said. 'Depends how my murder enquiry goes. But the food won't be as good as the embassy's.'

'You won't see me there. I'm not important enough,' said Dave. 'Thank God.'

TEN

I t was three o'clock before Dave and I arrived at the first of the Aldershot addresses that Tom Challis had identified from the phone numbers in William Rivers's book.

'Mr Milner? Mr James Milner?'

'That's me.' Milner was a tall, grey-haired, slender man, probably in his late sixties or early seventies. He wore jeans and a T-shirt and, despite the warm weather, an old sports jacket in the buttonhole of which was a tiny facsimile badge of the Parachute Regiment. 'What's this about?' He spoke confidently, but looked suspiciously at the pair of us.

'We're police officers, Mr Milner. I'm Detective Chief Inspector Brock of New Scotland Yard and this is DS Poole. We'd like to ask you a few questions.'

'You'd better come in, then, after you've shown me some ID, although I don't know how I can help you London fellows.'

I produced my warrant card and the old soldier nodded his satisfaction.

'I understand you're a friend of William Rivers, Mr Milner,' I said, as we followed him into his sitting room.

'Yes, I know old Billy Two Rivers. What's he been up to?' Milner sat down opposite us.

I was about to tell him when a woman entered the room, looking surprised at seeing us there. 'Oh, I didn't know we'd got guests, Jim,' she said.

'This is the missus,' said Milner, as we stood up. 'These gents are from the Met Police, Sue.'

'It's not about your pension, is it?' Susan Milner's face adopted a worried expression.

'Now why on earth should two CID officers from the Yard come here to talk about my pension, love?' said Milner. He saw my puzzled expression and explained. 'I left the army after five years, joined the Hampshire Constabulary and did my thirty, Mr Brock. But Sue here's got some crazy notion that the pension's going to be docked, what with all the cutbacks the government's making.'

'Your husband's pension is quite safe, Mrs Milner,' I assured her, 'but I'm not too sure about mine.' Milner laughed and I joined in. Dave did not appear amused.

'Right, now we've got that out of the way, what can I do for you?' asked Milner. He glanced at his wife. 'A cup of tea wouldn't go amiss, love,' he said, but then glanced at me. 'Unless you'd like something stronger.'

'No, tea will be fine, Mr Milner. Now, about William Rivers; we found your telephone number in his address book.'

'Something's happened to him, hasn't it?'

'I'm afraid so. He committed suicide in a Brighton boarding house.'

'Why the hell did the old boy top himself?' Milner seemed genuinely surprised. 'And in Brighton, of all places.'

I felt that I could be more open with Milner as he was an ex-policeman, and explained about the scam to which Rivers had fallen victim. 'At first,' I continued, 'I thought that losing that much money might've been too much for him to bear. Or even admit to.'

'Doesn't sound like the Billy Rivers I knew,' said Milner, with a shake of the head.

'But it turned out that he was suffering from incurable pancreatic cancer. The pathologist's diagnosis was that he'd only got days to live.'

'Poor old bugger,' said Milner. 'He must've been in a hell of a lot of pain. What did he do, hang himself?'

'No, he shot himself with a two-two pistol.'

'Where the devil did he get that from? I suppose he must've "liberated" it on some operation. Typical of Billy, is that.'

'How did you come to meet him? As far as we know he was in the SAS, but you were a Para, weren't you?' I nodded at his lapel badge.

'That's true, although he kicked off his career in the Paras. It was later, well before I met him, that he transferred to the SAS, but then he came back to our battalion as regimental sar'nt major. I'd just made it into the sergeants' mess and Billy put the fear of Christ into us young sergeants and into the whole battalion. A real tartar was Billy, and the Paras weren't exactly shrinking violets, if you know what I mean. Anyway, he was only there for about a year before he took his pension.'

'Any idea how he acquired that much money, Mr Milner?' queried Dave.

'Now you're asking, Skipper,' said Milner with a crooked grin, 'but it won't hurt to tell you now he's dead. He was in the army of occupation in Germany straight after the war was over. He must've been about nineteen then. In those days you could make a killing on the black market. From what I heard most of the squaddies were at it. Flogging all sorts of things to the natives: fags, coffee, soap and Scotch; in fact anything that might bring in a bit of cash. There was bartering going on an' all. I heard of one corporal who'd bought a Mercedes for twenty cigarettes, and a quartermaster who acquired a house for two bottles of Scotch. That sort of gear was the currency, you see, because after the war the Reichsmark had collapsed and the new Deutschmark wasn't really up and running. But the Germans never smoked the fags or drank the Scotch; they just used the stuff to trade.'

'Wasn't it risky?' asked Dave.

'Very. If you got captured by the military police it was a court martial and a stretch in the glasshouse. But Billy got away with it and so did a lot of the others. But I do remember that our cook-sergeant got done for flogging army rations to the Germans. He was busted down to private and did six months in Bielefeld military corrective establishment. And his German wife got done by the German police for receiving. Serve 'em right; flogging the lads' rations was a definite no-no. It was OK nicking army property off each other, but personal property and rations were definitely taboo.'

'And you?'

'I wish! It was all over by the time I got out there. The West Germans had got their sovereignty back and were better off than we were.' Milner sighed, presumably at regret for having missed that sort of opportunity. 'But how did this all come about? I mean, Billy falling for a scam of that sort. Doesn't sound like the Billy I knew. He might've run a scam or two, but I never thought he'd've got caught by one.' He broke off as Susan Milner entered with a tray. 'Ah, the tea.'

Mrs Milner poured the tea and handed it round before returning to the kitchen. Now that she was satisfied that her husband's pension was secure it appeared that she had no further interest in why we were there.

I decided to level with Milner and told him about the three murders we were dealing with. 'It crossed my mind, Mr Milner, that Rivers, being ex-SAS, might've decided to take the law into his own hands.'

'Not a chance.' Milner scoffed at the idea. 'Billy might've sold fags and coffee to the Germans, but that was it. Mind you, he must've been well into his eighties by the time he died. What does surprise me though is that he didn't report this scam to you lot.'

'We only found out as a result of a report from the German police,' I said. 'But d'you think he might've mentioned it to one of his SAS mates who decided to take revenge on Rivers's behalf?'

Milner shrugged. 'Your guess is as good as mine, Mr Brock,' he said.

'Any idea why your phone number was in his address book?'

'That was one of those funny things that sometimes happens.' Milner stopped to offer us cigarettes and light one for himself. 'After he packed in the army, I got a Christmas card from him out of the blue and we exchanged them from then on. It became a sort of ritual. Every now and then he'd ring me up and ask how I was getting on and how the lads in the battalion were. Not that I could tell him; I hadn't seen him in years and I'd been out of the army for a long time by then. But I got the impression that his mind was going a bit, so I humoured him by telling him that everything in the garden was lovely. But he did come down here to Aldershot – to Browning barracks – for a reunion in about, what, nineteen ninety, I suppose, but I never actually met him again after that. We kept meaning to make a meet, but somehow it never came off.'

'Thanks for your time, Mr Milner,' I said, as Dave and I stood up. I gave him one of my cards. 'If you think of anything else, perhaps you'd give me a bell.'

'Yes, I will. If you hear when the funeral is, I'd be grateful if you'd let me know. I'd like to see the old boy off.'

'Yes, of course, and thank Mrs Milner for the tea.'

The next two old soldiers we visited in the Aldershot area had each been in the Parachute Regiment, but neither of them was able to tell us as much as James Milner had done. And neither of them appeared capable of killing anyone. Not now. That left the one in Bordon.

It was about thirteen miles from Aldershot to Bordon and Dave covered it in a terrifying twenty minutes.

The woman who answered the door must've been at least seventy, and was grey-haired and stooped.

'Yes, what is it?'

'Would you be Mrs Crabtree, by any chance?'

'Yes. What d'you want?' Mrs Crabtree peered closely at us, as though she was short-sighted but too vain to wear glasses. Or had forgotten where she'd put them.

'We're police officers, madam,' I said. 'Is Mr Crabtree at home?'

Mrs Crabtree gave a humourless cackle, revealing that she'd lost a few of her teeth. 'You've missed him.'

'Oh, is he likely to be back shortly?'

'Shouldn't think so,' said the woman. 'I buried him five years back. Is there anything I can help you with?'

'Oh, I'm sorry. I was wondering if he'd known a sergeant major called William Rivers. He was in the Parachute Regiment and later in the SAS.'

'My Sid was a Para, but he never mentioned anyone by that name. He never talked much about his time in the army. He only did his National Service and couldn't wait to get out, so he said. He hated the army.'

'I see. Well, I'm sorry to have bothered you, Mrs Crabtree.'

'That's all right, dear. I hope you find that Mr Rivers what you're looking for.'

'Thank you,' I said.

'I wonder why Crabtree was in Billy Rivers's address book,' said Dave, as we drove away.

'Anybody's guess,' I said, 'but Milner did say he thought that Rivers's mind was wandering. One thing's certain though: Crabtree couldn't've topped our three victims.'

'What about Milner, guv?' asked Dave. 'Or the other two. D'you think they could've had anything to do with the murders.'

'No chance, Dave. Milner's an ex-copper, and although a murdering policeman wouldn't be a first, I very much doubt it. And like the other two, he's too old to go about topping people.'

'Perhaps so,' said Dave reluctantly.

We drove on for a while and then I said, 'I think we'll let the SAS know about Rivers's death, Dave, and then we'll go the funeral. It's just possible, if my theory is correct, that a closer friend of his than we've discovered already might turn up.'

'Are you thinking that one of those friends might be our killer, guv?'

'Funnier things have happened, Dave,' I said.

'Yeah, and right now we need something to happen.' Dave swung on to the A31, put his foot down and overtook a Polish articulated lorry.

Horst Fischer called back early on Friday morning.

'We have searched the apartment at Glockestrasse in Kettwig, Harry, the address you found for Trudi Schmidt on the bank statements that were in Adekunle's safe.'

'Anything of interest, Horst?' I asked.

'Nothing to connect her with the fraud, Harry.' Fischer chuckled. 'But we did find three or four DVDs featuring Trudi doing naughty things. It would appear that she'd been a pornographic actress at some time, and from what I could see, she was quite good at it.'

'D'you think that she was an innocent party in this fraud?'

'I don't think so, Harry. I spoke to the manager of the bank that issued the statements, and he told me that she had opened the account a year ago. Of course, she produced her passport and other identifying documents in accordance with the law, but she never visited the bank after that. All transactions were carried out electronically.'

'It looks as though she opened the account on Eberhardt's instructions, and that he or Adekunle handled it thereafter.'

'That was my thinking. She must have known why the account was being opened and why she wasn't to have anything to do with it,' said Fischer. 'I spoke to the official who deals with the opening of new accounts and he told me that Trudi Schmidt was accompanied by a man at the time, but this official didn't know who he was. He couldn't describe him either. I also learned from the bank that every month they sent an email to Adekunle in the UK informing him that account-holder Schmidt's latest statement was available online.'

'Didn't the bank query why those emails should be going to the United Kingdom?'

'I asked the manager about that. He told me that it wasn't the business of the bank to query a client's instructions and that the account holder could have the emails sent wherever she wanted. I also raised a query with our Vice Squad about the DVDs that Schmidt appeared in.'

'I presume they weren't able to add anything useful.'

'Nothing at all really, apart from a few comments about her performance,' said Fischer, with a guttural laugh. 'They told me that the company was quite legitimate. They also checked with the tax authorities and that the company that made the DVDs paid its taxes, which is all that seemed to worry the tax people.'

And that, I thought, showed how similar Britain and Germany were when it came to fiscal matters. And pornography.

I told Horst Fischer that Detective Sergeant Flynn was working on the bank statements and that I'd let him know the results as soon as possible.

'I doubt they'll tell us much, Harry,' said Fischer. 'The money will be out of reach now anyway.'

We were now getting desperate in our search for the killer, and I wondered if there was anything in either Hans Eberhardt's house or Trudi Schmidt's apartment in Germany that would shed some light on our murders. I decided that only a personal look at those residences would satisfy me.

Horst Fischer had proved that he was undoubtedly a capable detective, but he was concentrating his interest on the investigation of the frauds insofar as they affected Germany, rather than searching for something that would point to a killer in England. It might be that some item of evidence that had meant nothing to him might mean something to me.

Taking a metaphorical deep breath, I tapped on the commander's door.

'Yes, Mr Brock?' The commander peered at me over his half-moon spectacles and closed the file on his desk with, it seemed, a degree of reluctance.

'I have come to the conclusion that it will be necessary for Sergeant Poole and me to go to Germany, sir.'

'Whatever for?' The commander's face assumed a suitably appalled expression, and he took off his glasses.

I explained about the complexity of the murders that, I

suggested, had been made even more complicated by the death of Samson Adekunle, and wrapped up my submission with as much CID gobbledegook as I could muster. I trotted out the usual phrases like motive, means and opportunity and threw in a bit about scenes of crime and scientific evidence. I was pleased to see that the boss didn't understand a word of it, even when I mentioned the pornography.

Nevertheless, he pretended that he'd followed what I was talking about, and appeared to consider my request for some moments before coming to a decision. Of sorts.

'I think it's a matter that the deputy assistant commissioner will have to decide upon, Mr Brock,' he said eventually. 'Leave it with me and I'll let you know.' Oh well, no change there.

Ten minutes later I was summoned to return to the presence. Why the hell won't he use the phone other than to send for me? It was too much to hope that he'd descend from his paper mountain and actually come into my office.

'The DAC has agreed that it is necessary for you and Sergeant Poole to go to Germany, Mr Brock.'

I got the distinct impression that the commander was quite put out that the DAC had given the necessary authorization. The boss is well known for his parsimony, a miserliness that extends as far as the Commissioner's money. Even trying to extract a small amount of cash each week for his coffee was a monumental task. It's just as well he's unaware that our coffee machine is illegal in the eyes of the Receiver, an official who regards the unauthorized abstraction of Metropolitan Police electricity as one of the most serious offences in the criminal calendar.

I returned to my office and telephoned Horst Fischer in Essen.

'Horst, Sergeant Poole and I are coming to Essen.'

'Excellent,' said Horst. 'When can I expect you?'

'I'm afraid it'll have to be tomorrow,' I said.

'What's wrong with tomorrow, Harry?'

'Well, it is a Saturday.'

'I work on a Saturday,' said Horst. 'Don't you?'

'Most of the time, Horst, yes. And even on a Sunday sometimes.'

My ex-wife Helga's uncle had been a superintendent in the Cologne police, but he had a cushy office job that required him to work only on weekdays, nine-to-five, with Saturdays and Sundays off. Consequently, Helga's parents didn't believe that I frequently had to work over the weekends and thought that I was seeing another woman. At least, Helga's mother did.

'*Ja*, me too. I suppose you'll be arriving at Düsseldorf Airport.'

'Yes, that's so. I'll send you an email with my ETA.'

'Good, I'll be there to meet you.'

Walking out to the incident room, I asked Colin Wilberforce to get in touch with the department that arranged travel and to book flights for Dave and me for the following day.

ELEVEN

After an early start, much too early for my liking, our flight touched down at Düsseldorf Airport at just before ten, local time.

As the door of the aircraft opened, we were confronted by a German police officer in uniform.

'*Herr* Brock?' he enquired. He had a grave expression on his face and his hand rested lightly on his pistol holster.

'Yes, that's me. I'm Brock.'

'You are to come with me, *mein Herr. Herr* Fischer is waiting for you. Please to make no trouble so that I don't have to use the handcuffs.'

It was a statement that caused the previously self-assured, pretty young flight attendant to lose some of her cool. She raised her eyebrows and forgot to say that she was looking forward to seeing us again. In the circumstances, she probably assumed that she *wouldn't* be seeing us again.

Horst Fischer, a rotund, jolly man with huge moustaches, was waiting at the end of the jetway. His hands were on his ample stomach and he was laughing uproariously. He looked rather like an out-of-control Father Christmas.

'I hope you didn't mind my little joke, Harry,' he said, still chuckling as he shook hands.

By this time I was laughing too. 'This is Dave Poole, my sergeant,' I said, pleased to discover that there were some German policemen who shared our sense of humour. But over the years I've found that most coppers do have a rather bizarre sense of the ridiculous.

Fischer shook hands. 'Welcome to Germany, Dave,' he said. It seemed that he spoke a little English, but I was sure that I'd finish up interpreting most of what he said for Dave's benefit. And so it proved as the day wore on.

'Pleased to meet you, sir,' said Dave.

'You must call me Horst, Dave.' Fischer waggled a finger of admonition. 'And now I have a car waiting.' With a few terse words he brushed aside the low-key immigration and customs controls that existed at the airport, hurried us through to the concourse and out to a waiting police car. Telling the driver to turn on the blue lights and the two-tone horn, he glanced over his shoulder. 'I'm in a hurry for my first beer of the day, Harry,' he said, by way of explanation.

We covered the twenty-three miles to Essen in considerably less than twenty-three minutes.

Our first stop was at Horst's favourite *Gasthof* in the centre of Essen where he was greeted like an old friend and valued customer. Both of which I'm sure he was.

'Hello, Horst.' A bosomy young waitress appeared at our table. She was attired in a sort of Bavarian costume; but the skirt was much too short to be authentic and I doubted that high heels were a part of the traditional outfit. 'I see you have brought some friends with you today.'

'These gentlemen are from the famous Scotland Yard, *liebchen*.' Horst turned to me. 'This is Nadine, the sexiest waitress in all of Nordrhein-Westfalen. Three beers, Nadine, there's a good girl.' As she turned away he gave her a playful slap on her bottom.

'Coming right up,' the girl replied, and paused to glance at me. 'Are you English policemen the same as Horst?' she asked, with a giggle.

'Yes,' I said. 'We're all quite terrible people, especially him,' I added, pointing at Dave.

My comment produced another giggle and Nadine hurried away to fulfil the order.

Once three huge steins of *Bräu Hell* beer were in front of us, we got down to business.

'I thought we would go first to my office, Harry, where you can see exactly the evidence we have accumulated. Then I think it will be time for lunch, and in the afternoon you would like to have a look at the house of Eberhardt and the apartment of Schmidt, *ja*?' Horst laughed. 'And then dinner somewhere and a few beers, eh?' He seemed to regard our visit as a bit of a jolly.

The first thing that Fischer produced when we arrived at his office was one of the DVDs he had seized from Trudi Schmidt's apartment. He crossed the office and inserted the DVD into a video player.

The opening scene was of a naked woman lying on a bed. She was joined by a black man and they engaged in sexual intercourse. At first, the man's face was not visible, but a few frames later he turned to face the camera.

'The girl is Trudi Schmidt,' said Horst.

'Bloody hell, and that guy's Samson Adekunle,' exclaimed Dave.

'Ah, I think that is the name of one of your victims, *ja*?' said Fischer.

'Yes, he was the man whose body we found at a house in Paddington,' I said. 'He'd been severely beaten and then shot. It's our belief that he was tortured to reveal Eberhardt's email address, and that the murderer then sent an email to Eberhardt persuading him to come to England. And you told me that you'd found those emails on Eberhardt's computer, Horst.'

'*Ja*, that is so.'

In the next scene a young white man climbed on to the bed and joined in the fun with Adekunle.

'I wonder who he is,' said Dave.

I turned to Fischer. 'Is there any way of finding out that man's identity, Horst?' I asked.

'I'll speak to the Vice Squad again, Harry. They're in touch with the company that made the videos and they might know who he is. I'll let you know.'

From Fischer's office, we visited Trudi Schmidt's apartment at Glockestrasse. Fischer had done a good job in searching the place, but Dave and I spent an hour going through everything that was there. Regrettably, we found nothing that would further our investigation.

Hans Eberhardt's house was interesting, but failed to reveal anything that we didn't already know about. We examined the sophisticated printing press and it was clear that no expense had been spared in setting up the boiler-room scam. But given that this little team had extracted millions from gullible punters they could obviously afford the best.

'A fingerprint examination of this place and that of Trudi Schmidt did not reveal any prints of use,' said Fischer, anticipating my next question.

That evening Horst Fischer took Dave and me to a restaurant in the centre of Essen where we had a sumptuous dinner. Once again, he seemed to know the waitress who served us and engaged in his usual banter with her. To add to our enjoyment there was a cabaret, and we drank far too much German beer.

The next morning, our host drove us to Düsseldorf Airport and poured us on to an aircraft. Dave and I were suffering terminal hangovers, and I determined that I would never drink German beer again. But such vows tend to be forgotten with the passing of time. We thanked Fischer for his hospitality, but he shrugged and assured me that it hadn't cost him personally a single euro. The Essen police, he said, would cover all the costs, even for the hotel in which we had stayed, albeit briefly. I wish his boss could meet my boss.

All in all, we had learned little, but I was prepared to tell the commander that the visit had been extremely beneficial to our enquiry. I just hoped that a murder conviction would eventually back up that assertion.

Our first job on Monday morning was to attend Samson Adekunle's post-mortem.

As usual, Henry Mortlock had almost finished by the time Dave and I arrived.

'As far as I can tell, Harry, Adekunle had been dead about ten days.'

'That agrees with what we've learned since, Henry. Before Adekunle's body was found, the German police discovered evidence that he'd sent emails to Hans Eberhardt on the fifteenth of July, or was alive enough to provide his killer with Eberhardt's email address. So he was probably murdered very shortly afterwards.'

'Yes, that makes sense.' Mortlock pointed a pair of forceps at a stainless steel kidney-shaped bowl. 'That was the bullet I took out of him.'

'Looks like a two-two, guv,' said Dave. 'Same calibre as the ones that killed Eberhardt and Schmidt.'

Minutes after we'd returned to Curtis Green, Dave entered my office flourishing a message form.

'We've just had a call from the governor of Stone Mill prison, guv.'

'If someone's escaped, it's nothing to do with us,' I said. 'I've got quite enough on my plate dealing with three murders.'

'Not this time,' said Dave. 'This prisoner's still firmly banged up, and he told the governor that he has important information for us regarding the murders of Eberhardt and Schmidt.'

'Did he tell the governor what this important information was, Dave?'

'No, apparently he refused, saying that it was confidential and that he'd only tell the officer dealing with the case.'

'Sounds a bit dodgy to me. Did the governor at least tell us the inmate's name?'

Dave grinned. 'Yeah, it's our old friend Luke Dobson. So it's got to be a con.'

'But wasn't he supposed to be going straight, Dave?' I asked, with a jocular attempt at being surprised. 'What's he in for this time?' Dave and I had jousted with Dobson in the past, contests in which Dobson had always come second. A forty-two-year-old villain who specialized in serious robbery with violence, he had a string of convictions as long as the M1 motorway. But he was one of those likeable villains who bore no animosity towards the police when they captured him and succeeded in getting him banged up for a few years.

'I did a quick search on him in records. He's straight all right, guv, about as straight as a corkscrew. He was nicked by the Thames Valley Police some three years ago for a jeweller's shop blagging on Slough's ground. Apparently he and his cohorts emerged from the jeweller's to be confronted by a fully armed response unit. He's currently doing a nine stretch for that little job. They've obviously got some good snouts in Thames Valley.'

'Give the prison governor a bell, Dave, and ask him when we can see Dobson.'

'Already done that, guv. Any time today,' said Dave. 'By the way, the prison governor's a "her" not a "him".'

The governor's office was immediately above the gate at the front of the nineteenth-century, grim, grey edifice that is Her Majesty's Prison Stone Mill.

The governor was a brunette of about forty, attractively dressed in a navy trouser suit with a white jabot. Her long hair was dragged tightly away from her face and fashioned into a ponytail, a style that Dave described as a Croydon facelift.

'Welcome to Stone Mill, Mr Brock. Or to put it another way: this is Stone Mill and you're welcome to it,' she said, smiling mischievously as she crossed the office and shook hands with a firm grip. 'I've arranged for you to speak to Dobson in one of the interview rooms. Mr Reece will show you the way,' she added, indicating the prison officer who had escorted us from the main entrance. 'If you need any further assistance, do feel free to come back to me. I should warn you however, that these so-called prison cell confessions are commonplace, and usually turn out to be fiction. Prisoners like Dobson are very good at blowing smoke up your arse, if you know what I mean.'

'I know, Governor,' I said. 'I've been on the receiving end of all too many.'

Prison Officer Reece led the way along a labyrinth of corridors, through numerous locked gates and up an iron staircase until eventually we reached the interview room.

'I'll be outside, guv,' said Reece, unlocking the door. 'Give me a shout if you need me.'

I pushed open the door of the interview room, and Dobson, clad in a maroon tracksuit, immediately leaped to his feet.

'Blimey, I never knew it was you what was doing these toppings, Mr Brock,' he said, astonishment written large on his face. 'And you an' all, Mr Poole.'

'Life's full of little surprises, Luke,' I said, waving to Dobson to sit down. 'How's life treating you?'

'Up and down, like the proverbial fiddler's elbow, Mr Brock,' replied Dobson with a crooked grin. 'I don't s'pose you've got any snout on you, have you?'

'Are you allowed to smoke in here, then?' It was a facetiously rhetorical question to which I knew the answer. I tossed a cigarette to Dobson and handed one to Dave. It was one of the perversities of successive panicky governments that whereas the draconian smoking ban forbade smoking almost everywhere else, it allowed it in Her Majesty's penal establishments.

'Course I am,' said Dobson, accepting a light from Dave. 'They don't wanna breach me human rights, do they?'

'Perish the thought,' said Dave. 'You might sue them for damages.'

'Anyway, I dunno what all the fuss is about.' Dobson leaned back in his chair, relaxed and expelling cigarette smoke. 'D'you know what, Mr Brock? The biggest cause of death in this country in a few years' time will be worry. People are slowly worrying themselves to death. Worrying about what they eat and whether it's organic, what and how much they drink, whether they're breathing in pollution and whether there's nuts in anything. I'll tell you this much: the non-smoking, teetotal, vegetarian, wind-farm nutcases are taking over the world, and that's a fact. So there you are, guv'nor,' he added with a satisfied expression, certain that he'd diagnosed all the ills of mankind.

'Possibly,' I said, 'but now that we've had a helping of your porridge philosophy, Luke, can we get down to why you wanted to see me?'

'Ah, yes, well . . .' Dobson leaned forward, lowering his voice to a confidential level. 'It's this geezer, see, what come in last Friday, name of Emery, Kevin Emery.'

'Mean anything?' I asked, glancing at Dave, but he shook his head. 'Go on, Luke.'

'Well, he got banged up in my cell. He'd not been there longer than half an hour when he told me as how he'd done for them two in Richmond. You know, the camper van what was set on fire.'

'Why on earth did he tell you that, Luke?' asked Dave.

'Don't ask me, Mr Poole—' began Dobson.

'But I am asking you, Luke,' said Dave, with commendable patience.

'I asked him what he was in for, like,' said Dobson, being in no position to answer Dave's question about why Emery had taken him into his confidence. 'Well, you do, don'tcha? And he said as how he was on remand, having had his collar felt on Thursday for a blagging. But then he said he'd got hisself nicked on purpose to get out of the way because the Old Bill was looking for him for this double topping what you're dealing with. And he reckoned you'd never think of looking for him in the nick. Know what I mean?'

I was having doubts already. Nothing had been released to the media about the two victims having been murdered. As far as the general public was concerned Eberhardt and Schmidt had died as the result of an unfortunate fire. The inaccurate inference drawn by at least two of the crime reporters of Fleet Street was that a gas canister had exploded, and we'd done nothing to disabuse them.

'Is that it, then?' I asked. 'He didn't say how he'd done these toppings, or where he'd come from, or if he'd got form for violence? Nothing like that?'

'No, he clammed up after that. I s'pose he realized that he'd given up too much. He said that if it got passed on, whoever grassed would get striped. Well, I said to meself, that's all bullshit, so I thought I'd give you the heads-up, like.'

'Thanks, Luke.' I stood up and tossed him my packet of cigarettes. It wasn't too magnanimous a gesture; there were only three left in it.

'Be lucky, Mr Brock,' said Dobson, as I banged on the interview room door. 'You won't forget to mention to the governor that I've been helpful, will you?' he added as we left the room.

'Don't worry, Luke,' said Dave. 'We'll be sure to tell her all about it.'

'Everything all right, Mr Brock?' asked the attendant prison officer.

'Yes, thanks, Mr Reece, but I need to see the governor again.'

'Right you are. Follow me.'

We had to wait a few minutes while the governor finished a telephone conversation.

'Sorry about that, Mr Brock. The Department of Justice is a pain in the arse, always on the phone asking some damn-fool questions that they should know the answers to anyway. Now, how can I help you?'

'Dobson started off by saying he's sharing a cell with a prisoner called Kevin Emery.'

'Mr Reece?' The governor glanced at the prison officer.

'That's correct, ma'am,' said Reece. 'Dobson and Emery share a cell on number two landing in D Wing.'

'Dobson said that Emery was on remand for a robbery and went on to claim that he'd confessed to the two murders I'm investigating,' I said. 'I don't know how he knew about the murders though. We haven't released that information yet.' I knew, however, that the prison grapevine was extremely fast and extremely accurate when it came to learning about villainy in the outside world.

'We don't have any remand prisoners here, Mr Brock. They usually go to Brixton,' said the governor. 'When were these murders exactly?'

'Friday the eighteenth of July.'

The governor chuckled and crossed to a filing cabinet. Extracting a folder and returning to her desk, she donned a pair of heavy, black horn-rimmed spectacles and spent a few moments glancing through it.

'He's having you on, I'm afraid, Mr Brock,' she said, glancing up and removing her glasses.

'Who, Dobson? Or Emery?'

The governor laughed. 'One or the other, or both,' she said. 'Emery was transferred here last Friday from an open prison in Yorkshire. He's a sex offender who'd already served half a five-year term for grooming a young schoolgirl on the Internet and is being considered for day release. He's on the sex offenders' register and he'll be tagged if and when he's released. But at the moment it's a big if; he's to be interviewed by the Parole Board next week. So, there's no chance that he committed your murders. But I know what Dobson's up to. He wants his assistance to be noted for *his* Parole Board hearing. Not that that will occur for a few years yet. As I said earlier, prison cell confessions are all too common.'

'I know,' I said. 'It's not the first time I've been the victim of duff info. No wonder he didn't want to tell you why he wanted to see me. You'd've seen through it straightaway.' Dave and I rose to leave. 'Thank you for your time, Governor.'

'I'm sorry you've had a wasted journey, Mr Brock.'

'What'll happen to Dobson now?' I asked.

'I'll have them separated,' said the governor. 'I doubt that it would be a good idea to let him and Emery carry on sharing a cell even though I think it's unlikely that Emery said anything to Dobson about your murders. Nevertheless, prison gossip being what it is, Emery will know that Dobson's spoken to you and that'll worry Emery. It's the way the prison grapevine works. Don't ask me how it happens, but happen it does. Mr Reece will show you out.'

'I'll be having a few quiet words in Master Dobson's shell-like ear, guv'nor,' said Reece, as we reached the main gate.

'I wouldn't like to be on the receiving end of Mr Reece's "few quiet words",' said Dave, as we drove out of the gates and exchanged the prison's urine-laden air for the diesel-charged atmosphere of the outside world. 'D'you reckon Emery did tell Dobson that he was a double murderer?'

'I doubt he said anything. But whichever way it is, Dave, when Emery's in stir it's safer for him to admit to being a murderer than a sex offender. On the other hand, he could've been testing the water to see if his new cell mate was a grass. But the word on the landing being what it is Dobson probably knew that Emery was a sex offender and decided to put the bubble in. Unfortunately, he's not smart enough to tell a convincing tale.'

'Which is why he's doing nine for robbery,' said Dave.

And that was it; our visit to Stone Mill prison had been a complete waste of time. But it was an example of how the police are so often misled; even though I'd guessed from the start that it was a bum steer these things have to be followed up.

On Monday afternoon, Charlie Flynn told me what he'd discovered by checking through Trudi Schmidt's bank statements.

'I've set out the exact amounts in my report, guv,' said Flynn, handing me a document, 'but suffice it to say for the moment that large sums were paid in, but then went out again almost immediately. They all appear to have been sent by wire transfer to an account in the Cayman Islands. But there's no way of telling where they went from there, if they went anywhere.'

'Knowing how these guys work, Charlie,' I said, 'the funds won't have stayed in the Caymans for very long. I imagine that they were probably transferred all round the globe and I'd take a guess that at some stage they stopped off at the Bahamas. I doubt we'll ever be able to track them down.'

I spent a few minutes examining Flynn's report and sent a copy to Horst Fischer.

TWELVE

That afternoon I received a telephone call from Stella Kumar. She told me that her father's funeral would take place at eleven o'clock the following morning at his local cemetery in Pinner Road.

Even Colin Wilberforce's considerable skills and powers of persuasion failed to discover the telephone number of the SAS headquarters at Hereford. Eventually I attempted to call in a favour from an army officer at the Ministry of Defence with whom I'd had dealings in the past, but even he was unwilling to divulge this sensitive information, claiming that he didn't know it. He did, however, promise to pass on a message. I gave him William Rivers's details and the date and time of his funeral.

*   *   *

The day of the funeral was beautifully sunny with only the slightest breath of wind. Well in advance of the time set for the service Dave and I drove up the avenue leading to the tiny chapel and parked the car. We were hoping to spot some unusual faces. We didn't have long to wait.

At five minutes to eleven the cortège arrived: just a hearse and one car. Rivers's plain coffin was surmounted by a single wreath and the only mourners occupying the accompanying car were Stella Kumar herself and a man I took to be her husband Ram. There was no sign of William Rivers's grandchildren. I assumed that they were now adults and probably living away from home; possibly even abroad.

But then a BMW with civilian number plates drove into the cemetery grounds and parked next to our CID runabout. A man alighted and looked around. Although in plain clothes with a nondescript tie, his turnout and bearing were unmistakably those of a soldier.

'Excuse me,' the man said as he approached Dave and me. 'D'you know if this is the funeral of Mr William Rivers?'

'Yes, it is,' I said. 'Are you from the SAS?'

'What a strange question.' The man stared blankly at me.

'I'm Detective Chief Inspector Brock of New Scotland Yard,' I said, by way of offering a reason for my query.

'How do I know you're who you say you are?' Only then did the man smile, as though excusing his demand for proof.

I showed him my warrant card and he seemed satisfied.

'I'm here to represent the army, certainly. My name's Brown.'

'But you're not from the SAS?'

'I'm representing the army,' repeated Brown tersely, in a way that brooked no further discussion on the subject.

'I see. I only asked because William Rivers was in the SAS, many years ago.' I should've realized that members of the SAS never admit to it. I was once told by an infantry colonel that anyone who claims to be a past or present member of that illustrious regiment – and there were many who did – had most certainly never served with it. Secrecy, it seemed, was second nature to these tough men. It rather surprised me that Rivers had displayed a shield of the regimental device in his living room, but perhaps he never expected anyone to see it. It was fortunate that Charlie Flynn had had the foresight to take a photograph of it, otherwise we might never have known.

'So I believe,' said Brown, 'but what's your interest?'

I glanced at my watch. 'Perhaps we could speak afterwards,' I said. 'The service is about to begin. If you want to make your number with Rivers's daughter, that's the lady over there.' I pointed at Mrs Kumar who was dressed soberly in a black suit and hat.

'Thanks, I'll do that,' said Brown, and hurried to catch up with Rivers's only daughter. He and Mrs Kumar had a brief conversation and then entered the chapel together with Ram Kumar.

Moments later another small car drew up and a smartly-dressed James Milner alighted. He was wearing a blazer with a Parachute Regiment badge on the pocket, a regimental tie and a maroon beret with a Paras badge on it.

'You made it, then,' I said.

'Like I said, I thought I'd come and bid the old boy bon voyage. I did think about asking the Royal British Legion for a guard of honour, but it was not really my place to do it.' Milner pointed towards the sky. 'Billy spent a lot of his time up there and now he's up there permanently,' he said, and together we hurried into the chapel.

The service was short and apart from Dave and me there were only the four mourners: Mr and Mrs Kumar, James Milner and the mysterious Mr Brown. But there was a surprise before the coffin was removed for interment. Brown crossed to the lectern at the front of the chapel and, presumably with Mrs Kumar's acquiescence, recited from memory a few lines from a poem.

> *We are the Pilgrims, master; we shall go*
> *Always a little further: it may be*
> *Beyond that last blue mountain barred with snow,*
> *Across that angry or that glimmering sea . . .*

There followed a brief silence and then the pall-bearers removed the coffin and carried it slowly to the burial ground. Dave and I watched the committal from a distance and after Mr and Mrs

Kumar had left in their car, Brown walked over to where we were standing.

'You said you had an interest in Billy Rivers, Mr Brock.'

'Yes, but perhaps you'd tell me the significance of that poem you recited?'

'It's on the memorial to the SAS dead at their depot at Hereford.'

'How did you know that, Mr Brown?' asked Dave, in an attempt to persuade Brown to admit that he was a member of the SAS.

Brown afforded Dave a brief glance. 'I heard it somewhere,' he said. 'Now,' he continued, facing me again, 'you were going to tell me why you're so interested in the funeral of Billy Rivers.'

I explained about the swindle to which William Rivers had fallen victim, and the three murders that evidence indicated were connected to it.

'It did cross my mind that some of his former comrades might've heard about it and decided to exact revenge,' I continued.

'Most unlikely I'd've thought,' said Brown. 'From what I've heard of the SAS they might be trained killers, but they're highly disciplined *and* law abiding.' He glanced at his watch. 'If there's nothing else I can assist you with, Mr Brock, I do have another appointment.' With a nod and those few words of dismissal, he turned on his heel, crossed to his car and drove away. I had convinced myself, despite Brown's denials, that he faced the long drive to the SAS headquarters at Hereford.

'Another bloody waste of time, guv,' said Dave.

'It's in the nature of our calling in life, Dave,' I said airily.

'Yes, sir,' said Dave.

The murders of Eberhardt and Schmidt were now eleven days old, and despite our largely unproductive visit to Essen we were getting nowhere.

Dave and I had a quick lunch on the way back from Rivers's funeral and arrived at the office just after two o'clock. There was a message waiting for me from Joe Daly at the American Embassy. He had news, it said. We set off for Grosvenor Square immediately.

*   *   *

We were followed into Daly's office by Darlene bearing the obligatory coffee, and settled down to hear what the FBI agent had to say.

'This Lucien Carter guy hasn't vanished as you suggested might be the case, Harry. He's got an apartment on East 92nd Street in New York which was the address on the letter your realty agent received. Seems a bit careless that he allowed himself to be traced that easily. What's more he seems to be tied up in your scam.'

'Had he previously come to the notice of the FBI, then, Joe?' I asked.

'Sure thing. His name came up in an ongoing investigation that has links to the Bahamas. And the business of the Buenos Aires IT company has cropped up as well. But the Bureau didn't know he was in New York until I passed them your information.'

'Is he still there? In New York, I mean?'

'Sure is,' said Daly with a laugh. 'But as of now he's not at his apartment.'

'Where's he gone, then?'

'The Bronx or, to be precise, Rikers Island.'

'He didn't get bail, then.'

'No chance, Harry. The Bureau raided his apartment, found a whole load of fake share certificates and the judge sent him straight to Rikers.' Joe switched his gaze to Dave. 'That's the Big Apple's favourite prison, Dave.'

'Yes, I know,' said Dave. 'There's about fourteen thousand prisoners there. You've obviously been very busy in New York City.'

Daly laughed. 'You *have* heard of it, then.'

'Yes, I watch *Law and Order* on TV,' said Dave, and glanced briefly at me. 'When I've got time to sit down and watch TV.'

'Did the New York office tell you anything about those certificates, Joe?' I asked, ignoring Dave's veiled suggestion of oppression on my part.

'They sure did, Harry.' Daly turned in his chair. 'Darlene honey,' he shouted, 'bring in those copies of the share certificates we got in the diplomatic bag from Federal Plaza, there's a doll.'

Moments later, Darlene appeared with a sheaf of documents. 'That's everything the New York office sent us, Joe,' she said.

'There you go, Harry.' Daly handed me the copies of the certificates that the FBI had found in Carter's apartment. 'This guy seems to be the mastermind behind this boiler-room scam. They've already got a list of vics who'd gotten ripped off by him.'

There were some certificates I didn't recognize, but others, as Daly had said, were for the same bogus Buenos Aires IT company in which Lady Fairfax and William Rivers had invested. There were also some for an oil company whose tanker was supposedly leaving Nigeria in the near future, similar to the ones that had been found in Adekunle's study.

'Does your New York office know if Carter's been in the States for some time, Joe?'

'Looks like it. He's a Brit, by the way. They seized his passport, but there was nothing in it to indicate that he's been abroad recently. The last entry stamp was two years ago when he landed at JFK from Heathrow via the Bahamas. He also appeared to have paid a short visit to Paris some time ago. They're checking it out with the Immigration and Nationality Service. Chances are he's overstayed his landing conditions and that's why he didn't get bail. D'you have a reason for asking?'

'Yes, I was wondering if he could've had anything to do with my three murders.' I was interested that the Bahamian connection had come up again. Horst Fischer had told me that, according to Wilhelm Weber, in whose camper van Eberhardt had met his death, Eberhardt had visited the Bahamas several times.

'I don't think he'd want to get his hands dirty, Harry, unless your three vics had double-crossed him, but you never know. I'll send an email across and get our boys to put it to him.'

'Was there anything to indicate that he actually owned the property at Clancy Street, Paddington? The information we had was that he did own it, but as I said before, he was believed to be resident in France.'

'I'll put that on the list of questions,' said Daly. 'Have you been in touch with the French police?'

'Didn't seem much point, Joe,' said Dave. 'We didn't have an address for him there.'

'But in view of what you've found out, Joe,' I said, 'it might be a good idea for me to have a word with the French. He might be on their most wanted list.'

'Do they have one?' asked Joe.

'Yes,' said Dave. 'Mostly Americans.'

Daly laughed. 'Get outta here.'

I thought it was time that I brought the commander up to speed about my enquiries if for no better reason than to worry him with the possibility that Dave and I might have to go overseas again.

'Ah, Mr Brock, have you made an arrest yet?'

Oh, the naivety of the man. 'I fear we've got quite a long way to go before we start knocking-off suspects, sir.'

The commander wrinkled his nose at my use of the term 'knocking-off', but this time he didn't query it. Perhaps he's given up trying to rid me of criminal slang.

'Has this enquiry presented you with some problems, then, Mr Brock?' With a sigh of exasperation, the commander took off his glasses, placed them carefully in the centre of his blotter and gave me one of his superior stares.

Problems? Ye Gods! There are times when I find it hard to believe that this man is a policeman, let alone pretending to be a detective.

'International ramifications have manifested themselves, sir,' I began. Dave would've been pleased with that sentence.

'Oh? What sort of international ramifications?'

I sensed that the commander had immediately started to worry about expenses.

'Our enquiries have now spread to New York, France and to the Bahamas, sir. In addition to Germany.'

'Good heavens!' The commander shook his head and assumed an expression of grave concern. 'I trust that you and Poole will not be gallivanting half way round the world, Mr Brock,' he said sternly, as if daring me to contradict him.

'That remains to be seen, sir. It's possible that some of our enquiries may have to be carried out in person. There is some slight suggestion that the man in the custody of the FBI might be our murderer. His name's Lucien Carter and he's currently in Rikers.'

The great man raised his eyebrows. 'Is he suffering from some sort of illness, then?'

I wondered if he'd confused Rikers with a hospital. 'Rikers is a prison, sir. In fact, it's *the* prison for New York. As to whether he's ill, I can't say, but his health might've been affected by his inability to obtain bail.'

'A prison? I see. But isn't there a hospital of the same name?' The commander sniffed; he hated being wrong-footed. 'The Americans do give their prisons the most extraordinary names,' he said, in some forlorn attempt to justify his mistake. 'I believe there's one called Sing Sing. Presumably because they have a well-known choir there.'

I was tempted to say that Wormwood Scrubs wasn't exactly a commonplace name, but I thought I'd chanced my arm far enough for one day.

'I'll keep you informed, sir.'

'Yes, do that, Mr Brock, and do try to avoid going abroad again.'

Capitaine Henri Deshayes of the *Police Judiciaire* HQ at the quai des Orfèvres in Paris was my contact for all French criminal matters. We had liaised on several occasions, sometimes in London, sometimes in Paris, ostensibly to discuss pressing police business. And to enjoy the occasional meal with Gail and Gabrielle, Deshayes' gorgeous wife.

Although it was getting on for six o'clock, I knew that Deshayes, like those of us at the sharp end, was a real detective, and would still be at work. After several attempts in pidgin French to locate him, I was eventually connected to his extension.

'*Bonjour*, 'Arry. Are the London police once again in need of 'elp from the best police force in the world?'

'In your dreams, Henry, and *Bonjour* yourself.' I always emphasized the aitch of his name to compensate for him omitting it from mine. Unfair perhaps, but coppers of all nationalities tend to engage in a bit of badinage with each other. 'How is Gabrielle?' Deshayes' wife was an attractive and vibrant woman who had once been a dancer with the famous *Folies-Bergères*. She had much in common with Gail and when they weren't discussing the rigours of being a professional dancer, they were talking about fashion.

'She is well. And Gail?'

'She is well also, Henry.'

'*Bon*. When are you and Gail coming to Paris again? It's time we had a meal and a few cognacs, eh? While the girls are raiding the fashion shops.'

It was a feature of our occasional visits to the French capital that Gabrielle and Gail used it as an excuse to raid the haute couture establishments of the city. Henri and I managed to avoid these incredibly boring excursions by making an excuse of exchanging information about urgent police matters. We would then disappear to Henri's favourite bar where we would sink a few beers and put the world – and our respective police forces – to rights.

'I have a problem, Henry. Several problems in fact.' I explained in some detail about the triple murder enquiry that I was investigating, and told him about Lucien Carter. 'From what we've learned so far, Henry, it would seem that Carter is at the centre of this operation. I was wondering whether the name had come to your notice for involvement in similar frauds in France. There was a suggestion that he lived there at some time, but we've largely discounted that.'

'Leave it to me, 'Arry, and I'll get back to you as soon as I can. You can give me details for this man, *oui*?'

I provided Deshayes with the particulars that had been passed on to me by Joe Daly and which the FBI had obtained from Carter's passport.

'*D'accord!*' said Deshayes. 'Perhaps tomorrow I will be able to tell you if this man is of interest to the French police.'

My next job was to contact the Bahamian police, but that was something that could wait until tomorrow. I rang Gail and suggested dinner somewhere local.

We strolled hand in hand from Gail's townhouse along the bank of the river Thames into Kingston town centre. It had been a blazing hot summer and this evening was no different with the temperature still in the high seventies and not a breath of wind.

Gail was attired in a white linen trouser suit and her long blonde hair was loose. Her only jewellery was a set of discreet earrings that I'd bought her for her last birthday. At one stage she stopped to admire a bare-chested senior eight from a local school that was rowing upriver in perfect harmony.

'Cor blimey!' exclaimed Gail excitedly in the mock Cockney accent she was so good at. 'Just look at those lovely boys. Every one of them with a six-pack.'

'Why am I never lucky enough to see eight gorgeous women rowing along here stripped to the waist?' I asked.

'You always did like women oars,' said Gail enigmatically, and gave me a playful punch. 'You should be so lucky.'

I'm usually pessimistic about trying new places to eat, but to my surprise the restaurant, a newly-opened bistro, had an excellent menu. Never adventurous when it came to selecting something to eat, I followed Gail's lead. She chose smoked mackerel pâté followed by grilled sea bream, fondant potatoes and French beans, rounding off the meal with Eton mess. And so did I. We finished a bottle of Californian Zinfandel rosé, oddly described on the label as White Zinfandel, and wickedly saw off another half bottle.

'Harry darling . . .' Gail began somewhat pensively.

I knew that appealing voice. 'You're not taking to the boards again, are you?' Every once in a while, Gail displayed a hankering to return to the theatre. Mostly it had been a half-hearted ambition, and although she'd been offered one or two parts she'd subsequently turned them down. Not that she had to work; her millionaire father George gave her a generous allowance. Nevertheless, I suspected that Gail missed the grease-paint and bright lights.

'No, nothing like that. I've been thinking—'

'Careful,' I said. 'Harm can come to a young girl like that.'

'Just be serious for a moment, darling. Anyway, I'm not that young.' Gail gave a self-deprecating shrug and then voiced an idea that she'd obviously been harbouring for some time. 'Why don't you move in with me? Permanently, I mean.' She spoke rapidly, almost as if she regretted allowing the question to escape her lips.

'Whoa! Hang on just a minute.' I was completely taken aback

by her suggestion, one that she'd never even hinted at before. 'We always said that living apart ensured that we wouldn't get in each other's way. Does this mean you want to get married?' I tried to laugh it off. 'Are you proposing?'

'No, of course not. Anyway, it's not February and it's not a leap year. I don't see any point in getting married, not again, but if you think about it, living together makes sense. We'd share the cost for a start. It seems silly for each of us to have our own place.'

'Well, I don't know, Gail. It might spoil a beautiful relationship.' I was still trying to make light of her idea, as well as stalling for time, but only because the suggestion had come as something of a shock.

'If you don't want to, just say so.' She pouted at me. It was a very petulant pout.

'Let me think about it, darling.'

'Does that mean that you're not dismissing it out of hand, Harry?'

'No, I'm not, but there's a lot to talk about. For instance, what would we do with my furniture? There wouldn't be room for all of it at your place, and naturally there are some pieces I'd want to keep.' And then I played what I thought was my trump card. 'But what about Mrs Gurney?' The thought of losing my wonderful 'lady who did' would be too much.

'I'm sure she'd be delighted to come and work for us,' said Gail innocently. 'I don't have a cleaning lady at the moment.' She glanced out of the window. 'It wouldn't be a problem for her, surely? Your flat and my house are less than a mile away from each other.'

'Ah, I see,' I said. 'So when it comes down to it, this is all a ploy to hijack the services of my Mrs Gurney.'

Gail laughed. At last. 'Oh, you've guessed,' she said.

'I'm not averse to the idea at all,' I said, still loath to make an immediate decision. In truth, I was delighted that Gail had floated the suggestion. Although I'd thought about it from time to time, I'd always hesitated to propose it, and was agreeably surprised that it was she who'd done so. 'But let me think about the practicalities.'

'Wonderful!' exclaimed Gail. 'Let's celebrate.'

'We've just had dinner and it's getting late. How are we going to celebrate? Anyway, it's not a done deal.'

'I've got champagne in my bedroom fridge,' said Gail. 'That'll do for a start.'

'And then?'

'Use your imagination, silly.'

'Miss Gail Sutton,' I said, 'you're one wicked woman.'

'And ain't you glad o' that, Mr 'Arry Brock?' she said, again assuming her Cockney accent and running her tongue seductively around her lips.

Back home in Gail's bedroom we opened the champagne, but it was quite warm by the time we got around to drinking it.

THIRTEEN

FBI Special Agents Brendan O'Grady and Hugo Fernandez, both experienced Bureau veterans from the office at the Big Apple's Federal Plaza, entered the prison interview room on Rikers Island in the State of New York.

Lucien Carter, wearing rimless glasses and clad in the correctional facility's standard jumpsuit, was already seated on the other side of the table to which one of his wrists was shackled. He was a small man and had the appearance of a mild bookkeeper rather than a criminal mastermind. Not that he needed muscle in the particular line of criminality upon which he'd embarked. Just brainpower. But that was about to be tested.

'We know a lot about you, pal.' O'Grady, the senior of the two agents, threw down a dossier marked LUCIEN CARTER in large letters. 'And now you're going to tell us a lot more.'

'Aren't you supposed to caution me?' asked Carter, in his unmistakably refined English accent. He stared apprehensively at the dossier, unaware that it contained nothing but blank sheets of paper.

'Yeah, sure. You have the right to remain silent, blah, blah, blah. If you've been watching TV here in Rikers, you'll know the rest of Miranda. Take it as read.'

'Shouldn't I have a lawyer?'

'You think he's going to sweet talk the judge out of giving you twenty-five to life?' asked Fernandez, wildly exaggerating any sentence that Carter might receive for his misdeeds.

Carter paled significantly, but remained silent.

'You're in shtook up to your neck, Carter,' said O'Grady. 'Your three pals, Eberhardt, Schmidt and Adekunle have all been murdered back in little old England.'

'What?' exclaimed Carter, unable to keep the telltale signs of shock from his voice, or the fact that the three victims were known to him.

'Getting to be too much trouble, were they? What did you do? Send someone to rub 'em out, huh?'

'I don't know anything about these people. Who are they?'

'You're a real piece of work, Carter, you know that?' O'Grady glanced at Fernandez and grinned. 'He doesn't know anything about 'em, Hugo.' He opened his briefcase and pulled out another dossier. This one *did* contain information. Taking out a copy of the letter that Joe Daly in London had sent to the New York office he placed it in front of Carter.

'That letter is a reference for the property in Paddington, London, England that you sent to a realty agent. You own that house, Carter, and that's where the butchered body of your pal Samson Adekunle was found shot to death. So, what've you got to say about that?'

'I don't know anything about any of this,' protested Carter, but his face belied his statement. His brain went into top gear as he tried to distance himself from these shocking events.

'He says he doesn't know squat, Brendan,' said Fernandez, an expression of contrived astonishment on his face as he turned to O'Grady and spread his hands. He faced Carter again. 'My advice to you, pal, is to get yourself an attorney pretty damn' fast. He might just persuade the DA to plea-bargain you down to fifteen to twenty. On the other hand, mister, you might just do yourself a favour and tell us all you know.'

'He's right, you know, Carter,' said O'Grady. 'Right now it's a toss-up between spending the rest of your life here in Rikers or getting extradited back to the UK.'

'What d'you want to know?' Carter suddenly realized that

there was no way out of his predicament. If he didn't tell these hard-nosed federal agents the truth, they'd just keep coming back until he was old and grey and still on remand. Not that that was likely, but Carter was not conversant with the legal system of the United States.

'Tell us everything and we'll sort out what we don't want.'

'All right, so I ran a boiler-room scam, but I didn't kill anyone. Why would I do that?'

'You knew these three guys that gotten wasted, then?'

'Yes, of course I did. They were my operatives in the UK.'

'And where's all the moolah stashed?'

'The what?'

O'Grady raised his eyebrows. 'The money, you dumb fuck.'

'Here and there,' said Carter.

'Listen, motherfucker,' said Fernandez, banging the table with the flat of his hand. 'If you want our help, you're going to have to give us something.'

'It's in offshore accounts in different parts of the world. We moved the cash around between the Cayman Islands, the Bahamas, Lichtenstein, Dubai and Belize.' Carter shrugged. 'I don't even know myself where it is right now.'

'Are you telling me you ran this operation, but you never kept a handle on where the green stuff went?' Fernandez didn't believe him and his face and the tone of his voice registered that disbelief.

'Certainly I did. But I relied on Eberhardt, Schmidt and Adekunle. They knew better than to play fast and loose with me. But now they're dead, I don't know where the money's gone. They kept moving it and informed me whenever they did, but if they'd moved it just before they were murdered, there's no telling where it is now.'

O'Grady thought that Carter was probably right about that, but it didn't help him to answer Joe Daly's questions. He stood up and hammered on the interview room door.

A corrections officer appeared immediately. 'You guys finished in here?' he asked.

'Sure,' said Fernandez. 'Take this useless bozo back to his nice warm cell and make him comfortable. He's likely to be there for the next hundred years.' And with that empty threat he and O'Grady left Carter to the tender ministrations of the Rikers guards.

Once back at Federal Plaza, O'Grady sat down and composed a report for Joe Daly in London.

Next day, I tried to put aside Gail's suggestion of moving in with her. It wasn't that I was averse to the idea, but the complications were too much for me to cope with while I was dealing with the three murders that I was attempting to solve. Added to which were the complexities of the international fraud that we'd discovered as a result.

I spent an hour or two reading and rereading all the statements that had been taken in the hope that they might throw up something that I'd missed. They didn't. Allowing for the time difference, I left it until the afternoon before attempting to speak to the Bahamian police.

Colin Wilberforce interrogated his computer and came up with the name and telephone number of the officer in charge of the Central Detective Unit of the Royal Bahamas Police Force in Nassau.

I went back to my office to make the call.

'Good afternoon. This is Detective Chief Inspector Harry Brock of the London Metropolitan Police, phoning from New Scotland Yard,' I began. 'Is that Superintendent Duncan Gould?'

'Yes, it is, and a very good morning to you, Mr Brock,' said Gould with a chuckle. 'How's your weather over there?' He had a rich voice that made me think of mahogany.

'This afternoon it's a fine sunny day with temperatures in the seventies, sir.'

'Is that all? Must be damn' chilly over there, old sport. It's ninety-two here and raining like hell.' Gould emitted another throaty chuckle. 'Are you an Old Bramshillian by any chance?'

'A what?'

'Have you been to the Police College at Bramshill?'

'Oh, Bramshill. Yes, I was there a few years ago, sir.' I'd wasted a few months in the depths of Hampshire and spent most of my time listening to classroom coppers lecturing me on things I knew already. And drinking in the local pubs, of which there were far too many for the good of my liver. But I did forge a friendship with Jock Ferguson, now a detective superintendent in the Hampshire Constabulary. Being a local he knew the best hostelries in the area and since then had proved to be a useful contact on more than one occasion.

'I was there too, a year or so back,' said Gould. 'Great fun and good pubs, but I didn't learn much. Now, Harry, how may I help you?'

'It's a long story, sir.'

'I like long stories, Harry, and call me Duncan, why don't you?'

'Right, Duncan.' I explained, as succinctly as possible, about our complex investigation, the scam we'd uncovered and the possible link between Lucien Carter and the Bahamas. Just for good measure I threw in the names of the three murder victims and that of Wilhelm Weber. I included Weber because he'd told Horst Fischer about Eberhardt's trips to the Bahamas. And the Essen police still hadn't discovered whether he knew more than he was telling. 'Carter was recently arrested by the FBI in New York, and is currently being held in Rikers prison pending further enquiries,' I said. 'But I wondered if he had come to the notice of the Royal Bahamas Police Force. Or, for that matter, whether any of my victims had.'

'I can't tell you immediately, Harry, old boy. These islands are full of crooks. Remind me to tell you about the murder of Sir Harry Oakes one day, the one the Duke of Windsor interfered with.' Gould paused to laugh uproariously. 'I'll have to search the records. Give me your phone number and I'll get back to you.'

'Thanks, Duncan, I appreciate it.'

I'd no sooner replaced the receiver than a call came in from Henri Deshayes. Things were certainly humming today.

'*Bonjour*, 'Arry.'

'And good day to you, Henry. Have you got something for me?'

'Not directly, 'Arry, but we've had reports of dozens of share frauds involving this same Buenos Aires information technology company. We've also received complaints from about twenty people who've lost a total of some three million euros between them, but there are bound to be others who are too ashamed to come forward.'

This was always the problem with boiler-room scams, so called because of the high pressure salesmanship that went with the fraud. People who have been defrauded will often stay quiet for fear of what other people, including the police, will think of their stupidity at falling for a silver-tongued con man at the other end of a telephone.

'It sounds as though Lucien Carter is at the back of it, Henry,' I said.

'Maybe. The *brigade financière* – our fraud department – followed up the address in Paris that the letters purported to come from, but it was no surprise that the address didn't exist. Their investigators also found out that the funds could not be traced, and that was no surprise either. A lot of wire transfers all over the place, it seems, but they couldn't tell where the money finished up. I've put Lucien Carter's name into our central computer. If his name comes up anywhere, I'll let you know. Can you give me the telephone number of the FBI office dealing with him?'

'It's the New York office of the FBI, Henry,' I said, and gave him the details. 'The special agent in charge there has been in touch with Joe Daly, the FBI agent at the American Embassy in London. I've also made contact with the police in the Bahamas.'

'*D'accord.* I'll come back to you if I get anything else, 'Arry.'

Once again the enquiry had ground to a standstill pending information from sources beyond my control.

I had no sooner finished my conversation with Henri Deshayes when Kate Ebdon appeared in my office doorway. 'I've spoken to the Border Agency, guv,' she said. 'They have no record of a Samson Adekunle having entered the UK.'

'As I thought, he's an illegal immigrant. Either that or their records aren't reliable.'

'Surely not,' said Kate, with mock disbelief. 'But the Border Agency wants to know what we're doing about it.'

'What *we're* doing about it? Bloody sauce. What did you tell them, Kate?'

'I said they could have his body once we'd finished with it.'

'Joking aside, Kate, what does happen to him, once the coroner releases the body?'

'As I understand it, the local authority is responsible for burying him. At the taxpayers' expense, of course.'

'Of course,' I said, 'but don't tell Dave. That sort of thing gets him all hot and bothered.'

'I also had a word with the Nigerian High Commission, but they didn't know anything and didn't want to know.'

'And that, Kate, is par for the course,' I said. 'Nigeria is the centre of the scam world.'

No sooner had Kate disappeared than Tom Challis appeared in my office clutching an open stationery book.

'I've tracked down the Deacon family, guv.'

'Who the hell are they, Tom?' I was becoming totally confused with the ever increasing number of names that continued to crop up in our enquiry.

'You remember asking me to track down William Rivers's relatives?'

'Right, I'm with you. What about them?'

'George Deacon is William Rivers's great nephew and the grandson of Rivers's sister Gladys. As he's aged twenty-five, I thought he might be a likely runner for the toppings. I can't see his parents getting involved in a triple murder, and the grandparents are both dead.'

'Have you got an address for him?' I never ceased to be amazed at the detective skills of my younger officers. In common with other coppers of my generation, we misguidedly thought that we were the best detectives there were or ever had been.

'Yes, guv, he's living at Ealing.'

'I'd better have a word with him, I suppose. Thanks, Tom.'

'D'you want to go now, guv?' asked Dave.

'No, we'll leave it till this evening. He's probably at work.'

It was about half past three that afternoon when Joe Daly strolled into my office.

'Joe, what brings you here?' I asked.

'I've just been across at the Yard enjoying one of your senior officers' lunches,' said Daly.

'Is "enjoy" the right word, Joe?'

'The food was fine, but your commander sure knows how to shoot the breeze. I reckon he went on for about twenty minutes or more.'

'Is that all?' I said. 'That's quite brief for him.' I'd wisely pleaded pressure of work to avoid joining the commander's audience.

'At least I was sitting next to Alan Cleaver,' Daly continued. 'He's got a few good stories to tell.'

Dave, having been alerted to Joe Daly's presence, appeared in my office with three cups of coffee. 'Not as good as your embassy coffee, Joe,' he said, 'but we're an impoverished nation now.'

'Remind me to send you a food parcel, Dave.' Daly took a sip of coffee and grimaced. 'Yeah, I see what you mean.' He put his cup and saucer on the corner of my desk and didn't touch it again. 'The reason I've called in, Harry,' he said, 'is that a couple of agents from the New York office interviewed Carter this morning in Rikers.' He took an email from his pocket and handed it to me.

'And you've got it already?' I queried, as I began to read O'Grady's report.

'New York is five hours behind us, sir,' said Dave smugly, the 'sir' implying that I should have been aware of this widely known fact.

'I reckon your sergeant's a wise-ass, Harry,' said Daly, treating Dave to a high-five.

'You don't know the half of it,' I said, skimming through the email. 'This report doesn't say much that we didn't know already,' I added, returning the brief report to Daly. 'I reckon Carter knows exactly where the money is, but isn't saying.'

'That was my take on it, Harry. After all, what's he got to lose? He probably thinks he's going to spend the next twenty years in a federal facility, so why give anything away. In fact, Fernandez probably gave Carter his usual spiel about shaping up for twenty-five to life. I know Fernandez and he's got a big mouth, and sometimes he's too smart at making comments of that sort. One of these days he'll come up against a defence attorney who'll take him to pieces on the stand.'

*   *   *

George Deacon's apartment was in a modern block in Ealing, and Dave and I arrived there at a little after six o'clock that evening.

The barefooted well-endowed girl who opened the door of the flat looked to be no older than twenty, if that. She was wearing a pair of white shorts and a tee shirt that bore the single word 'YES' followed by an exclamation mark.

'Mrs Deacon?' I asked, being fairly sure that she was not.

The girl laughed. 'Not yet. I'm Tricia Hardy, George's fiancée. Did you want to see him?' She spoke with what I thought was, and was later confirmed as, a Canadian accent.

'If he's in,' I said.

'Sure. Come on through.' Tricia Hardy seemed quite happy to admit two complete strangers into the apartment without querying who we were or why we were there. No wonder crime in London is rife.

'Hey, Deacon, get off your butt. There's a couple of guys here to see you,' said Tricia, addressing a young man reclining on a sofa. He too was attired in shorts and a tee shirt, although his bore 'CALGARY' in large letters.

'Who the hell are you?' demanded George Deacon, tossing aside the book he'd been reading. Slowly and apparently in some pain, he stood up and gazed suspiciously at Dave and me. I thought I sensed an element of fear in his appraisal. Either that or he was more aware of crime in the capital than was his fiancée.

'We're police officers, Mr Deacon,' I said, and effected introductions.

'From Scotland Yard, you say?'

'That's correct, sir,' said Dave.

'Well, I haven't got a car, if that's what you're here about. I go everywhere on a bicycle.'

Funny,' I thought, *how people always assume that a visit from the police has something to do with an infraction of traffic law.*

'How very green of you, sir,' said Dave.

'What's this about?' Deacon asked. He waved at the sofa. 'Take a pew.' He squatted on a beanbag and Tricia sat on the floor with her legs crossed. She moved with enviable suppleness and looked as though she might be good at yoga.

Dave picked up the book that Deacon had been reading and glanced at the title. '*Crime and Punishment*. Good luck! I always found Dostoevsky a bit heavy going.'

'So do I,' said Deacon, apparently unsure what to make of a detective sergeant with a knowledge of Russian literature, 'but I'm doing an Open University degree.'

'I understand that you're related to William Rivers, Mr Deacon,' I said, steering the conversation back to the purpose of our visit.

'Who?'

'William Rivers. I believe he's your great uncle. He lived in Pinner.'

'Oh, him. I never met him. Bit of a recluse according to my mother. From what she told me, he was a bloody-minded old soldier. I gather that he didn't have much to do with the rest of the family. I heard that my Auntie Stella had a blazing row with him, all because she married some Indian guy. Anyway, why have you come to see me about him?'

'He's dead, Mr Deacon. He committed suicide in Brighton just over a week ago.'

'As a matter of interest, Chief Inspector, why are you telling me all this?' Deacon was unmoved by the news of his great uncle's death, but as he'd never met him that was understandable.

'We have reason to believe that he was defrauded of some ten thousand pounds.'

'Where on earth did he get that much money from?' Deacon's face registered a shock similar to that displayed by Stella Kumar when we'd told her the amount of money her father had accumulated.

'I've no idea,' I said, declining to pass on what James Milner had told me about Rivers's black market activities in Germany at the end of the Second World War. 'The only reason I'm here is to find out whether you knew anything about this fraud.' *And to see if you were responsible for my three murders.*

'I'm afraid I don't know anything about it.' Deacon shook his head. 'Mind you, I might've got to know him if I'd found out he was worth that much. Might even have gone to the funeral. But I suppose that's taken place.'

'Yesterday, as a matter of fact, sir,' said Dave.

'Oh well, we wouldn't've made it anyway. Trish and I only got back last night.'

'Got back?' I queried.

But it was Trish Hardy who answered. 'We spent almost the whole of July in Calgary, Alberta. It's my home town and I thought I'd better show Deacon off to my folks before I agreed to marry him.' She laughed. 'He decided to have a go at the rodeo, that's why he's aching all over,' she volunteered. 'I told him not to, but he's bloody-minded when the mood takes him, but not as bloody-minded as the mustang was.' She seemed devoid of any sympathy for her fiancé's escapades, and laughed.

'Sorry I couldn't help you with this fraud business,' said Deacon, as he limped to the door to show us out. 'But as I said, I never met the old boy.'

And that crossed George Deacon off our list of suspects. Subject, of course, to the usual checks.

FOURTEEN

It turned out that Joe Daly's flying visit earlier that afternoon wasn't the end of the Lucien Carter affair, although in another sense it was. The question of Carter and where he'd put the money ended abruptly with a telephone call from the London FBI agent just after Dave and I returned from interviewing George Deacon. And after I'd given Colin Wilberforce the task of confirming George Deacon's story that he and Tricia Hardy had spent the whole of the last month in Calgary.

'Harry, can you come across to the embassy? I've got some bad news, although you might not think it's bad.'

'What sort of bad news, Joe?'

'I'll tell you when you get here, but I've just opened a bottle of Jim Beam that might help to ease the pain and suffering.'

I didn't like the sound of that, and Dave and I hastened to Grosvenor Square without further delay.

*   *   *

We were joined in Joe Daly's office by Darlene. It seemed that it was Daly's close of play relaxation when he and his secretary enjoyed a few drinks.

Joe poured substantial measures of his Kentucky whiskey into chunky tumblers and handed them round. 'You guys want ice?' he asked.

'Certainly not, Joe,' said Dave. 'We're British.'

'So, what's this bad news?' I asked, having taken a sip of Daly's whiskey.

'Lucien Carter's dead.'

'*Dead?* What happened?'

'First reports say that he was murdered by another inmate, but enquiries are ongoing.'

'I'll bet they are,' said Dave quietly.

'How the hell did he get topped in Rikers?' I asked. 'I thought that prison was as tight as a drum.'

'Sure it is,' said Daly, 'but these things happen. If some inmate decides to take another one out, he'll do it somehow. According to the information that O'Grady of our New York office was given, Carter was in the exercise yard when another remand prisoner stabbed him.'

'Do we know who this other guy was?'

'Not yet. I'm waiting on more details, but I'm wondering if whoever killed Carter had gotten paid to take him out.'

'Yes, so am I,' I said thoughtfully as I considered this latest twist in my murder enquiry. 'Are your guys doing the investigation?'

'No, Harry. Investigations like that are done by the New York Police Department. They won the fight with the Bureau and the Department of Corrections. Believe me, if you think you've got turf wars here, you ain't seen nothing.'

The following day, I sat in my office mulling over what we knew so far. It wasn't much beyond that the fact that I had three unsolved murders on my hands and no idea how to solve them.

Dave and I went out for lunch at our favourite Italian restaurant, and I spent the afternoon trawling through the mass of paperwork that had been mounting up since a week ago last Friday.

I made a decision. 'We need to talk, Dave,' I shouted through my open door. 'Grab some coffee and come in.'

'On its way, guv.' Five minutes later Dave appeared with two cups of coffee, and kicked the door shut with his foot.

'Take a pew, Dave. I've been thinking that we'll have to go public with these damned murders because we don't seem to be getting anywhere.'

'True, sir,' said Dave. 'But that won't help with Carter's murder in Rikers.'

'We've got enough of our own murders without worrying about that,' I said. 'Anyway, that's down to the NYPD.'

'But surely there's a connection with our murders,' said Dave.

'I shouldn't think there's any doubt about it, but getting to the bottom of that particular topping rests with our American friends. It's nothing to do with us.'

'But we could take a trip over there, guv,' suggested Dave. 'We might find out something that they've missed.'

I gave the impression of giving the matter some thought. 'Good idea, Dave. I could go over there on my own and leave you here to oversee the UK end of things. I doubt that the commander would sanction both of us going.'

'Thank you, *sir*,' said Dave.

I rang the head of Press Bureau at the Yard.

'Bob, I want to release details of my three murders to the media.'

'I fielded a few enquiries about the camper van fire just after it happened, Harry, but interest seems to have died down. These things don't stay in the news longer than about twenty-four hours at best. All that was released at the outset was that there was an unfortunate fire at Richmond in which two people lost their lives. And the media seems to think that the Adekunle murder was a random burglary gone wrong. D'you want to tell the world about all three of them now?'

'I think it's the only way we're going to get any help, Bob,' I said, and went on to give him chapter and verse about the deaths of Eberhardt, Schmidt and Adekunle, but without any mention of the share scams that appeared to be the motive for their murders. I didn't say anything about the death of Lucien Carter in Rikers. I doubted that anyone in the UK would be able to offer any information about that, not that there would be much I could do with it if they did. Except to pass it on to the NYPD.

Then I sat back, metaphorically, and awaited the flood of information that would undoubtedly be forthcoming from concerned and helpful members of the public. If only!

'D'you think we *will* get anything out of the press release, guv?'

'I hope so, Dave, but don't hold your breath.' I glanced at my watch. 'It's damned near half past seven. Go home, and give Madeleine my regards.'

'She's on tour in Russia, guv. She's currently at the Mariinsky Theatre in St Petersburg where the Kirov ballet company usually performs. She won't be back until Sunday morning. Looks like another microwave supper.'

The murderer picked up the newspaper and stared in horror at the front-page article about Eberhardt, Schmidt and Adekunle. He wondered if it had also been on the TV, but as he had no access to a television set, he didn't know.

He firmly believed that he'd covered his tracks and that the original press stories about the two deaths in the camper van being an unfortunate accident had meant an end to it. But now he saw the frightening announcement that the police were regarding them as murders.

Even more unsettling was that Scotland Yard was now linking those deaths to the murder of Samson Adekunle. He'd been sure that his anonymous and deliberately belated telephone call to the police had given them the impression that it was a random killing resulting from a bungled burglary. Press reports had thought so, too.

His mind went back to the old fool with the dog who'd seen him shooting at a tree in Richmond Park, and wondered if he'd told the police what he'd seen. Not for the first time he cursed himself for his foolishness. After all, he'd had enough practice at the German gun club; he didn't have to do more in public. That was just bravado accompanied by a firm belief that he wouldn't be caught.

Fortunately, he hadn't given the secretary of the gun club in Birmingham his real name, and the ploy of taking a room with

Mrs Patel would have made it more difficult for him to be found. However, he was confident that his theft of the firearm from the gun club near Essen would not be discovered by the British police, even though he'd been obliged by the nit-picking Germans to give his real name and produce his passport.

But now it seemed that his initial confidence was unfounded.

He went downstairs and sought out the landlord.

'I'm leaving,' he announced.

'You'll have to pay to the end of the month,' said the disgruntled landlord, irritated that he'd now have to find a new tenant.

'That should cover it,' said the murderer, and peeled off a couple of twenty-pound notes from a roll he took from his pocket.

'What d'you want me to do with any mail that arrives for you?' asked the landlord.

'There won't be any,' said the murderer, and hastening back to his room threw his few possessions into a battered holdall.

His next problem would be finding somewhere to live until he could flee abroad. Preferably back to Germany.

The landlord pondered the sudden departure of his lodger and idly wondered if it had anything to do with the three murders that had been reported in that morning's newspapers and on the previous evening's television news. But he didn't wonder for long. Once his erstwhile tenant had driven off in his Volkswagen Polo, he walked down to the local police station.

I arrived at the office on Friday morning, full of hope that the press release might yield some helpful results. Like hell! Last night's evening papers and television news bulletins had carried lengthy reports about our triple murder enquiry, and today's national newspapers published similar items. One enterprising journal had managed to acquire a photograph of Adekunle's house in Paddington, and also reproduced a picture of a Volkswagen camper van similar to the one in which Eberhardt and Schmidt had been murdered. Another paper had produced a photograph of Guy Wilson's house in Bendview Road, Richmond, describing it as 'The house of antiquarian book dealer Guy Wilson, opposite which the brutal slaying had occurred.' It was a photograph that produced the first complaint arising out of our enquiries.

But there were no telephone calls from people who knew the murderer and were about to tell us where he lived.

'Good morning, Harry.' No sooner had I got my first cup of coffee in front of me than Alan Cleaver wandered into my office. I'd already been told by Colin Wilberforce that the commander had taken the day off and that Cleaver was acting in his place.

'Morning, guv.' I made to stand up, but Cleaver waved me down, at the same time sinking into my armchair.

'We've had an official complaint from a bloke called Guy Wilson, Harry.'

'What's he banging on about? It was him who called the fire brigade to the camper van where we found the bodies of Eberhardt and Schmidt.'

'Yeah, I know. Well, a photograph of his house appeared in one of this morning's tabloids together with details of what he did for a living.'

'Yes, I saw it.'

'I know it's nothing to do with us,' Cleaver continued, 'but he's got this bee in his bonnet that police leaked details to the press. Can you spare a few minutes to go down there and disabuse him?'

'I suppose so, guv.' I was disinclined to make apologetic overtures to the egotistical Wilson, particularly as I knew the information had not come from us, but Alan Cleaver must've had a good reason for asking me.

'It'll save time in the long run, Harry. The local CID told me that Wilson claims to have influential friends and is threatening to write to his MP. Frankly, I think it's all bluster, and anyway I couldn't give a toss about his grievance. But nipping this thing in the bud would save us having to deal with a parliamentary question if some idiot Member of Parliament did happen to raise it in the House. Or if the said Member wings it across to the Independent Police Complaints Commission.'

I glanced at my watch. 'I'll go down there now, guv,' I said.

'Thanks, mate,' said Cleaver. 'Let me know how you get on. Give me a ring if it's more convenient for you.'

Oh, what a refreshing change from the commander.

*   *   *

'And about time.' Guy Wilson threw open his front door and retreated into the house, leaving Dave to close the door. 'You'd better come into the study.'

Wilson sat down behind his desk, but didn't invite us to take a seat. We did anyway.

'I understand that you have a complaint about press coverage, Mr Wilson,' I began.

'Too bloody right I have.' Wilson snatched at a copy of a tabloid newspaper that was open on his desk. 'Have a look at that. The offending article is on page three.'

'I've seen it,' I said.

At that moment a woman whom I presumed to be the Wilsons' housekeeper entered the study. She was wearing an overall coat and her face wore a bland expression. 'Do you wanting coffee, Mister Wilson?' she asked in an accent that seemed to indicate that she originated from an Eastern European country.

'No,' snapped Wilson, 'and close the door. I'm not to be disturbed.'

The woman, her face still expressionless, withdrew silently and shut the door behind her.

'What exactly is your complaint about, Mr Wilson?' I asked.

'I want to know how the press got hold of all those details about my personal life,' Wilson said. 'And that gutter rag in particular.' He gestured at the newspaper.

'I'm afraid I haven't the faintest idea,' I said. 'Have you tried asking them?'

'I don't have to. It was the police, wasn't it? I know you chaps are hand in glove with the media. Helping them to hack into people's emails and that sort of thing.'

'I'm sorry to disappoint you, Mr Wilson, but the last thing I wanted was to see details about you or your house appearing in the press. That sort of thing can very often be counterproductive to our enquiries.'

'Well, someone must've told them.'

'In our experience, Mr Wilson,' said Dave, 'journalists are extremely resourceful people. It would not have taken much working out that your house was opposite the crime scene. And it is but a short step from there to discovering what sort of trade you're in.'

'I'm not in trade,' snapped Wilson, riled by Dave's remark. 'I'm an antiquarian book dealer.'

'The usual method that these people employ is to talk to your neighbours . . . or to the people who work for them . . . or for you,' said Dave, unconcerned about annoying Wilson even further. 'It's surprising how easily a few pounds will unlock tongues. It's called cheque book journalism.'

'Are you suggesting that a member of my staff spoke to the newspapers?' Wilson bridled at the suggestion.

'That's entirely a matter for you to discover, Mr Wilson,' I said. 'You know your people much better than we do. Do you employ many people?'

'None of your damned business,' said Wilson irritably, but I imagined that his only member of staff was the woman who had offered him coffee a few minutes ago. For a moment or two, he toyed with a letter opener on his desk. 'If it was counter-productive to your enquiries, as you suggested it was, why didn't you stop them publishing those details, Chief Inspector?'

'Because, Mr Wilson,' said Dave, despite the question having been directed at me, 'we pride ourselves on freedom of the press in this country. There's no way in which we could exercise any sort of censorship, or would wish to.'

'I shall sue them.' Wilson was disgruntled that we were refusing to accept responsibility for the offending article.

'As far as I can see, there's nothing libellous in the article,' I said.

'Then I shall sue for breach of privacy.' I got the impression that Wilson was determined to seek redress from one quarter or another. 'And I'll write to my MP. For all I know these people have been listening to my phone calls.'

The door to the study opened and Wilson was about to bark a reproof when he saw that it was his wife Helen. This morning she was attired in an expensive Chanel grey trouser suit that most women would've died for.

'Oh, I'm sorry, Guy,' said Helen Wilson, 'I didn't know you had clients.'

'They're not clients, darling,' said Wilson, suddenly becoming syrupy polite to his trophy wife. 'It's the police. They're denying telling this damned newspaper what I did for a living.'

'They didn't tell them,' said Helen.

'What?' Wilson's face expressed concern. 'What d'you mean? How d'you know it wasn't the police?'

'It was me, darling,' said Helen. 'He was an awfully nice young man who called here, and I thought that for people to know that you dealt in rare books might help you to expand your client base. After all, it's free advertising in a national newspaper, isn't it?'

Wilson rose from behind his desk, red in the face, and I sensed that we were on the threshold of what we policemen like to call 'a domestic'.

'Unless there's anything else, Mr Wilson, we'll be on our way,' I said, as Dave and I hurriedly rose from our seats. 'We'll find our own way out.' I noticed that Dave was doing his best to stifle a laugh.

Wilson dismissed us with a wave of the hand. There was no apology for his unfounded accusations, but I didn't expect one.

'Oh dear!' said Dave, finally erupting into unrestrained laughter as we got into our car and made our way back to central London.

I rang Alan Cleaver on my mobile. 'Wilson's withdrawn his complaint, guv,' I said. 'More or less.'

'What was the outcome?' asked Cleaver.

'It turned out that it was his wife who spoke to the press, guv.'

There was a roar of laughter from Cleaver's end. 'Nice one, Harry.'

On our return to Curtis Green, I decided to call it a day and Dave and I went for a quick beer in the downstairs bar of St Stephen's Tavern on the corner of Bridge Street. We picked this pub rather than our usual haunts of the Red Lion or the Clarence, mainly to avoid journalists who wanted information rather than giving it. A mistake.

'Hello, Mr Brock. Long time no see.'

The sleazy, permanently sweating, overweight individual occupying a stool at the far end of the downstairs bar was known to most members of the CID as Fat Danny. He was the worst crime reporter for the most disreputable tabloid newspaper known to man and, believe me, that was no easy reputation to acquire.

'I don't suppose you just happened to be here on the off chance that I might drop in, Danny,' I said. 'Or was it an overwhelming desire to buy me a pint if I did happen to appear?'

'Always a pleasure to buy you a drink, Mr Brock, and you too, Mr Poole.' Danny promptly ordered two pints of best bitter, and another large Scotch for himself.

'Pay attention to what happens next, sir,' said Dave. 'You are about to witness a reporter putting his hand in his pocket and paying for a round.'

'*Journalist*,' muttered Danny as he pushed our two pints along the bar.

'I take it you want something, Danny,' I said, taking the head off my beer.

'These three murders, Mr Brock. What's the SP?'

'Exactly what you wrote in that gutter rag you work for, Danny.'

'Yeah, but there must be a bit more to these toppings than that. I mean, that was the standard press release, yeah?' Danny paused in mid-sip. 'It was, wasn't it?'

'Oh, there is more, Danny,' said Dave. 'The name of the murderer. I thought you'd dropped in here to tell us who he is and where we can find him.'

'Leave it out, Mr Poole. What's the German connection? Drug smugglers were they? International art thieves? Terrorists? Surely you can give me a bit more.'

'As soon as we find out anything, you'll be the first to know, Danny,' I said.

'After we've told every other crime reporter,' muttered Dave.

'*Journalist*,' said Danny again. 'I'm a *journalist*.'

'Was it you who did that piece about Guy Wilson in your rag, Danny?' I asked.

'Not a chance,' said Dave. 'Mrs Wilson said that the reporter who called was a nice young man.'

It was gone eight o'clock before I opened the door of my flat. It was, as usual, clean and tidy. But this was in no way anything to do with me. I've already mentioned my wonderful cleaning lady called Gladys Gurney, an absolute diamond whom Gail now seems intent upon kidnapping. But only if I move in with her, a proposition I'm still turning over in my mind.

Mrs Gurney comes in three times a week and miraculously transposes the unbelievable chaos of my abode into something approaching civilized living. I've no idea how she manages it, but I do know that she's worth every penny I pay her.

As was so often the case, she had left me one of her charming little notes.

> Dear Mr Brock,
>   That window cleaner of yours come in today and done the windows. He had the cheek to charge six pounds what I give him. But I also give him a piece of my mind because I thought it was a scandal what he was charging.
>   Yours faithfully
>   Gladys Gurney (Mrs)

I left ten pounds on the kitchen worktop with a note of thanks. Gladys is well worth the extra few quid that I give her from time to time. After all, she's only supposed to clean the flat, but she does more, much more. She washes and irons my shirts and changes the bed. Moreover, she frequently launders the underwear that Gail somehow manages to leave strewn about the bedroom floor, and parcels it up in tissue paper that she brings with her.

I switched on my answering machine, but there was only one message and that was from Gail. It seemed that we'd been invited to join Bill and Charlie Hunter for a barbecue at their house at Esher the following afternoon. 'If,' Gail had added sarcastically, 'you can tear yourself away from your murder mystery games.' She has become much more cynical about my job since I first met her.

Just to make the situation clear, I should explain that the 'Charlie' of the duo is not a bloke but a woman called Charlotte, a thirty-something actress and long-standing friend of Gail. Charlotte Hunter is not her stage name and although Gail had once told me what it was, I could never remember it.

Charlie's husband Bill sits behind a desk somewhere in the

City and makes a lot of money quite effortlessly. Or so it would appear.

I rang Gail and told her that I'd be delighted to visit the Hunters, if for no better reason than to have a sight of Charlie in her minimal bikini. But I didn't tell Gail that.

'Why don't you come round for supper,' suggested Gail. 'I think I can manage to cobble something together.'

'I'll be there in half an hour,' I said enthusiastically. I'd sampled Gail's 'cobbled together' meals many times before and they weren't to be missed.

I arrived within the promised time span, bearing the obligatory bottle of champagne. I don't know why I bother really; Gail's two fridges – one in the kitchen and one in the bedroom – are always fully stocked with Heidsieck.

The meal, a selection of cold dishes, was delicious and we drank far too much Sauvignon Blanc.

'The champagne's in the bedroom,' said Gail suggestively, once the meal was over. 'D'you intend staying the night?' she queried, in an offhand sort of way.

She knew bloody well I would.

FIFTEEN

It was five o'clock the following afternoon when we arrived at the Hunters' palatial residence in Esher. One of half a dozen similar houses situated on a gated estate, it was a modern property set in its own grounds. Gail had once told me that it boasted six bedrooms, each with an en suite bathroom.

The swimming pool was enclosed in a purpose-built wooden chalet in which there were electric heaters and floodlights, not that either was switched on today; the temperature was still in the seventies. At one end there were cabins for changing, and showers. One side of the chalet consisted mainly of wide sliding doors that gave on to a patio and a state of the art charcoal barbecue. Like everything else that the Hunters did, no expense had been spared. There were many occasions, like now, when I thought that choosing the Metropolitan Police for a career had not been the smartest move I'd ever made.

Bill was attired in Hawaiian-pattern swim shorts, flip-flops and an apron that bore the ludicrous depiction of a human skeleton.

It's a curious custom of the British that at the first sign of sunshine they feel impelled to drag their food out of doors and set fire to it.

Bill was no exception. He was already hard at work burning sausages, chunks of meat and all the other bits and pieces that Englishmen think should comprise an alfresco meal. From time to time, he paused to sip at a glass of red wine.

Charlie, in a microscopic bikini, bless her, was reclining on a poolside lounger slowly lowering the level of liquid in a tall glass of Pimms.

Gail promptly disappeared into one of the changing cabins to reappear moments later in a cerise bikini that was bitchily designed to outdo Charlie's in terms of minimalism.

'I see you've got a few murders on your hands, Harry,' said Bill, as I joined him at his barbecue. 'I read about it in yesterday's paper. Surprised you had the time to join us.' He turned over a couple of steaks that were in danger of going beyond the well-done stage, and topped up my glass with wine.

'Take more than a few murders to miss one of your feasts, Bill,' I said, although what I really meant was that I'd hate to miss the sight of Charlie's gorgeous near-naked body disporting itself by the pool. 'Just to make matters worse, they seem to be mixed up with a boiler-room scam.'

'Oh, that's bad news,' said Bill, turning from his haute cuisine duties and waving a pair of kitchen tongs. 'If I can help at all, give me a ring. I had a client last year who was seen off with some offer that was too good to miss. I told him that if it was too good to miss, then he should miss it, but it was too late. The damn' fool had already invested. Lost about twenty grand, I think.'

'Thanks all the same, Bill, but I've got the Fraud Squad on standby.' What I didn't say was that accountants – and I included Bill in that category – always wanted to make the books balance, whereas the Fraud Squad had an overwhelming desire for them *not* to balance. And then began to dig.

Once we'd eaten, Bill and I relaxed on loungers and consumed chilled Beaujolais while the girls played about in the pool.

'How's business, Bill?' I asked.

'Hand to mouth, old boy,' said Hunter, but had the good grace to smile. 'Struggling to make ends meet. Well, you know how it is. Had to forgo a new car this year.'

'What appalling bad luck,' I said sarcastically. If only I had the chance to 'struggle' to make ends meet to the same degree as Bill, I'd be a happy man, but on a chief inspector's pay there wasn't much chance. And my BMW was five years old.

Charlie hailed us from the pool. 'Aren't you two layabouts coming in?' she asked, and as if to make the request irresistible she tossed her bra on to the tile surround. To be quickly followed by Gail doing likewise.

'Not even that'll tempt me, Charlie love,' rejoined Bill, and stood up to pour stiff measures of Courvoisier XO into two brandy balloons.

'Misery,' cried Charlie, and turned away to have a quiet conversation with Gail at the far side of the pool.

'That's a bit more like the old Charlie,' said Bill, handing me the cognac and sitting down again. 'She used to be like that all the time.'

It was a remark that seemed to indicate an undercurrent of tension in the Hunter ménage, but I said nothing. I'd always imagined them to be the perfect couple.

'It was fine when we each had our own place,' confided Bill, 'but once we'd got married and started to share a house, the awful spectre of domesticity crept in. You'd be surprised how things like that can change a relationship.' But he seemed to realize that he'd said too much and clammed up. Neither he nor Charlie had ever discussed their marriage before and even now I suspected it was the alcohol talking. Nevertheless, it made me think.

Despite several further attempts by Charlie and Gail to entice us into the pool, Bill and I remained resolutely where we were and got slowly drunk.

Consequently, it was almost midnight by the time we'd managed to get a taxi and roll into bed. At Gail's house.

Monday brought the first positive piece of information we'd received since the start of the enquiry.

'We've just had a call from a Mr Cyril Jefferson who lives in New Malden, sir.' Colin Wilberforce came into my office clutching a message form. 'He telephoned to report that he'd seen a man shooting at a tree in Richmond Park. He saw the piece in Friday's newspapers about the murders at Richmond and Paddington and wondered if there was a connection.'

'Did he say when this shooting took place, Colin?'

'On Friday the fourth of July, sir.'

'Perhaps the shooter was an American celebrating Independence Day,' said Dave in an aside.

'Oh, well,' I said with a sigh, 'I suppose we'd better go and see him, but I've no doubt it'll be another dead end. Have you got a phone number for this Jefferson?'

'Yes, sir.'

'Give him a ring, then, and ask if he's willing to see us.

Ten minutes later, having been assured that Cyril Jefferson was at home, Dave and I ventured forth to New Malden.

Jefferson was in his sixties and was a beige man: beige trousers, beige shirt, beige socks and beige shoes. And I'd've put money on him wearing a beige anorak when he went out.

'I'm Detective Chief Inspector Brock and this is Detective Sergeant Poole, Mr Jefferson,' I said. 'You telephoned my office to say that you'd seen a man shooting at a tree in Richmond Park early last month.'

'I'm glad someone's taking an interest at last. Please come in.' Jefferson showed us into a small but comfortable room. 'I rang Kingston police station straight after the incident and told them what I'd seen. They asked if the man had gone, and when I said he had, they told me that they'd make a note of it.'

'Wonderful,' commented Dave quietly. 'Police work at its finest.'

'I understand that this was on Friday the fourth of July,' I said.

'That's correct. It must've been about eleven o'clock in the morning.' Jefferson leaned forward, elbows on knees, hands linked. 'I was out walking the dog at the time.'

'Seems a long way to go from New Malden to walk the dog,' I said.

'I often drive out there and park the car. Raffles likes a bit of fresh air and the chance to romp around, don't you, boy?' Jefferson leaned down to tickle the ears of a large red setter. 'He's my only companion since the wife died,' he said, looking up again.

'Do you remember exactly where in the park this shooting took place, Mr Jefferson?'

'No, I'm afraid I can't describe it for you.'

'If we took you back to the park would you be able to show us?'

Jefferson thought about that for a moment. 'Yes, I think I would,' he said eventually. 'D'you want to go now?'

'If that would suit you,' I said, surprised at the man's willingness to assist.

'Yes, that's fine,' said Jefferson, and despite the warm weather, donned a beige anorak. 'All right if I bring the dog?'

'Of course,' I said.

Dave parked the car inside Richmond Park's Kingston gate and Jefferson led us off the road for about half a mile. Then he paused and looked around.

'That was the tree, Chief Inspector.' Jefferson pointed at an old oak.

'Can you be certain, sir?' asked Dave.

'Oh yes. I always follow the same route when I take the dog for a walk. He likes this particular part of the park, don't you, boy?' Jefferson stooped to stroke the dog's head. The dog ran off a few yards and started to sniff the ground.

We moved nearer and examined the tree that Jefferson had indicated. On close examination, I could see that there were at least three bullets embedded in its bark.

'From what I can see, sir,' said Dave, 'I'm pretty sure that these are point-two-two calibre. But there are no shell cases anywhere.'

'Either he was using an automatic pistol or he collected the cases or someone else did,' I said. I didn't mention in Jefferson's presence that point-two-two was the calibre of round that had killed Eberhardt, Schmidt and Adekunle. But knowing our luck it would probably turn out to be a coincidence.

'I'll see if I can get a local SOCO to come out, sir. There are some stationed at the Surbiton lab in Hollyfield Road,' said Dave, taking out his mobile. He still refused to call scenes-of-crime officers by their latest title of forensic practitioners. Probably because he guessed that it would soon be changed again by the funny names and total confusion squad at the Yard. 'Might be a good idea to get one of them to extract the rounds from the tree. If I did it with a penknife it might damage them. And we'd better have a photographer take a few shots of the tree.'

It was a good point. One has to cover all the bases before giving evidence at a trial. Defence counsel have a nasty habit of asking completely irrelevant questions, and it's always satisfying to confound them by having an answer.

'And get on to the local nick to send a car out here to take Mr Jefferson home.'

'There's no need for that,' said Jefferson. 'I can catch a bus.'

'It's no trouble, Mr Jefferson,' I said. 'I'm very grateful to you. I'm sure that this will prove to be useful evidence.' Whether it did or not, it was always a good thing to encourage those rare members of the public who assisted the police. 'Did this man see you watching him?'

'No, I don't think so. I was over there,' Jefferson said, indicating a clump of bushes with the stem of his pipe. 'But Raffles barked when he heard the shots and the man ran off. The shots weren't very loud. I'd've thought they would've been louder.'

'Did you see what happened to this man after he saw you, Mr Jefferson?' I asked.

'Not really. I followed at a discreet distance.' Jefferson gave a rueful laugh. 'One doesn't want to get too near to a man with a gun.'

'Very wise. But presumably you didn't see where he went.'

'Not with any degree of certainty, but as I reached the road,

I saw a Volkswagen Polo driving out of the park at quite high speed. At least, I'm pretty sure it was a VW. But I'm not sure if the man I saw shooting at the tree was the man driving it.'

'I don't suppose you managed to get the number, did you?' Dave asked hopefully.

'No, I'm terribly sorry, I didn't.' Jefferson sounded very apologetic at what he perceived to be a failure on his part. 'But I did notice that the window at the back was broken. There was just a piece of cardboard there and it looked as though he'd fixed it in place with sticky tape.'

'Was it the back window or a side window, sir?' asked Dave, busily making notes in his pocketbook.

'The nearside,' said Jefferson promptly. 'Some years ago I had a VW Polo, and one of those windows went on mine. It was a devil of a job to get a replacement. Mind you my old car was knocking on a bit.' He chuckled. 'Bit like me.'

'Was the car you saw about the same age as the one you owned, Mr Jefferson?' I asked.

'I couldn't tell you. I only caught a fleeting glimpse of it. But as I said, I'm not completely certain it was a VW.'

Dave invited Mr Jefferson to sit in our car and took a statement from him about what he had seen. A few minutes later a car arrived from Kingston police station to take our informant back to New Malden.

'Once again, thank you for your assistance, Mr Jefferson,' I said, and shook hands.

Fortunately a forensic examiner had been available at the Surbiton laboratory when Dave's request went out, and ten minutes later a guy called Pearson arrived. He spent some time photographing the tree and the surrounding area, and finally extracted the rounds from it.

Dave went through the necessary paperwork to maintain continuity of evidence and we were about to leave the park when officialdom arrived.

'What's going on here, then?' demanded a park keeper. 'This is Crown property you know, and you have to have a licence to take photographs of the trees in this park.'

'I've got a licence,' said Dave, and thrust his warrant card under the park keeper's nose.

'Oh, right you are, guv'nor,' said the park keeper and promptly retreated from the scene.

We left the park and made our way back to Curtis Green.

'D'you think there's anything in the fact that it was a Volkswagen, guv,' asked Dave, as we joined the A308 for London. 'Given the German connection. Or that it wasn't far from Richmond.'

'You're clutching at straws, Dave,' I said.

'There aren't any to clutch at,' said Dave.

Back at Curtis Green, I arranged for a force-wide message to go out asking for any sightings of a Volkswagen Polo with a broken nearside window. I asked for details to be reported, but that the driver was not to be stopped or questioned. Being a realist, I held out little hope of it being traced, particularly as Cyril Jefferson had not been altogether sure that it was a VW.

I also asked Colin Wilberforce to enter the details on the police national computer in case nationwide checks on vehicles might identify the vehicle in question. It was always possible that an automatic number plate recognition unit would check the vehicle against the PNC. Although ANPR units did constant checks on moving traffic they were mainly searching for uninsured vehicles and other road traffic violations. But, as I've said before, Uniform Branch patrols often found someone for whom the CID had been searching for months. I lived in hope.

'I checked George Deacon's story, sir,' said Wilberforce. 'He and Miss Hardy did arrive at Heathrow when they said they did, and the Royal Canadian Mounted Police confirmed their story of staying in Calgary.'

'I'm not surprised,' I said. 'I got the impression that they were telling the truth.' That was another one off the list.

The murderer decided to get as far away as he could from his last address in Isleworth. He selected Greenwich for no better reason than that it was nearer to the Channel ports than central London. He intended to leave from Dover in the very near future and make his way back to Germany. Failing that, he would go to Harwich and thence to the Hook of Holland. He'd not been to the Netherlands before, but had heard that its people had a laissez-faire view of life, and that would suit him ideally.

He arrived in Greenwich and stopped at a newsagent's shop. Intent upon finding somewhere to live, and once again relying on a local newspaper for advertisements of accommodation, he found what he wanted. He made his way to a general stores in a street not far from Trafalgar Road.

'Can I help you, sir?' A man in a brown warehouse coat was standing behind the counter of the empty shop.

'I understand that you've got rooms to let.' The man pointed at the appropriate entry in the paper. 'According to this ad.'

'That's right. I'll be happy to show you. I've got no one else staying here at the moment so you've got a choice.' The shopkeeper, who introduced himself as Mr Martin, took a bunch of keys from a hook next to the computerized cash register. He led the way through a door at the back of the shop and up a flight of stairs to the first floor.

That there were no other people occupying the accommodation suited the murderer ideally.

'There are two rooms and a bathroom on this floor, and one on the top floor at the front,' said Martin. 'But there's a separate bathroom next to that one, so you might prefer that, having that floor all to yourself, so to speak.'

The murderer didn't have to think twice about making a choice. He'd rather be alone on the top floor and have the benefit of a bathroom that other tenants, if any arrived, would be unlikely to use. The fewer people who saw him the better.

'I like top floors,' the man said unconvincingly. 'Can I have a look at that one?'

'Certainly.' Martin, followed by the murderer, mounted the second flight and unlocked a door.

The accommodation was minimal: a large rug on bare boards, a bed, a table with an upright chair, and an armchair that had seen better days. 'I'm afraid there's no TV,' he said apologetically.

'Doesn't matter,' said the murderer. 'There's never very much to watch these days. I'll take it.' He reached an agreement with Martin and paid a week's rent in advance.

'I'll give you a rent book later on,' said Martin. 'What's your name?'

The murderer didn't hesitate. 'Derek Ford,' he said.

'Incidentally, I don't live on the premises,' said Martin, pausing at the door. 'I'll give you a key to the side door, but please make sure you lock it if you go out, and when you come back. There are a lot of criminals in this area these days.'

'So I've heard,' said the murderer.

No sooner had I finished briefing Wilberforce about Jefferson's discovery than another call came in. This time from Hounslow police station. A man named Donald Ives had called in that morning expressing concern about one of his tenants who had left with what he told the police was 'unseemly haste'. Ives wondered whether it had anything to do with the three murders that had been reported in the press.

This report was, I suspected, one of many we were likely to receive and would probably be irrelevant, but it had to be followed up. That, I'm afraid, was one of the penalties of telling the press that you wanted help from the public in finding a murderer.

'What's the address, Colin?'

'This is it, sir.' Wilberforce handed me a slip of paper bearing Donald Ives's particulars.

'Here we go again, Dave,' I said.

'We decided to let the room,' said Ives, admitting us to his house, 'once our daughter got married and fled the nest. We thought we'd make a few bob now that it was no longer being used.'

'Tell me about the man who lived here, Mr Ives,' I said.

'He'd only been here for a couple of weeks and the agreement was that he'd stay for at least a month, but he suddenly decided to up sticks and leave. I have to say that I was a bit put out by it and I told him he'd have to pay to the end of the month.'

'And did he?' queried Dave.

'Oh yes, he didn't jib at all. Just took out a roll of notes and paid me without a quibble. But I knew he'd seen the morning paper and it seemed that what he saw in it caused him to take off in a hurry. You know, the bit about the murders.'

'What was this man's name?'

'Derek Ford,' said Ives.

'Did he leave a forwarding address?' asked Dave.

'No. He said that there wouldn't be any mail for him.'

'Perhaps we could have a look at his room,' I said.

'Of course.' Ives led us upstairs to a comfortable room at the back of the house, and stood back while we looked around. There was nothing in the room to excite our interest, no personal belongings, no clothing. In fact, nothing. Nevertheless I decided to have a forensic examiner give it the once over.

'D'you mind if I have a fingerprint officer examine the room, Mr Ives? It's just possible that your late tenant might be the one we're looking for.' I didn't think for a moment that we'd struck that lucky, but stranger things have happened. Not that finding fingerprints would help, unless there was a set on record to compare them with.

'Of course,' said Ives enthusiastically. No doubt he was delighted to be at the centre of a major murder investigation. That, of course, carried risks of undesired publicity. And for that matter, the possibility of risks to himself.

'I'd be grateful if you didn't mention this to anyone at the moment, Mr Ives, particularly the press. You wouldn't want to alert this man to our interest, would you?'

'No, of course not,' said Ives, but I sensed that I'd just dashed his hope of making a few pounds from a crime reporter. And there was no doubt that Fat Danny, if he heard about it, would be hotfooting it to Isleworth as fast as his little legs would carry him.

We waited an hour for a fingerprint officer to arrive, and he spent another hour spreading powder over all the likely surfaces. He then spent ten minutes explaining to a disgruntled Mrs Ives the best way of removing it.

'Perhaps you'd let Linda Mitchell have the results,' said Dave.

'Who?' asked the fingerprint officer.

Dave sighed and gave him Linda's details.

SIXTEEN

On Tuesday morning I received the ballistics examiner's report. She was prepared to testify that the rounds that were removed from the Richmond Park tree were a match with those taken from the bodies of Eberhardt, Schmidt and Adekunle. It looked as though Cyril Jefferson had witnessed our killer engaging in some target practice prior to carrying out the murders. But whether the Volkswagen Polo with the broken rear nearside window that Jefferson had spotted leaving the park was the murderer's car remained to be seen. But as he'd admitted, he might have got the make of the vehicle wrong. So far nothing had come in reporting a sighting of a vehicle matching his description.

The ballistics examiner had the foresight to mention the legislation that had followed the Dunblane massacre, and her report went on to express the tentative view that the two-two calibre pistol was most likely to have been illegally obtained. Or had even been smuggled in from abroad. Finally, she mentioned that the rounds did not match any found at other scenes of crime.

I walked through to the incident room.

'Colin, send out a circulation to all forces asking for details of any reports regarding the theft of a two-two pistol. Within, say, the last two months.' I held out little hope of a positive reply. If the weapon had been illegally held, or if the loser was a villain, it was unlikely that the theft would have been reported to the police.

'Right, sir.' Wilberforce turned to his computer and announced that the message had been sent before I'd left the room. All we had to do now was to wait.

At two o'clock that afternoon, Wilberforce came into my office with a computer printout.

'A report from West Midlands Police, sir. It doesn't mention any stolen weapon, but their Birmingham East Local Policing Unit received a report regarding the curious behaviour of a man who applied to enrol in their club. Apparently he was never seen again after his first visit.'

'When was this, Colin?'

'The report was lodged at the Stechford police station on Wednesday the twenty-fifth of June, sir.'

'The date would be right if the same man was the man that Jefferson saw,' I said. 'And no other reports have come in from anywhere else?'

'No, sir.'

'I suppose I'd better look into it,' I said, 'and that means a trip to Birmingham.' I was, however, convinced that I'd be wasting my time. But, as I've frequently mentioned, such matters have to be followed up.

I waited until the following day to make sure that we'd not received any reports about stolen weapons or other examples of odd behaviour, and Dave and I set out for Birmingham by road. As usual it was tricky getting out of central London, but once on the M1 we had a reasonably clear run.

We arrived at Stechford police station in Station Road just before midday.

'I'm DCI Brock, Metropolitan, Sergeant,' I said to the officer on counter duty. 'I telephoned earlier to say that I'd be calling in.'

'Come through, sir,' said the sergeant, lifting the flap of the counter. 'The inspector's office is this way. He is expecting you.'

The inspector already had the report on his desk.

'Harry Brock, DCI, Metropolitan,' I said, shaking hands. 'This is Dave Poole, my sergeant.'

'What is your interest in this strange business, Mr Brock?' asked the inspector.

I explained about the triple murder we were investigating and that the ballistics report had indicated the likelihood of a target pistol having been used.

'I understand from your email that a man applied to join a shooting club up here,' I continued, 'but was not seen again.'

'That's so. The secretary of a local gun club reported that a man had applied for membership, but that he disappeared once he'd fired a few rounds,' said the inspector. 'He didn't take up membership and he didn't return.'

'Do you have a name and address for this mysterious gun club applicant, Inspector?'

'He gave his name as Derek Ford and the address where he was staying is a lodging house in Sheldon.'

Derek Ford was the name that Donald Ives' lodger had given. This was beginning to look interesting.

'Sheldon is near the airport, isn't it, sir?' asked Dave. It wasn't immediately clear to me why he'd asked that question.

'Yes, about three miles or so,' said the inspector.

'Was the secretary able to give you any more information about this man Ford?' I asked.

'Only that he was satisfied as to the man's identity, sir. Gun clubs are supposed to be very strict about membership and they're obliged by law to demand documentary proof. Ford apparently produced a rent book for the address in Sheldon. I have the details here. Personally I think they should've asked for more than a rent book, but as he didn't take the matter any further I don't suppose it matters.'

'I think I'd've asked for more than just a rent book, too,' I agreed.

The inspector shrugged, apparently at the failure of the club to demand proper identification. He gave me the address at which Ford had rented a room, together with a copy of the original report. 'We made an enquiry at the address, but weren't able to find out any more about him than I've already told you. We had no other address for him and there was little more we could do. After all, he applied to join the club but then changed his mind. It's not really a matter for the police. But in view of your circulation about the murders in London and possible stolen firearms, I thought it might be of interest to you.' He smiled. 'We have quite a lot of much more important things to do here than follow up things like that, Mr Brock,' he added.

'I'm sure you do,' I said, 'and thank you for your help so far. I'll visit Ford's address in Sheldon, in case there is any more to be learned. Perhaps you'd give my sergeant directions.'

'Would it be easier if I sent a local officer with you, or do you know this part of Birmingham?'

'A local officer would be very helpful,' I said. 'I'm a stranger here.'

'I'll make sure he's in plain clothes,' said the inspector, and used his telephone to make the necessary arrangement.

Mrs Patel, Derek Ford's erstwhile landlady, was a tall, slender woman attired in a sari. She gazed somewhat suspiciously at the three of us. 'Are you wanting rooms?'

'No, madam,' I said. 'We're police officers.' It was a statement that did little to lessen her suspicion.

'What is the problem?' demanded Mrs Patel, maintaining a firm grip on the edge of the front door. 'We are all law-abiding persons in this house. No drugs, no bad people, no loose women.'

'I'm sure you're right, Mrs Patel,' I said, 'but I was hoping that you could tell me something about a Mr Derek Ford who, I understand, stayed here for a while.'

'Ah, Mr Ford, yes. A policeman was here about him a while ago.' Mrs Patel opened the front door wide and invited the three of us into her sitting room. 'He was only here the once, you know. A bit of a strange fellow.'

'Really? But I thought he took lodgings here,' I said, even though I knew that he hadn't stayed.

'That is quite correct.' Mrs Patel took a book from a side table and flicked through the pages. 'Yes, here we are. Mr Ford took a room here on the second of June, but he didn't even stay for that one night. He paid for a week, but never came back here again.' She glanced up. 'I told the other policeman who came here all about it.'

'Did this Mr Ford leave anything here, Mrs Patel?' asked Dave. 'Any luggage or other belongings?'

'No. Once he had paid me, he said that he would go to New Street railway station and collect his bags from the left luggage office, but he never came back. Most odd behaviour. To tell you the truth I didn't know whether to let the room again.'

'Did this Mr Ford have a car, Mrs Patel?' asked Dave.

'Not that I saw,' said the woman. 'I certainly did not see any such vehicle outside when he called here. Anyway, he said he was going to the railway station to collect baggage, so perhaps he came by train.'

You should've been a detective, Mrs Patel, I thought.

We obtained a description of the errant Derek Ford from Mrs Patel, but it wasn't much help. An ordinary man in his mid-twenties was all she could tell us.

We next paid a visit to the gun club in search of the secretary who had told the police about Derek Ford and his rather odd disappearance.

Fortunately for us, both the secretary and the armourer were there when we called. That certainly saved us another journey from London.

'What can you tell me about this man Derek Ford who applied to join your club, but didn't pursue it?' I asked, once introductions had been effected.

'He seemed a responsible sort of fellow, Chief Inspector,' said the armourer. 'I asked him a few questions about his standard of shooting, and he told me he was ex-army and knew all about guns.'

'Did he produce any evidence of that?'

'No, I'm afraid not. Not evidence of having been a soldier. Anyway, I took him out to the range and he fired quite competently. He obviously knew how to handle a weapon, but he did admit to being unfamiliar with the pistol he was firing.'

'What was the weapon, sir?' asked Dave.

'A Rohm Twinmaster Action CO_2-charged target air pistol,' said the armourer promptly. 'It's a German job and very reliable.'

'As a matter of interest,' said the secretary, 'may I ask why officers from Scotland Yard are so interested in this man? We reported it to the local police, but they didn't seem to attach too much importance to it.'

'They were probably right not to do so,' I said. 'But it's just possible that Ford might be able to help us with our enquiries into a matter we are investigating in London.' I had no grounds for saying that, at least not yet, but in the course of an investigation as complex as a triple murder anything might help. Even so, I decided against mentioning the murders to either of the officials. The temptation to earn a few pounds by speaking to the press about a visit from Scotland Yard homicide officers would be too much for them to keep to themselves. That sort of publicity was more likely to hinder than help.

'What documentary evidence of identity did you demand of Mr Ford?' asked Dave, a question not designed to suggest that the officials had acted competently. And he knew the answer anyway.

'He produced a rent book for an address in Sheldon,' said the secretary. 'It's a local address, and he told us his landlady was a Mrs Patel.'

'We know. We've interviewed her,' said Dave. 'But did you visit the address or telephone her for confirmation?'

'Er, no,' said the secretary. 'The rent book seemed genuine enough, and I looked up Mrs Patel in the phone book. The address tallied with the one on the rent book.'

'I see.' Dave paused long enough to imply unspoken criticism of such a cavalier approach to security, especially where firearms were concerned. 'Can you describe Ford?'

'About twenty-five or so, I suppose,' said the armourer. 'Five-ten, perhaps even six foot. Neat haircut, clean shaven and dressed in a blazer and light-coloured slacks. Oh, and he was wearing a tie that looked as though it was a regimental one.'

'Any idea which regiment?' asked Dave.

'No, I didn't recognize it. I was in the Royal Air Force Regiment, but it looked like an army tie. On second thoughts I suppose it could have been an old school tie.'

'As I understand it, the reason you reported this man to the police was that having applied to join, he changed his mind and never came back.' I was beginning to think that Dave and I had wasted our time in travelling to Birmingham. Except for the coincidence of the name Derek Ford.

'There was a bit more to it than that,' said the armourer. 'When I took him out to the range, I handed him the Rohm air pistol I mentioned, but he asked if we had any automatic pistols he could fire, like a Walther or a Beretta. I explained about the legislation that followed the Dunblane massacre, but he didn't seem to know anything about it. He said he'd been abroad for a long time.'

'And that was definitely the last you saw of him, was it?'

'Yes, he never came back. I did suggest that if he wanted to practise with an automatic, he'd have to go to another country. I suggested Germany. There are a lot of gun clubs there using all manner of weapons.'

'Did this Ford character have a car, sir?' asked Dave.

'Not that I know of,' said the secretary, 'but I don't have a view of the road from my office.'

'Thank you for your assistance, gentlemen,' I said. The armourer's suggestion that the disappearing Derek Ford might try Germany for practice made me wonder if he had done so and if any weapons had been reported stolen there. But that was something I'd have to take up with Horst Fischer.

In order to round off our Birmingham enquiry, Dave and I called at New Street railway station.

The clerk in the left luggage office greeted us by grumbling about pressure of work, the bloody-mindedness of the public and Network Rail, the organization that managed this particular part of the railway. I don't know what he thought the police could do about it.

That out of the way, the clerk condescended to thumb through a couple of books and told us that there was no record of any one called Derek Ford depositing any baggage in June or at any time afterwards. But I got the impression that the left-luggage clerk was not the most conscientious of record keepers.

We returned the West Midlands policeman to his station and made for London. We were on the M6 before Dave mentioned this latest twist in our investigation.

'It strikes me that this Derek Ford took the room with Mrs Patel so that he'd have an address in the Birmingham area if the gun club checked. I don't think he ever intended to stay there.'

'It certainly looks like it, Dave. Although it seems as though they didn't bother to follow it up, or ask any pertinent questions.'

'And that is why I asked the local police the question about the airport, guv. I reckon that Ford established himself as a resident at somewhere near the gun club to provide the secretary with bona fide proof of identity, but actually intended to travel to the club from wherever he lived. In the event he didn't bother to join and that was possibly because he couldn't get his hands on an automatic.'

'But he did suggest to Mrs Patel that he'd be going to New Street station to pick up his baggage.'

'I know, guv, but he didn't, did he? So far, all we can be certain of is that he's a liar.'

'All we have to do now is find out his permanent address, if he has one,' I added gloomily. The task of trying to find a man named Derek Ford somewhere in the United Kingdom was a mammoth one.

'If Derek Ford is his real name,' said Dave.

'And if he hasn't taken up the club armourer's suggestion of going to Germany,' I said.

'But at least we know that there was a Derek Ford staying in Isleworth until quite recently,' said Dave. 'So he could be a Londoner, if it's the same guy.'

Waiting until Mr Martin, the shopkeeper, had locked up and left for home, the man calling himself Derek Ford made his way downstairs. He tried the communicating door to the general stores on the ground floor and was delighted to find that it was unlocked.

Spending a few minutes searching the crowded shelves, he eventually found what he was looking for: a claw hammer and a jemmy.

Returning to the second flight of stairs he took off his jacket and began the laborious task of removing every other tread. In the event it wasn't too difficult; the wood was old and even rotten in some places. *It was positively criminal, renting out a dangerous place like this*, he thought cynically. Finally, he eased one of the remaining treads, but left it in place so that it would creak if anyone stepped on it.

When he'd finished, he took the tools he'd borrowed back to the shop, left them on the counter, and returned to his room, carefully avoiding the missing treads while holding on to the rickety banister rail.

Once back in his room, he checked his automatic pistol and

loaded it, just as he'd been taught to do at Sandhurst. Not that he thought he'd need to use it. He was planning to cross the Channel in the next few days and eventually make for Brazil, as Ronnie Biggs of the infamous Great Train Robbery had done in 1970. But he was labouring under the mistaken belief that he couldn't be extradited from there.

We arrived at Curtis Green at about five, having stopped off at Toddington Services on the M1 motorway for a belated bite to eat.

Assuming for the moment that Derek Ford was a strong suspect for our three murders, I sat in my office for an hour pondering the problem of finding him. There were quite a few channels of enquiry open to me, among them the General Register of Births, Deaths and Marriages; the Passport Office; and the Driver and Vehicle Licensing Agency. Not that the latter would have recorded details of a broken window on a Volkswagen Golf. Unfortunately. And that was assuming that the VW Cyril Jefferson had seen was being driven by the killer.

But each of those sources was likely to throw up a fair number of men named Derek Ford, even those in their mid-twenties, and it would take days if not months to interview each of them because they could be anywhere in the country. And even then we might not find him if the name he'd given was not his real name. It was a possibility that Dave had suggested on our way back from Birmingham. In fact the more I thought about it, the more likely it seemed that he had used a false name. No murderer in his right mind would apply for membership of a gun club and use his real name when approaching its officials. That said, I've always believed that murderers are not of sound mind anyway.

In theory, the club should've demanded some substantial documentary proof of identity, but I knew that such requirements were more often honoured in the breach. The fact that he'd produced the rent book with which Mrs Patel had provided him was not in my view sufficient to meet legal requirements.

In the meantime, of course, and still assuming Ford was the killer, there was a very good chance that he would by now have fled abroad. And if he had any sense it would be to somewhere that did not have an extradition treaty with the UK. Like Congo, Mali, Syria or Iran. But he'd have to be mad to go to any of those places.

For the time being, however, I told Colin Wilberforce to make a PNC entry giving details of what additional information we knew of the mysterious Derek Ford.

'And when you've done that, Colin,' I said, 'perhaps you'd see if you can trace any flights in and out of Birmingham Airport that he might've taken from, say, the first of June.'

'Right, sir. Incidentally, there aren't any direct flights between London and Birmingham, but I'll see what I can do.' Wilberforce turned to his computer. 'Of course,' he said, swinging back to face me again, 'if he lives in the London area, it would have been quicker for him to go by train. Or he could drive. He could have done it in about two and a half hours. You'd waste that much time checking in and going through security at an airport.'

'Yes, I know, Colin,' I said. 'Dave and I just did that drive. But Ford could live anywhere in the UK.'

'Or the world,' put in Dave. 'Unless, as I suggested, he's the same Derek Ford who did a runner from Isleworth.'

I'd only been in my office for ten minutes when Colin Wilberforce came in.

'There are over twenty airlines using Birmingham International Airport, sir, but fortunately the airport keeps a central computer record of all passengers passing through the airport. It's something to do with anti-terrorism.'

'Thank God for that,' I said.

'However, sir,' said Wilberforce, 'they have no trace of a Derek Ford going in or out of the airport at any time after the first of June.'

'Thanks, Colin. No more than I expected. But it does seem to point to his having arrived there by train or driven there from London. Perhaps in a Volkswagen Polo,' I added hopefully, but that was too much to expect. No one had seen Ford in a car in the Birmingham area, but that didn't mean he hadn't arrived there in one.

I sent for Dave and Kate Ebdon and brought Kate up to date on the result of our Birmingham enquiries.

'Have a word with the Ministry of Defence, Kate, and see if they can give you any information about this Derek Ford. He told the armourer at the gun club in Birmingham that he was ex-military, but if he gave them and Mrs Patel a false name we aren't going to get anywhere. It's worth a shot, though.'

'To coin a phrase,' muttered Dave.

I telephoned Horst Fischer in Essen and told him about our enquiries in Birmingham.

'If this man Ford did go to Germany with the intention of acquiring a gun, Horst, I was wondering if you had any reports of a stolen weapon in, say, the last couple of months.'

'Let me have a look, Harry,' said Fischer, and once again I heard the telltale tapping of a computer keyboard. 'We've had reports of seven firearms stolen nationwide since the beginning of June. Six were from private property, but one was from a gun club on the outskirts of Essen. But losers don't always report a loss, especially if they're criminals.'

'We have a similar problem, Horst.'

'I'll make some enquiries and call you back, Harry. You say the man gave the name of Derek Ford?'

'That's the name he gave the club in Birmingham, Horst, but I doubt that it was his real name.'

SEVENTEEN

Horst Fischer rang me back the following morning.

'A bit of luck, I think, Harry. I've spoken to officials at the gun club here who reported the loss of a firearm, and they had a new English member. And he gave the name of Douglas Forbes.'

'Can they be sure, Horst?'

'There can be no doubt about it. He produced a British passport as evidence of his identity. He attended only a few times, but after the last time he was there, the armourer found that a point-two-two calibre High Standard Supermatic Trophy pistol was missing. They reported it to us, and details of Forbes were circulated to Interpol, but we've heard nothing since. I suppose they'll send out a green-corner circular in due course.'

'I hope so, Horst,' I said, not having much faith in the ability of Interpol to move with any degree of alacrity. A green-corner circular is sent to member nations asking for certain criminals to be watched. But no such Interpol information had appeared on the PNC. If it had, Wilberforce would've spotted it immediately.

'By the way, Harry, we've released Wilhelm Weber, the man who lent his camper van to Eberhardt,' said Fischer. 'I'm satisfied he didn't know anything about Eberhardt's activities.'

It was after that conversation with Fischer, that Kate Ebdon came into my office.

'No luck with Derek Ford at the Ministry of Defence, guv, but—'

'Doesn't matter, Kate. Try this one.' I gave her the details of Douglas Forbes that Fischer had passed on.

Half an hour later she returned. 'I think we've got a result, guv,' she said, waving a sheet of paper. 'The army turned up Douglas Forbes in their records with the same date of birth; he's now aged twenty-five. Apparently he was accepted for the Royal Military Academy six years ago, but after two months at Sandhurst turned out not to be up to their exacting standards. They didn't specify what his shortcomings were, but as a result he was returned to his unit and discharged from the army.'

'We're getting somewhere at last, Kate.'

'And some, guv. I interrogated the General Register Office's computer at Southport and came up with some interesting connections.'

'Well, don't keep me in suspense.'

'Douglas Forbes is the only son of Philip and Nancy Forbes.' Kate looked up with a wide smile and an expression of triumph on her face. 'And Nancy Forbes, née Fairfax, is the daughter of Catherine, Lady Fairfax and the late General Sir Michael Fairfax.'

'Got him!' I exclaimed, although I was doubtful that it had been that easy. 'Well done, Kate.'

'Unfortunately I haven't been able to find an address for Douglas Forbes, or for his parents.'

'At least we know where Lady Fairfax lives, Kate. That'll be a good starting point, but I don't know how we're going to break it to her that we suspect her grandson of being a murderer.'

'If he is,' said Kate.

'He's got to be, Kate. His grandmother was swindled out of forty grand. If that's not a motive, I don't know what is.'

'Unless someone assumed his identity, guv.'

'But why should they do that?'

'Perhaps Lucien Carter masqueraded as Forbes,' said Kate, throwing cold water on her own discovery. 'Assume for a moment that Carter had been swindled by Eberhardt, Schmidt and Adekunle. He might've decided to take them out. And he'd've known who Forbes was. Carter's little firm had seen Forbes's grandmother off for forty grand.'

'Unfortunately, that's not now easily resolved,' I said. 'And I doubt that Carter would've known of Douglas Forbes's existence. Anyway, Carter's dead. Someone topped him in Rikers, but I suppose the FBI agents in New York found out what he'd been up to before he was stabbed to death. Although Joe Daly said that according to Carter's passport, he hasn't been out of the States for some years. No, it's got to be Forbes in person.'

'D'you think Lady Fairfax will give up her grandson?' asked Kate.

'There's one way of finding out.' I glanced at my watch. 'You and I will pay her a visit this afternoon.'

During the drive out to Pinner, I'd been turning over in my mind how best to broach the thorny subject of Douglas Forbes. By the time we arrived at Lady Fairfax's house, I'd formulated a rough plan.

Catherine Fairfax might've been in her late seventies, but she was still very alert and recognized me immediately.

'Chief Inspector, do come in. Have you got some good news for me?'

'I'm afraid not, Lady Fairfax,' I said, as we followed her into her sitting room.

Catherine Fairfax glanced at Kate, and I effected an introduction.

'This is Kate Ebdon, Lady Fairfax, one of my detective inspectors.'

'How d'you do, my dear.' Lady Fairfax shook hands.

'Ripper, m'lady, thanks.' Kate always interpreted that quintessential English greeting as if it were a genuine enquiry into the state of her health.

For a moment or two, Lady Fairfax seemed slightly bemused by Kate's response, but then she smiled. 'You're Australian,' she said.

'Yeah, how did you guess, ma'am?'

'My husband and I spent three years in Australia when Michael was military attaché at the high commission in Yarralumla in Canberra. It's a lovely country.'

'Canberra's not so dinkum, but Queensland's the place to live. Port Douglas just north of Cairns is real beaut.'

'Is that where you're from, my dear?'

'Sure is, ma'am. It's a great place with weather good enough for me to go skinny-dipping in the Coral Sea a lot of the year.' Kate sighed. 'But then I decided to come to the Old Country.'

'It must've been idyllic,' said Catherine Fairfax, seemingly unsure how to respond to Kate's unembarrassed claims of nude bathing. She turned to me. 'However, Chief Inspector, I'm sure you didn't come here to talk about this young lady's home town.'

'No, Lady Fairfax. It's a rather delicate matter and concerns your grandson.'

'Douglas? What's he been up to now?'

'You don't sound surprised,' I said.

'He was always a difficult child, but we thought he'd be all right after deciding to follow his grandfather and his father into the army. It didn't work out, though. At Sandhurst, he assaulted a sergeant. That's the death wish to a military career, of course, and he was returned to his unit and discharged. But by that time Michael was already dead, thank God. Heaven knows what he'd've had to say about it.'

'D'you know where your grandson is now, Lady Fairfax?' asked Kate.

'I'm afraid not, my dear, but his parents might be able to help you. I'll give you their address.' Catherine Fairfax struggled across to her escritoire and ferreted about for an address book. 'There it is,' she said, pointing to an entry.

Kate made a note of the Buckinghamshire address.

'Might I ask why you're interested in speaking to Douglas, Chief Inspector?' asked Catherine Fairfax.

'We think he might've stolen a pistol from a gun club in Germany.' In fact, I was now satisfied that there was little doubt about it.

'Oh dear!' Forbes's grandmother did not seem at all surprised by this revelation. 'What on earth would he have done that for?'

'We're not sure, Lady Fairfax, but clearly it's something we have to follow up.' I decided not to tell her that her grandson was a front-runner for three murders, and might even have been implicated in a fourth, that of Lucien Carter.

'Of course you must look into such things. There's so much crime these days.' Catherine Fairfax shook her head. 'I don't know what'll become of Douglas,' she said sadly.

I could've answered her question, but decided it was politic to say nothing.

It was about 15 miles from Pinner to Stoke Poges. Catherine Fairfax had told me that Philip Forbes was no longer a serving army officer, so there was a good chance of him being at home. Fortunately both he and his wife were there.

'Colonel Forbes?'

'Yes, but I don't use the rank now that I'm retired. Don't hold with that sort of nonsense.' Forbes was dressed in a Paisley shirt and khaki linen trousers. His upper lip was adorned by a clipped and greying, guardee moustache and he wore heavy horn-rimmed spectacles.

'I'm Detective Chief Inspector Brock of New Scotland Yard, Mr Forbes,' I said, 'and this is Detective Inspector Ebdon.'

'You've come to see me about Douglas, I take it, Chief Inspector.'

'Yes, but—'

Forbes smiled. 'My mother-in-law telephoned me just after you'd left her. It's an old army habit to share intelligence, you know.' He conducted us into his living room and indicated a middle-aged woman, clearly of the twinset-and-pearls class, who was seated in an armchair. 'This is my wife Nancy, Douglas's mother of course.' He crossed the room and switched off the television. 'Now then, tell me how I can help you.'

'It's a rather delicate matter, sir,' I began, repeating the phrase I'd used to Lady Fairfax.

'There's no need to beat about the bush, Chief Inspector,' said Forbes, inviting us to take a seat. 'Both my wife and I know that Douglas has turned out to be a bad egg. What's he done this time?'

'We have reason to believe that he might have stolen an automatic pistol from a gun club in Germany, Mr Forbes,' I said, thankful for Forbes's refreshing and no-nonsense reaction. 'In Essen, to be precise.'

'So my mother-in-law told me. That sounds like par for the course as far as Douglas is concerned.' Forbes brushed at his moustache and shook his head. 'Let's have it, then.'

I explained what we'd learned from our trip to Birmingham and told him of the report I'd received from the German police.

'Why d'you think he wanted this weapon? Allowing, of course, that it was in fact Douglas who stole it.'

'At the moment, sir, we haven't discovered a reason.' It didn't seem a good idea for me to accuse Forbes's son of being a murderer; we didn't have any direct proof. Yet.

But Forbes was ahead of me. 'D'you think he might've murdered someone?'

'I suppose it's a possibility,' I said cautiously.

'Good God, man, what other reason does one have for going about stealing firearms?'

'What can you tell me about your son, sir?' asked Kate.

Forbes raised his eyebrows at Kate's Australian accent, but didn't comment on it. 'As Lady Fairfax probably told you, Inspector, he got the sack from Sandhurst. The bloody young fool struck a directing staff NCO in front of several witnesses. In my day that would've merited a court martial, but instead he was discharged with ignominy. Sufficient punishment in itself, I suppose.' He shook his head at the apparent leniency of the modern army.

'What did he do after the army discharged him, Mr Forbes?' I asked.

'He spent a year or two hanging around in the West End of London doing God knows what, but I'm sure he got in with some bad hats. Then he went to Germany and spent a year or two there.'

'Whereabouts in Germany?' asked Kate, her interest suddenly aroused.

'Hamburg, I believe. We know he got mixed up with some German girl over there, even talked about marrying her. But then he found out that she was taking part in pornographic films and he said that that was too much for him. I suppose he did have some standards, but I have to say they were damned difficult to find.'

'D'you happen to know the name of this woman, sir?' Kate asked.

'I certainly can't think of it offhand, Inspector.' Forbes glanced at his wife. 'Can you remember her name, my dear?'

'It was Trudi Schmidt.' Nancy Forbes had no problem immediately recalling the woman's name.

'Are you sure about that, Mrs Forbes?' I asked.

'Positive. On one of the rare occasions Douglas did drop in to see us, he showed us a photograph of her. She looked like a tart.' Mrs Forbes was scathing in her dismissal of someone whom she would have loathed having as a daughter-in-law.

'Is that name of some significance, Chief Inspector?' asked Forbes, and paused to glance at his wife. 'D'you think she had something to do with this swindle that was perpetrated on my mother-in-law?'

'We're considering every possibility, sir,' I said, unwilling to divulge too much about our enquiries, 'but until we can speak to your son we can't rule it out. Do you know where we can find him?' I wanted to avoid further discussion about the fraud.

'The last we heard of him he was living in some sleazy bedsit in Pimlico, but we don't keep in touch.' Forbes paused. 'Well, the truth of the matter is that he doesn't bother to keep in touch with us.'

'He doesn't even send us a Christmas card,' said Nancy Forbes sadly. It was obvious that her errant son's behaviour affected her more than it did her husband. 'To be honest, the only time we see him these days is when he wants money.'

That, and the revelation that her son might be in serious trouble, had almost reduced her to tears, but not quite. If she was anything like her mother she was of the stiff upper lip class.

'And he doesn't get any cash,' said Forbes. 'Not any more.'

'Do you happen to have your son's exact address, Mr Forbes?' asked Kate.

Philip Forbes picked up a Filofax from a nearby table and jotted down the address on a blank page. Tearing it out, he handed it to Kate. 'That's the last address we had for him, Inspector. As I said, it's in Pimlico, but that was a year ago. I somehow doubt you'll find him still there.'

'D'you know if your son owns a car, Mr Forbes?' I asked.

'Probably,' said Forbes, 'but I've no idea what it is.'

'Do you really think he stole this gun, Mr Brock?' asked Nancy Forbes.

'Everything seems to point to it, Mrs Forbes,' I said.

We thanked Douglas Forbes's parents for their frankness and assistance and took our leave.

'I'll see you out, Chief Inspector,' said Forbes, and accompanied us to the front door, making sure that he closed the sitting room door. 'I didn't mention it in front of my wife, but isn't Trudi Schmidt one of the people who was murdered in Richmond in that camper-van fire?'

'That's correct, sir,' I said.

Forbes nodded. 'I read it in the newspaper, but fortunately my wife rarely watches the news on television and only ever scans the *Daily Mail*. But I quite understand that you can't say any more. Sub judice and all that.' He was clearly a man who joined up the dots very quickly and had probably concluded that we wanted his son for murder.

'Looks like Douglas Forbes is our man, guv,' said Kate, on the way back to Curtis Green.

'Maybe,' I said cautiously. 'It's one thing to have our suspicions, but I've a nasty feeling that we're going to have one hell of a job finding him.'

'D'you think his involvement with Trudi Schmidt has any relevance?' asked Kate, braking sharply to avoid a cyclist who seemed to think that traffic lights didn't apply to him.

'Could it have anything to do with the fact that she was a porn actress?'

'In what way, Kate?'

'An act of revenge for betraying him by having it off with other blokes on film.'

I laughed. 'I doubt it, but that wouldn't explain why Eberhardt and Adekunle were killed, unless Eberhardt was unlucky enough to be in the wrong place at the wrong time. And certainly wouldn't be a motive for Lucien Carter's murder. In fact I'd go further. I wouldn't mind betting that Forbes was the unidentified sexual athlete that Dave and I saw on the DVD when we went to Essen.'

I left it until the following morning to make a start on tracking down Douglas Forbes. But from what his parents had said, it wasn't going to be an easy task. And so it proved.

The address that Philip Forbes had given us for his son turned out not to be the sleazy bedsit he'd suggested it was, but a good quality flat in a Georgian three-storied townhouse.

I pressed the bell-push and waited.

'Looks like he's done a runner, guv,' said Dave.

'If he was ever here in the first place,' I said, hoping that Dave would be wrong.

I pressed the bell-push a couple more times. We were just about to give up and make enquiries at other apartments in the house when the intercom buzzer sounded.

'Who is it?'

'The police,' I said.

'Oh God! You'd better come on up, then. It's one flight up. Door on the right.'

We ascended the stairs to the first floor. The door to the apartment was opened by a twenty-something languid blonde who looked as though we'd roused her from a deep sleep. She raised her left arm high on the edge of the door for support so that her black silk wrap parted to reveal a matching camisole and shorts.

'What time is it?' she asked, running a hand through her untidy hair and yawning.

'Five past eleven,' I said.

'In the morning,' added Dave.

'Good God, is that all?'

'We're police officers,' I announced again.

'So you said. What's happened now? Has someone stolen my bloody car?'

Oh, not again, I thought. *What is it about the police and the public's precious motor cars?*

'We're looking for Douglas Forbes,' said Dave.

'You and me both, darling. He owes me two hundred quid,' said the blonde, casting a lingering eye over Dave. 'You'd better come in. I'm just about to make some coffee.'

Uninvited, Dave and I sat down in a couple of armchairs that I suspected had been chosen for their style rather than their comfort. The blonde stationed herself behind a counter that separated the kitchenette from the seating area and fiddled about with an electric kettle and a cafetière. Eventually she poured coffee into three bone-china mugs and handed them round before sitting down opposite us.

'Are you Mrs Forbes, by any chance?' I asked, sipping at the coffee that I was pleased to note was excellent.

'Not bloody likely, darlings. I'm Lavinia Crosby.' Her cultured, drawling voice matched what I'd always thought to be an upper-crust sort of first name. 'I haven't seen Dougie for over two months now, maybe longer.'

'Were you two an item?' asked Dave, employing modern day parlance to describe living together.

'We were shacked up for a year, but it seemed like ten. Are you from the local cop shop?'

'No, I'm Detective Chief Inspector Brock of New Scotland Yard and this is Detective Sergeant Poole.'

'Oh, the big guns. Sounds as though Dougie's in some sort of deep mire.'

'We shan't know until we talk to him, Miss Crosby,' I said.

'It's *Mrs* Crosby, actually.' Lavinia drew out the last word with an affected drawl. 'Not that it matters a damn. Bertie buggered off a couple of years ago. Not set eyes on the ratbag from that day to this. He went to live in Switzerland I think. Or was it Austria?' She glanced at her elegant Baume & Mercier wristwatch. 'I'm glad you woke me up, actually. I'm supposed to be meeting a guy for lunch.'

'Have you *any* idea where Douglas Forbes is, Mrs Crosby?'
I asked, tiring of her irrelevant responses.

'Not a clue, darling,' said Lavinia. 'Dougie lived here for
about a year, as I said, most of the time living on my money
before he buggered off. Daddy didn't approve of him, but then
Daddy doesn't approve of any of the guys I shack up with.
Probably because he doesn't like the way I spend the allowance
he gives me.' She shrugged at what she clearly thought to be
gross parsimony on her father's part.

That came as no surprise. It sounded as though 'Daddy' was
a shrewd judge of character if what we knew of Douglas Forbes
was anything to go by. And that caused me to wonder what sort
of wastrel Bertie Crosby must've been. And where he'd really
gone and why, not that that was any of my business. But it did
prompt a thought.

'Was Bertie Crosby a stockbroker by any chance?'

'A stockbroker?' Lavinia laughed. 'Bertie wasn't anything,' she
said. 'A leech is the only description that comes readily to mind.'

'When did Douglas Forbes leave?' I asked.

'About six weeks ago, I suppose. I woke up one morning
and there he was gone. Not seen him since.' Although giving
the impression of being a dizzy blonde bimbo, Lavinia Crosby
was shrewd enough not to mention Forbes's recent flying visit.

'Did Douglas have a car?' asked Dave.

'He drove my Porsche most of the time, but he did have an
old banger.'

'What sort of car was this old banger?'

'A VW I think. I know that one of the windows was broken,
but he never got the bloody thing fixed. He was like that, you
know. Just couldn't be bothered. But that was Dougie all over.'

'Which window?' Dave too was beginning to get ratty with
her meandering chatter.

'Oh, I don't know, Sergeant dear. I think it was the little one
at the back. On the left-hand side. He'd never have got me out
in the bloody thing, that's for sure. More coffee?'

'No, thanks.' Dave took out his pocketbook. 'D'you happen
to know the number of his vehicle?'

'Good God, no. I don't collect car numbers. I don't even
know my own.'

'If he should happen to reappear, perhaps you'd ask him to contact me as a matter of urgency, Mrs Crosby.' I handed Lavinia one of my cards, knowing full well that Forbes wouldn't return or that if he did he'd disappear again like early morning mist in the rising sun. It was actually a waste of one of my cards.

EIGHTEEN

Back at Curtis Green, Dave got straight on to the Driver and Vehicle Licensing Agency's computer at Swansea.

'Bingo!' he exclaimed. 'We've got an index mark for Forbes's Volkswagen.' He switched to the PNC and fed in the number. 'Aha! It's flagged up for no insurance. What a surprise. I wonder why he hasn't been stopped by the Black Rats. They're obviously not trying hard enough. They should've spotted him by now.'

'Perhaps his car's in a garage somewhere,' I said, 'or he's flogged it or it's been broken up. But if Forbes still has it, the traffic police have got every justification for stopping him and seizing his car. Make an entry on the PNC asking for him to be arrested, but not to be questioned other than regarding traffic offences.' I paused. 'And add the caveat "may be armed and dangerous".'

I retired to my office and embarked upon a series of phone calls.

First of all, I contacted Horst Fischer in Essen and told him what we'd learned of Douglas Forbes.

'He's the obvious suspect for our murders, Horst,' I said. 'Furthermore, we've learned that he lived with Trudi Schmidt for a while in Hamburg.'

'That's interesting, Harry. D'you remember when you came to Essen that you saw a white man in the pornographic DVDs?'

'Yes, I certainly did, Horst.

'I've since spoken to the producers of those films and they identified that man as Douglas Forbes. At least,' Horst added cautiously, 'a man giving the name of Forbes.'

That came as no surprise. Philip Forbes had obviously been

wrong in assuming that his son had any acceptable standards of moral behaviour.

I wondered if Forbes's split with Trudi was not that she was a porn actress, but that she shared her favours with several other men, albeit on camera. But I dismissed that thought immediately. From our viewing of the DVD, we knew that Forbes, Adekunle and Trudi Schmidt had all been in shot at the same time. We also knew that Trudi had convictions for unlicensed prostitution, although Forbes probably didn't know that. Or if he did, he didn't care. The man was obviously a dissolute wastrel.

'We're attempting to find Forbes, Horst,' I said, 'but he's proving to be somewhat elusive.'

'It's the way of criminals, Harry.' Fischer and I clearly took a similar jaundiced view of the criminal fraternity. 'Perhaps you'd let me know when you have arrested this man, then I can clear up all my loose ends. You know how it is with the paperwork, *ja*?' He gave another of the raucous chuckles with which we'd become familiar during our stay in Essen.

'Only too well, Horst. But from what we've learned, he might be in Germany.'

'Give me his details and I'll have him circulated on our national computer network.'

'I'll send you an email,' I said, and promptly got Colin Wilberforce to do it.

My next call was to Joe Daly at the American Embassy. I explained how far we'd got in our search for Douglas Forbes, and asked him if he'd received any further information about Lucien Carter's murder in Rikers.

'The NYPD have gotten zilch, Harry,' said Joe. 'There were twenty-five prisoners in the exercise yard when it happened. The correction officers saw nothing, and, believe it or not, all the prisoners went shtum.'

'Oh, surely not, Joe,' I said sarcastically.

'Yeah, I know. It's unbelievable,' said Daly, matching my cynicism with his own. 'Anyhow, straight after the incident the governor ordered an immediate lock-down and the COs did a thorough search, but no weapon was found. The autopsy report stated that Carter was killed with a single stab wound and died instantly. Anyway, that's one more perp out of circulation.'

'Looks like it'll be another unsolved, then.'

'I guess so. The received wisdom is that whoever was the top man among the prisoners saw Carter as some sort of threat and had him taken out. But I doubt we'll ever know why.'

Bearing in mind the time difference, I waited until three o'clock that afternoon before ringing Superintendent Duncan Gould of the Royal Bahamas Police Force.

'Good afternoon, Duncan,' I said, when Gould picked up. 'It's Harry Brock in London.'

'Good morning to you, Harry. How's your weather?'

'The climate's OK, Duncan, but the police work's getting a bit complicated.' I'd concluded from our previous conversation that Gould was obsessed with the weather. I told him about the murder of Lucien Carter in New York, but this was not news to him.

'Yes, I heard, Harry. I've been in touch with the FBI and they filled me in. Still that's one more criminal off the books,' said Gould, echoing Daly's reaction to Carter's death. Policemen across the world took the same negative view of villains. 'I've still got the matter of the frauds to deal with, though. We've come across quite a few people who've been swindled, probably by Carter. And we're talking hundreds of thousands of Bahamian dollars here. Our dollar comes out to about two-thirds of a pound sterling, but it's still a lot of money. However, that's my problem. I hope you get your man, Harry.'

'Oh, I will, Duncan. Rest assured of that,' I said, and replaced the receiver.

Despite my confident reply, I was by no means sure that I would be feeling Forbes's collar in the near future. He could now be anywhere in the world, especially if he'd been tipped off, possibly by the languorous Lavinia Crosby who, I thought, had probably seen him more recently than she'd claimed to have done. I doubted though that Forbes's father would've warned his son of our interest, even if he knew more than he'd told us about Douglas Forbes's current whereabouts.

But at least I didn't have to worry any more about the world-wide boiler-room frauds for which Carter, Eberhardt, Schmidt and Adekunle had been responsible. That was a problem I would happily hand over to the Fraud Squad. Once our man was in custody.

All we could do now was to sit back and wait. Very irritating, but once again the progress of our enquiry was in the hands of other people. I sent the team home for an early night with the proviso that if Forbes was located that evening or over the weekend, some of them would be called back to duty.

I telephoned Gail and suggested dinner somewhere. Much to my delight, she suggested staying in and offered to prepare a meal at home.

As I was in good time, I called in at a store in Kingston and bought Gail some Chanel Cristalle, her current favourite. Nothing like an expensive smelly to put a girl in a good mood.

The weather still being hot and humid, I dropped by my flat and changed into a shirt and chinos.

Gail had obviously taken the same view of the heat. Barefooted, she was wearing a saffron kaftan and, as I later discovered, nothing else.

Both sets of French windows in her first floor sitting room were wide open, but it had made little difference to the temperature. I poured a large whisky for myself and prepared a gin and tonic for Gail.

'I don't suppose you've given any more thought to my suggestion of moving in with me, have you, darling?' asked Gail, glancing impishly at me. She placed her glass on the coffee table and ran her finger down the side drawing a line in the condensation.

'To be perfectly honest, darling, I've not had much time.' Although I rarely talked about the Job when I was with her, I went on to explain about the discovery that Douglas Forbes was probably our murderer. 'It all hinges on him being found,' I said. 'But I will give your idea some thought.'

'I take it that you haven't dismissed it, then,' said Gail, repeating what she'd said to me at the bistro just over a week ago.

'No, not at all.' I'd made Douglas Forbes the excuse for not making a decision. But I knew that, once made, it would be irreversible and I didn't want to rush into it. However, the signs of dissatisfaction I'd detected during my conversation with Bill

Hunter were uppermost in my mind. Had I told him of Gail's suggestion I'm sure he would have cautioned me against any precipitate move on my part. And that prompted a thought.

'Does Charlie Hunter ever play away?' I asked.

Gail stared at me. 'Whatever made you ask that?'

'Nothing really. It was just that Bill sort of hinted that everything in their expensive garden wasn't exactly lovely.'

'Shall we have dinner first?' Choosing not to continue a conversation about her friend, Gail stood up, pulling open the top of her kaftan and wafting air down the front. 'Or later.'

I knew exactly what she meant, and she knew that she'd posed a question that was only slightly less difficult for me to answer than whether I was to move in with her.

'I think we'd better have dinner first,' I said.

'Good, then we won't have to rush.'

I presumed she meant rushing what else we both had in mind.

It was on the following Wednesday, five days later, that the first sighting of Douglas Forbes's car was reported. Once again it was a vigilant constable who'd made the discovery, and she'd sighted it in Greenwich, in a backstreet not far from Trafalgar Road. The premises consisted of a general stores with a number of rooms above it.

The woman officer had made purposely vague enquiries in the shop and had been told by an assistant that he thought the man who lived in one of the rooms above was the owner of the car, but his name was Derek Ford. At that point, the officer decided that she would report the matter to a senior officer and await further instructions.

It turned out to be a very wise decision.

The local detective chief inspector rang me and asked what action his people should take, given that Forbes was a suspect for three murders. I told him to do nothing other than to have a discreet eye kept on the premises, and that I would be there with my team ASAP. The DCI promised to have a few uniforms placed unobtrusively nearby.

For a start, I assembled Kate Ebdon, Dave Poole, Tom Challis and John Appleby.

'What about firearms?' asked Dave.

I shook my head. 'There isn't the time to get authorization,' I said. 'Anyway we'll leave that to an armed response unit if we need to. I don't want to get into a shoot-out with this guy if he turns nasty.'

Forbes's car, still with its broken window, was outside the shop. At least, the car registered in Forbes's name was there. It was possible that Forbes had disposed of it and failed to notify the DVLA of the transfer, but I hoped not.

Dave and I entered the shop, leaving Challis and Appleby in one of the two cars that had brought us to Greenwich. The territorial support group was parked a few yards down the road and Kate Ebdon went to brief the inspector in charge on the current state of play.

'Are you the owner of these premises?' I asked the man behind the counter, once I'd identified myself.

'Yes, I am. Is there some trouble?'

'You could say that,' said Dave laconically. 'What's your name?'

'Martin. Frederick Martin.'

'And do you own this entire property, Mr Martin?' I asked.

'Yes, I do. Why?'

'Is one of your tenants a Douglas Forbes?'

'There's no one of that name here. There's only one man living here at the moment and his name's Derek Ford. He's got a room on the top floor.'

'Is that his car outside?' Dave asked.

'Yes, I believe it is, but if it's not licensed or anything like that, it's not my responsibility.'

Here we go again, I thought. *We're not here about anyone's bloody car.*

'What's he look like, this Derek Ford?' persisted Dave.

'I only saw him once. That's when he moved in the day before yesterday. He seems to stay in his room, at least while I'm here.' Martin furnished a description that could've tallied with Forbes. And a hundred others.

'Top floor, you said.'

'Yes. The room at the front.'

Dave glanced at me. 'Give it a go, sir?'

'How do we get up there?' I asked the shop's owner.

'There's a door at the side,' said Martin, 'but it's locked.'

'Very helpful,' said Dave, 'but can we reach the upstairs through the shop?'

'Oh, I see. Yes, this way.' Martin showed us through a door at the back and indicated a flight of stairs.

Douglas Forbes, who'd told Martin he was Derek Ford, had heard a car door slam. He'd moved quickly to the window and peered down at the street.

Two cars had been parked in the kerb outside the shop. Two men, one white and one black, each wearing a suit, and a woman in jeans and a white shirt, had alighted from one of them. They looked like police officers even though they weren't wearing uniform. The three of them had a brief discussion before the woman walked away. The two men then entered the shop.

Forbes glanced at the second car and saw that there were some men in it, but they showed no signs of getting out.

How on earth could the police – and he was sure that's who they were – have found him so quickly? Suddenly it looked as though his plans for an escape to the Continent were to be thwarted before they'd even begun.

Moving rapidly, he shifted the upright chair across the room and opened the door. Taking out his pistol, he checked it one more time to ensure that it was loaded.

He'd already killed three people and if he was caught alive, his sentence would be no greater for adding a few police officers to his score. And doing so might enable him to escape.

He waited. Minutes later he heard people coming up the first flight of stairs. He thumbed off the safety catch. And waited.

Dave and I ascended the first flight of stairs, but as we were about to mount the second flight, we got a surprise. The first of two surprises, that is.

'Half the bloody staircase is missing, guv,' said Dave.

I glanced up at the stairs and saw that every other tread had been removed, making it difficult, although not impossible, to reach the top floor.

Dave and I began our slow and careful way upwards, intent

on avoiding the gaps. We were about a third of the way up when I stepped on a tread that produced a loud creaking noise. We both froze.

Suddenly a shot rang out and a round hit the wall near Dave's head, chipping a chunk out of the plaster.

I couldn't see who'd shot at us, but I was pretty sure it would have been Forbes, alias Derek Ford. We retreated rapidly.

'I think the bastard's shooting at us, guv,' said Dave calmly, as we returned to the comparative safety of the first floor landing.

'Yes, Dave,' I said, 'I rather got that impression myself.'

We descended to the shop a damned sight faster than we'd gone up.

'There's no need for discretion any more, Dave. Tell Appleby to get the TSG to close the road and surround the building. Also they are to tell the people in the premises opposite to stay away from the windows. Then get on the air and tell central command control that I need an armed response unit here without delay. And we'd better have additional back-up.'

'As good as done, sir,' said Dave, and raced out to the street.

'How many people have you got working here, Mr Martin?' I asked the shopkeeper.

'At the moment there's just me and my assistant Ryan.' Martin indicated a spotty-faced youth with his hands in the pockets of an oversized warehouse coat. The spotty-faced one grinned.

'Right, I want you both out of the premises as quickly as you can.'

'But I'll need to turn off the till and lock up.' Martin gave me a baleful look, as though I'd taken leave of my senses. 'What on earth is happening?'

'Do *not* lock the shop, Mr Martin,' I said firmly. 'My officers will need to gain access to the upstairs and they're not going to break down any bloody doors in order to get there. Now, get out quickly.'

Dave reappeared. 'All wrapped up, sir.'

'What was that bang I heard just now, Chief Inspector?' asked Martin, as we hastened him from the shop.

'That, Mr Martin, was your lodger taking a pot shot at me.'

'By the way,' said Dave, 'your Mr Ford has vandalized your staircase.'

'Vandalized it?' Martin stared at Dave with a blank expression.

'Yes, he's taken half the treads away. Must've been short of firewood.'

'But there aren't any fireplaces up there. They were taken out years ago,' said Martin, apparently oblivious to the fact that it was seventy-four degrees in the shade outside, and that his tenant would have no need of a fire anyway. 'He must've done that during night, after I'd locked up and gone home,' he complained. 'I'll have to charge him for the damage.'

'Good luck,' said Dave. 'I'll let him know you'll be sending him a bill.'

We moved out into the street, taking Martin and his assistant Ryan with us. By now, the area had been cleared, and the blue and white tapes that these days were part of any form of police action were visible at each end of the street. I told Martin and his assistant to get beyond the tapes as quickly as possible.

Several distant police sirens blasted the air. The cavalry was arriving.

A familiar figure strode towards me. He was in shirtsleeves, but wearing body armour,

'PS Dan Mason, sir, CO19.' Mason was a sergeant with the tactical firearms unit. 'We meet again,' he said.

'Indeed we do, Dan. A warehouse near the Walworth Road early one winter's morning was the last time, I seem to recall.'

'At least it's a bit warmer today, sir,' Mason said.

'In more ways than one,' commented Dave drily.

'I understand that someone's been shooting at you, sir.' As was his custom, Mason was talking calmly about an armed confrontation that could lead to one or more of us getting killed. 'What's the SP on this one?'

'I'm as certain as I can be that the guy up there is Douglas Forbes, Dan,' I said, and outlined what we knew so far in relation to the present situation. I went on to tell Mason about the three murders we strongly suspected Forbes of having committed. 'Not that it matters a damn who he is; he started shooting at us the moment we started going up the second flight of stairs.'

Mason rested a hand on his holstered Glock pistol. 'If he's your murderer, sir,' he said, 'he's got nothing to lose if he tries to take a few of us out, then.' It was a realistic observation. The likelihood of Forbes receiving a sentence of more than thirty years – even if it were that long – was remote, however many murders he'd committed. The more limp-wristed members of our government had intimated to the Lord Chief Justice that he should set the guidelines accordingly. 'Are you thinking of sending for a negotiator, sir?'

'No, I'm not, Dan. I've a feeling that this guy is not in a negotiating mood. But I'd rather like to take him alive.'

Sergeant Mason pursed his lips. 'Might be difficult, sir,' he said. 'If he starts shooting at any of us again, my people will have to return fire. And they shoot to kill.'

'I hope it won't come to that,' I said. 'By the way, our man has removed part of the staircase leading to his room on the top floor.'

Mason shrugged. 'These things are sent to try us, sir.'

'A Uniform Branch chief superintendent's just turned up, sir,' said Dave. 'He'd like a word.'

'Where's he from?'

'No idea, sir. I don't think he's the local guv'nor. Could be from Area HQ or even the Yard, I suppose.'

'That's all I need,' I said, turning as an individual approached who looked young enough to have obtained his uniforms from Mothercare. I presumed he was a product of the accelerated promotion course, the Bramshill Police College forcing process that elevated officers to a point beyond their level of competence.

'Chief Inspector Brock, is it?'

'Yes, sir.'

'What's happening exactly, Mr Brock?'

I explained that a man believed to be Douglas Forbes was holding siege on the top floor, and had already discharged a firearm.

'I see,' said the chief superintendent. 'How are you proposing to deal with the situation, Mr Brock?'

'*Let's purge this choler without letting blood*,' quoted Dave quietly.

'I beg your pardon?' The chief superintendent turned to Dave. 'What are you talking about?' He cast a critical gaze at Dave.

'*Richard the Second*, Act One, Scene Two, sir,' said Dave. 'It's Shakespeare,' he added, just to complete the reference.

'Yes, of course. I thought I recognized it,' said the chief superintendent unconvincingly, as he rapidly reappraised his view of black detective sergeants. 'What are you proposing to do, Mr Brock?' he asked again, redirecting his gaze to me.

'I shall talk to him in kindly tones, sir, and attempt to point out the error of his ways and the hopelessness of his situation. And if that doesn't work Sergeant Mason will probably kill him.'

'I see.' The chief superintendent didn't seem at all happy with that solution. 'Well, be careful.'

'Oh, I shall, sir. It's always uppermost in my thoughts,' I said, restraining myself from making a really sarcastic retort.

Taking Dan Mason, his PC partner and Dave with me, we re-entered the shop and ascended the first flight of stairs.

'Douglas Forbes, we're police officers,' I shouted, keeping well out of range on the first floor landing. 'You may as well give yourself up. The only alternative will be that my officers will storm your room and take you dead or alive.'

'Just like a shoot-out at the OK Corral,' added Dave, loud enough for the gunman to hear.

My entreaty was greeted with another shot that hit a wall somewhere. Followed by yet another. Our assailant was obviously firing blindly.

Mason switched the Heckler-Koch carbine from his shoulder and made it ready. Slowly he moved to the bottom of the second flight of stairs and looked upwards. Mason's partner, his own H-K at the ready, moved to a position to the rear and right of Mason.

A further shot rang out, but once again, it hit the wall behind Mason harmlessly.

'Come on, you bastards, come and get me,' said a cultured voice from above. Standing at the top was a man in a defiant pose holding a pistol.

Moving out of the line of fire, Mason rested his carbine and took his Glock pistol from its holster. 'Make your way down slowly,' he ordered, 'and keep your hands where I can see them.'

'The hell with you, copper,' shouted the man and raised his pistol.

Switching his Glock to a double-handed grip, Mason discharged two rounds in quick succession.

It is the teaching of SO19, the firearms department, that shots should be kill shots, but the man's quick movement resulted in his being hit in the upper thigh.

With a cry of pain, the man dropped his pistol and tumbled down the stairs, landing in an ungainly heap at Mason's feet.

Dave and I dragged the man into an upright position, and Mason patted him down to ensure he had no other weapons on him.

'He's clean, sir,' said Mason.

'Are you Douglas Forbes?' I asked.

'Yes.'

'Douglas Forbes, I'm arresting you on suspicion of the unlawful possession of a firearm, and discharging that firearm with intent to kill.' I deliberately didn't mention the murders of which I strongly suspected him. If I'd done so I'd've been precluded from questioning him about them later.

'You do not have to say anything,' began Dave, 'but it may harm your defence if you do not mention when questioned something you later rely on in court. Anything you do say may be given in evidence.'

'I need a doctor,' said Forbes.

'I'll make a note of that,' said Dave. 'Needs a doctor,' he repeated, as he scrawled a few words in his pocketbook.

Someone had had the foresight to call an ambulance, and we escorted the limping Forbes into it. I deputed DS Challis and DC Appleby to accompany our prisoner to the hospital.

'Where are you taking him?' I asked the paramedic.

'Lewisham A and E, guv.'

'A satisfactory conclusion, Mr Brock.' The chief superintendent approached me from the end of the street.

'Conclusion, sir? It's only the beginning not the end,' I said, and went in search of the inspector in charge of the territorial support group.

'Yes, sir?' The inspector was standing close to one of his tenders.

'Come with me, Inspector,' I said, and led him back into the shop and up the first flight of stairs. 'You'll see that the prisoner removed every other tread. While he was standing at the top

PS Mason shot him in the leg and Forbes dropped his pistol. It's not on the remaining treads, so I think it must've fallen through one of the gaps where a tread was taken away. I need it found and preserved for evidence. And I don't want to find any of your guys' fingerprints on it.'

'No problem, sir.' The inspector grinned. 'We've recovered evidence before, you know.'

'Yes, of course. Sorry, it's been a busy sort of day.'

Remarkably it took the TSG men only a matter of minutes to find Forbes's weapon.

'It appears to have bounced off one of the remaining treads and through the banisters on to the first floor landing, sir,' said the inspector, handing me the weapon shrouded in a plastic evidence bag. 'I have taken the precaution of unloading the remaining rounds.' He handed me a second plastic bag, and gave me his pocketbook. 'Perhaps you'd sign for it all, sir. Continuity of evidence.'

Now it was my turn to grin. 'Touché,' I said, and signed for the pistol that the inspector had correctly described as a point-two-two calibre High Standard Supermatic Trophy pistol, and the spare ammunition.

Dave and I ascended to the room that Forbes had occupied and took a cursory look around.

'We'll get Linda Mitchell and her team to give it the once over, Dave,' I said, 'but I doubt she'll find anything useful.'

'Forbes must've used tools to take up the treads on the staircase, sir,' said Dave, as we reached the ground floor again. 'There aren't any in his room, so he must've used some from the shop. I noticed that Martin stocks that sort of stuff, like hammers and jemmies and screwdrivers. We might just find Forbes's fingerprints on them if we can locate them.'

'Fetch Martin back in here, Dave.'

Accompanied by Dave, the shopkeeper returned to his store, peering round apprehensively as though fearing the gunman might still be there.

'It's all right, Mr Martin, we've arrested him,' I said. 'Now then, when you came in this morning, did you notice anything out of place?'

'Yes, I did, as a matter of fact. A claw hammer and a jemmy.'

'Where are they?' asked Dave.

'I put them back on the shelf. They were on the counter, but I don't remember having left them there.'

'That's because you didn't, Mr Martin. Your lodger left them when he was in his do-it-yourself mode and attacking your staircase. Perhaps you'd show me which tools they were.'

Martin moved to take a hammer from a shelf containing a variety of basic tools.

'Don't touch them, just point them out,' said Dave, as he donned a pair of protective gloves.

Martin indicated the hammer and the jemmy and Dave placed them in a plastic evidence bag. 'Might be able to get some dabs off them, sir, even though Mr Martin's handled them,' he said to me.

'Are you buying those?' asked Martin.

'No, Mr Martin, I'm seizing them as evidence,' said Dave patiently. 'I'll give you a receipt and you'll have them returned in due course.'

'Will I be able to claim from the police for the damaged staircase?' Martin was clearly unhappy, not only about the seized tools, but the entire police operation.

'Unfortunately no,' said Dave. 'You see, Mr Martin, the staircase was not damaged by the police or at our request. I suggest you have a word with your insurance company.'

'But they'll put my premiums up,' whined Martin.

'I know,' said Dave. 'It's a cruel old world.'

NINETEEN

It was the following afternoon that I received the telephone call to say that Douglas Forbes had been discharged from Lewisham hospital. He was now at Charing Cross police station in Agar Street whence he had been escorted by the two officers who had been guarding him in the hospital.

Douglas Forbes, still wearing the bloodstained trousers in which he'd been arrested, limped into the interview room.

'I'm Detective Chief Inspector Brock of New Scotland Yard,' I said, 'and this is Detective Sergeant Poole. I would remind you that you're still under caution.'

Dave turned on the recording machine and announced the presence of ourselves and that of Douglas Forbes.

'I'm obliged to inform you that you are entitled to have a solicitor present.'

'No thanks. Waste of money,' said Forbes. He leaned back in his chair, his hands behind his head. 'Who grassed on me?' he asked, the criminal argot sounding incongruous in his educated tones. 'Was it Lavinia Crosby?'

'No, it wasn't. When we visited Mrs Crosby last Friday she denied having seen you for at least six weeks.'

Forbes smiled. 'Good old Lavinia,' he said. 'Then it must've been the old guy who saw me shooting at a tree in Richmond Park.'

'Not him either. He couldn't identify you.'

'How the hell did you find me, then?' Forbes appeared mystified that we had tracked him down.

'It's called dedicated detective work,' said Dave.

'Well, I suppose you want to talk to me about the murders of Adekunle, Eberhardt and Schmidt.' Forbes moved forward, rested his elbows on the table and smirked. 'That'll have taught the bastards not to swindle my grandma.'

The pistol recovered by the TSG officers from the Greenwich shop where Forbes had been arrested had already been examined by a ballistics expert.

She reported that the weapon was undoubtedly the firearm used to carry out all three murders and tallied with the rounds taken from the tree in Richmond Park. And the fingerprints on the weapon were those of Douglas Forbes. That collection of evidence proved to my satisfaction that we'd got our man 'bang to rights' as we say in the CID.

We didn't really need a confession, but one always helps to wrap up a case beyond all reasonable doubt. We'd also had confirmation that Forbes's fingerprints were found on the hammer and the jemmy seized by Dave. But even that didn't prove that he'd actually used them to destroy part of Martin's upper staircase. Not that we intended to charge him with criminal damage anyway.

'A statement of your part in it would be a start,' I said, surprised that Forbes seemed about to tell us all we wanted to know. Just to be on the safe side, I cautioned him again.

'I've no regrets,' said Forbes. 'As I said, those bastards swindled my grandmother out of her life's savings and left her practically destitute. They got what was coming to them. I was determined to make them pay. And I wanted them to know why I was killing them, and I wanted them to suffer. Particularly Adekunle.'

'Do you admit to killing them?' I posed the question formally.

'Of course I do. What's more, I thoroughly enjoyed killing them.'

'D'you want to tell me about it? Or make a written statement?'

'Both if you like.' Forbes continued to languish in his chair as though he hadn't a care in the world. He seemed to accept that he would be spending a large part of the rest of his life in prison.

'How did you know who was behind the scam?' asked Dave.

'As a matter of fact, I had a bit of luck, old boy. When I was in Hamburg, I shacked up with Trudi Schmidt, and she invited me to take part in some porn films that were being made in a studio there. The money was good and it's not often you get paid to spend all day screwing some good-looking German birds. They're very sexy, you know, German birds. Samson Adekunle was at it, too, and he seemed to have plenty of spare cash. He told me that he lived in England, but came across to Hamburg or to a place called Kettwig – it's near Essen – to keep an eye on the books for some guy called Lucien Carter. He told me of all the people he'd seen off, even mentioning that my grandmother had been one of his victims. And he mentioned her by name, not that I let on that she was my grandmother. But it was that admission by Adekunle gave me the idea to seek some retribution.'

'Did you ever meet Lucien Carter?' I asked.

'No. I couldn't find out where he was, at least not until I saw Adekunle in London. He told me that Carter lived in the States. In New York, he said.'

'Carter's dead,' I said. 'Murdered in Rikers prison in New York.'

'Oh, jolly good,' said Forbes, and laughed. 'Saved me the job. I hope he suffered.'

'Did you have anything to do with Carter's murder?'

'I wish I had, but I've never been to New York.'

'Go on, Mr Forbes.'

'Yeah, well, I asked Adekunle what his angle was and he quite openly told me about the scam he and Trudi were running along with a German guy called Eberhardt. In fact, he asked me if I wanted a piece of the action because they could always use a well spoken English guy to persuade punters to part with their spondulicks. He reckoned I'd got a good telephone voice. I don't know how he came to that conclusion; I'd never spoken to him on the phone.' Forbes laughed again; it was almost maniacal; he seemed to find some amusement in his murdering spree and unwittingly revealed his vicious side. 'Well, I'll do most things, but I drew the line at that sort of fiddle, mainly because my grandmother had been fleeced by some of these boiler-room bastards. But I made out I was interested.'

'How did you find Adekunle in England?' asked Dave.

'Easy. I told him I'd contact him when I was back in London. He gave me his address in Paddington. Clancy Street it was, and that's where I started. I called on him and after a little gentle persuasion he provided me with Eberhardt's email address.'

'I think it was a little more than *gentle* persuasion,' put in Dave.

'You could say that.' Forbes grinned. 'As for the rest, I guess you know it all. Once Adekunle had given up the address, I sent Eberhardt an email and suggested he came over. Then I told him to park in Bendview Road, Richmond, and that's where I killed him. I know that area rather well, you see; I lived in Petersham years ago. It was a bonus that Trudi was with him too.' He sounded quite proud of his ingenuity in luring his two victims to their death.

'And you claim to know nothing about the murder of Lucien Carter in Rikers,' I said.

'I might've murdered the three over here, Mr Brock, but I wouldn't know the first thing about setting up a contract killer to take out a guy in a prison in the Big Apple, if that's what you're suggesting. As I said, I've never been there.' Forbes was impeccably polite, as he had been throughout the interview, but I was not about to forget that he'd tried to kill Dave and me, to say nothing of Dan Mason.

'Why did you pick Guy Wilson's address when you told Eberhardt where to park his camper van?' I asked.

'Who the hell's Guy Wilson?'

'He lives at 21 Bendview Road, immediately opposite the place where you murdered Eberhardt and Schmidt,' said Dave.

'Really? It just happened to be a house with a suitable grass verge opposite it,' said Forbes. 'I didn't know anything about any Guy Wilson.' He laughed again. 'I'll bet you gave him a hard time.'

'By the way,' said Dave, 'there was ten thousand pounds in Adekunle's safe at the time you murdered him.'

'What?' Forbes appeared shocked. 'Christ, old boy, if I'd known about that, I'd've had it off him and given it to grandma.'

'As a matter of interest, Mr Forbes,' said Dave. 'Was there a reason for you picking the name Derek Ford as an alias?'

'Yes,' said Forbes. 'It was a name that had the same initials as my real name. I have monogrammed handkerchiefs, you see.'

'Bloody hell,' said Dave.

'D'you wish to make a written statement about all this, Mr Forbes?' I asked.

'Why not?' responded Forbes breezily. 'Passes the time.'

It took Dave six and a half hours to write down Forbes's account of the murders he had perpetrated, and when it was finished Forbes signed it without demur.

On the Friday morning, Douglas Forbes appeared before the district judge at the City of Westminster magistrates court in Horseferry Road. After a short hearing he was remanded in custody to appear at the Old Bailey eight days hence.

Now the really difficult part began: the preparation of the report for the Crown Prosecution Service. As I've often said, the paperwork's a damned sight harder than the investigation.

Before we got on with the matter in hand, I received a phone call from Joe Daly at the American Embassy.

Insofar as the murder of Lucien Carter in Rikers was concerned, the NYPD had been unable to discover who had killed him. Since the last speculative suggestion that it was a prison gang boss, the consensus now was that it was probably something as simple as Carter having looked at his attacker with the wrong expression on his face. Such are the vicissitudes of an inmate's psyche that a simple smirk can cost a man his life.

Fortunately it wasn't my problem.

Following his appearance at the magistrates court, the lawyers at the Crown Prosecution Service had decided to indict Forbes with all three murders. Usually they would have kept two of them up their sleeve in case he was found Not Guilty on the first, or a guilty verdict was overturned on appeal. Not a bad idea, considering how fickle English juries can be. But on this occasion they were as sure as they could be that he wouldn't be acquitted. The theft of the pistol from the gun club in Germany was 'left on file', the lawyers having decided that it would be too difficult to prove apart from being pointless.

TWENTY

'I reckon you must have a season ticket for this place, guv'nor.' The City of London policeman nodded as we entered the Central Criminal Court at Old Bailey, ready to do battle with Forbes's nit-picking defence lawyers. In my days as a uniformed constable we had to salute senior officers, but nowadays it appeared that a nod and a witty remark would suffice.

Dave and I sat down in the well of Number One Court, standing up again almost immediately as the Common Serjeant appeared to take his seat on the bench.

I glanced up at the public gallery and saw that Douglas Forbes's parents, Philip and Nancy Forbes, were there, but of Lady Fairfax there was no sign. That, however, didn't surprise me. Not only was she probably too infirm to travel from Pinner, but I imagined that the stress of the trial would have been too much for her to bear. It had always struck me in the past how protective grandmothers can be of their grandsons, no matter how wayward they were.

'Put up the prisoner,' cried the clerk in the theatrical tones that is a prelude to the unveiling of that tragicomic panoply that passes for British justice.

The tall figure of Douglas Forbes appeared in the dock between two prison officers. He was immaculately suited and clearly fully confident of himself. He half bowed to the judge, adjusted his tie and shot his cuffs.

'Douglas Forbes, you are charged with the wilful murder of Samson Adekunle in the County of London on or about the fifteenth of July. Against the Peace. How say you upon this indictment?'

'Not guilty, My Lord,' said Forbes in a strong voice, and glanced around the courtroom with a smile.

Presumably this plea of innocence had been made on the advice of his counsel. But I was cynical enough to believe that it was the barrister's way of stringing out his daily fee, known in the law trade as a 'refresher'.

The clerk put the other two indictments, the murders of Hans Eberhardt and Trudi Schmidt, and received that same plea of Not Guilty to each.

'Bring in the jury,' said the judge.

Dave and I left the court. We knew what would happen next and we'd seen it all before. Opposing counsel would do battle about which of the potential jurors was suitable and which was not. It was a racing certainty that anyone clutching the *Daily Telegraph* and wearing a tie, particularly one that appeared to denote something, would be peremptorily challenged by defence counsel. Not that that would be a terribly clever move on this occasion, given Forbes's background and upbringing. That said, however, such persons of substance are more likely to condemn one of their own who has erred, than not. But finally a jury of twelve 'upstanding' citizens that was more or less acceptable to both sides would be formally empanelled.

Prosecuting counsel would then open for the Crown, outlining what she proposed to prove, and that would be followed by defence counsel's opening address. If he felt like it. Sometimes the defence would reserve that right until later. No doubt there was a reason for this, perhaps even a legal requirement, but I was never too interested in the machinations of so-called justice.

It wasn't until the morning of the second day that I was called to give evidence.

Crown counsel, an attractive woman in her mid-forties with blonde hair that hung well beneath the back of her lawyer's wig, led me through the details of the interview I'd conducted with Forbes.

Defence counsel rose to cross-examine. 'Detective Inspector Brock . . .' he began.

'Detective *Chief* Inspector, sir,' I said.

'Ah, quite so. My apologies.' Forbes's barrister spent a few moments examining his brief while he absorbed this initial setback. It's always a good move to stop defence counsel dead in their tracks. It tends to throw them off balance just when they're poised to strike with their first debilitating question. Well, debilitating in their view.

'Now then, Chief Inspector.' Forbes's counsel quickly recovered from my interruption and afforded me what he imagined to be a disarming smile. 'It strikes me that my client confessed to these murders all too readily. I would suggest to you that it was strange that he should have done so.'

I felt like saying that he didn't have much of a choice, given the evidence stacked against him, but I confined myself to staring back at counsel.

'Well, do you have an answer, Chief Inspector?'

'If you have a question, sir,' I said, doing my thick copper impersonation. I noticed the whisper of a smile crossing the judge's face.

'Let me rephrase it as a question, then.' The barrister sighed audibly. 'I put it to you that my client was coerced in some way into making what seems to be a full and frank confession. Is that not true?'

'No, sir, it is not. The entire interview was recorded, as you will know, and the recording is available to the court should it so desire.'

'Yes, yes, but what went on before the recording machine was switched on?'

'Nothing evidential, sir.'

'Thank you, Chief Inspector.' Forbes's counsel took one or two more sideswipes about procedural points, but was unable to cast any doubt on the substance of my testimony. But he had to try, I suppose; that's what he was being paid for.

Dave followed me into the witness box and 'proved' the written statement he'd taken from Forbes.

Doctor Henry Mortlock gave his damning evidence, describing in lurid detail the injuries to Samson Adekunle's body he'd found when he'd examined it. Just to drive the point home, he sought the judge's permission to display, on a large screen, photographs taken at Clancy Street that showed the slumped and naked figure of Adekunle still secured to the kitchen chair in which he'd been found. The depiction of the Nigerian's butchered corpse produced expressions of revulsion on the faces of the jury. Two of the female members actually turned away from the horrific images.

And as if that were not sufficient, Mortlock then displayed photographs of the chargrilled bodies of Eberhardt and Schmidt in the camper van, and later on his slab at the mortuary, and went on to describe, in graphic detail, the cause of their deaths.

The expert witness in ballistics, a young woman named Dr Jo Clark, displayed photographs on the large screen and gave evidence of the rounds taken from the three bodies. She explained such mysteries as striation and rifling characteristics, muzzle velocity and calibre. She talked of examining the pistol seized at Greenwich and how she had arrived at the irrefutable conclusion that it was the weapon used in all three murders.

Defence counsel continued to prove that he was earning his legal-aid fee, and rose to query the testimony regarding the rounds recovered from the tree in Richmond Park.

'Could those rounds not have been damaged when they were removed from the tree, Doctor Clark?'

'No. They were removed by a forensic examiner experienced in such matters. That examiner can be called, if so required.' Jo Clark turned towards the judge as she said that.

'Are the rounds taken from the tree at all relevant to the murders?' asked the judge in a dry voice.

'No, perhaps not, My Lord,' said counsel, and sat down.

The remaining members of our little cast of players testified to their own particular area of involvement in the investigation, and so the trial dragged on to the eighth day and its inevitable conclusion.

'Members of the jury are you agreed upon your verdict?' asked the clerk, when the jury trooped back into court following its deliberations. It had taken them a mere forty-five minutes, and that had probably included a coffee break.

'We are,' said the foreman.

'On the first count on the indictment, that of the murder of Samson Adekunle, do you find the defendant guilty or not guilty?'

'Guilty.'

'And is that the verdict of you all?'

'It is.'

It came as no surprise that the jury also found Forbes guilty on the other two counts as well.

'Very well,' said the judge. 'The prisoner is remanded in custody to appear here in two weeks' time for sentencing. Take him down.'

Forbes half bowed to the judge, winked at the most attractive of the women jurors and descended the dock steps.

And two weeks later here we were again.

The Common Serjeant, his severe face seeming to imply regret that he no longer had the option of donning a black cap, gazed at Forbes for some seconds before speaking.

'Douglas Forbes, you have been found guilty of three of the most heinous crimes of murder that it has ever been my misfortune to try. Although your counsel made a half-hearted attempt to convey the impression that you were of diminished responsibility, I can see no justification for that submission. You set about, deliberately and with malice aforethought, to seek out your unfortunate victims and murder them in cold blood. As an example of premeditated killings it is difficult for me to recall a precedent. You will go to prison for life on each count of the indictment and shall not be considered for parole until you have served at least thirty years. Take him down.'

'Thank you, My Lord,' said Forbes. He bowed to the judge and turned to descend the dock steps for the last time.

Outside Court Number One, in the vast echoing Grand Hall, I encountered a sombre Philip Forbes comforting his wife Nancy who was dabbing at her eyes with a handkerchief.

'I imagine it to have been a foregone verdict, Chief Inspector,' said Forbes.

'I think so, sir,' I said.

'A case of our son's misplaced idea of justice for his grandmother, I suppose,' said Forbes, and he and his wife turned away.

Kate Ebdon, Dave and I crossed the road to the Magpie and Stump public house for a well-deserved glass of ale. 'Well, that's another one dealt with, guv,' said Dave.

I bought pints of best bitter for Dave and me, and a gin and tonic for Kate, and we moved to a quiet corner of the saloon.

'I understand that you're thinking about moving in with Miss Sutton, guv,' said Dave suddenly. Kate looked up, her face displaying great interest at this juicy snippet.

'Where the hell did you get that idea from?' I asked. I was surprised that he knew about it even though I was aware that Gail and Madeleine had fairly frequent phone conversations. But those calls were usually to compare notes about the difference between classical and modern dance.

'I'm a detective, sir,' said Dave. 'But have you decided whether you're going to move in with her, or not?'

I glanced at my watch. 'Time we were getting back to the factory, Dave,' I said.